Praise for

BLOOD ENGINES

"A fast-paced, thoroughly fun, satisfying read."
—Kelley Armstrong, author of *No Humans Involved*

"*Blood Engines* wastes no time: by page three I knew I was reading an urban fantasy unlike any I'd previously encountered. The characters and world are real, immediate, and unapologetically in-your-face, throwing you into a story that trusts you'll keep up with the fast pace without flinching. It charges along with crisp pacing, a fascinating range of secondary characters, and a highly compelling lead in Marla Mason—her ruthless pragmatism gives her a completely different feel from her fictional contemporaries. I genuinely look forward to the next book!"
—C. E. Murphy, author of *Coyote Dreams*

"Pratt is a deft storyteller whose blend of suspense, magic, and dry humor kept me entertained and turning pages. *Blood Engines* is one of the most absorbing reads I've enjoyed in a long time, gluing me to the couch. I adore Marla, her done-at-all-costs character is someone I can relate to and want to cheer for. Best of all, I didn't figure the ending out until I got there. It's a book widower, and I can't wait for the sequel."
—Kim Harrison, *New York Times* bestselling author of *For a Few Demons More*

"Brain-twisting, superb... Amazingly strange, fascinating ideas spring from the pages, one after another with surprising frequencies, blending a dozen or more schools of magical thought into a psychedelic tapestry of unexpected depth.... I've read a lot of urban fantasies, and believe me, *Blood Engines* is new and different and not to be missed."
—SFSite.com

"The first of what promises to be an exciting and compulsively readable new urban fantasy series. Pratt has a deft touch with characterization and plot, fusing magical elements with more mundane details easily and seamlessly."
—*Romantic Times,* four stars

"Strong overtones of both noir and steampunk... [and] the darkly witty dialogue is like what a reader might expect if Howard Hawkes had written urban fantasy, where the only way to tell the good guys from the bad guys is that the good guys get even sharper dialogue. In addition, Pratt plunders a plethora of pantheons and perspectives on magic, ensuring that the magical San Francisco is just as diverse as the non-magical version, counting amongst its citizens silicon mages, biomancers, and metalworking artificers, not to mention shamanistic sex magicians (who are well worth mentioning).... I would recommend *Blood Engines* to anyone who loves a fun and fast-paced fantasy adventure."
—*Green Man Review*

"An entertaining romp featuring a kick-ass heroine, a distinctive magic system, and lots of local color."
—*Locus*

Also by T. A. Pratt

BLOOD ENGINES
DEAD REIGN
SPELL GAMES

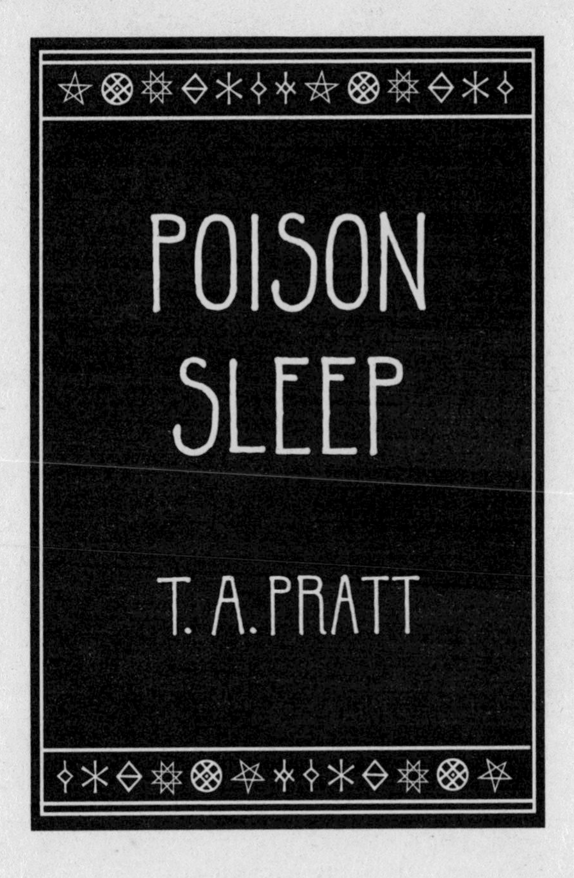

BANTAM SPECTRA

POISON SLEEP

A Bantam Spectra Book / April 2008

Published by Bantam Dell
A Division of Random House, Inc.
New York, New York

Cover design by Jamie S. Warren Youll

ISBN 978-0-553-58999-3

Printed in the United States of America
Published simultaneously in Canada

www.bantamdell.com

OPM 10 9 8 7 6 5 4 3

For Jenn,
who follows her dreams

"A dream has power to poison sleep."
—Percy Bysshe Shelley, *"Mutability"*

POISON SLEEP

1

The Bentley squealed to a halt at the top of the icy horseshoe driveway before the looming brick face of the Blackwing Institute. Marla leapt from the passenger side and rushed for the front doors, purple-and-white cloak billowing after her in the gusty winter wind. The blade of the slim dagger in her hand crackled with blue sparks of paralytic magic, and she held colored pebbles in her left fist, each capable of neutralizing one of the five senses. Even deaf, blind, paralyzed, and unable to smell, taste, or feel, Elsie Jarrow would be lethal, but Marla's charmed weapons would at least level the field.

Marla paused at the entryway. With her hands full she couldn't haul open the heavy wooden double doors, carved all over with symbols of calming and confinement, and she couldn't exactly clench the paralyzing knife in her teeth. Fortunately Rondeau caught up with her then. He had a butterfly knife in one hand, which would be about as useful for fighting Elsie Jarrow as a damp bath towel, but Marla appreciated the effort. Rondeau did have one magical weapon—he could Curse, blaspheming in the primal language that predated the fall of Babel, but the effects of such a Curse, while impressively destructive, were unpredictable, and Elsie Jarrow *fed* on chaos. Marla had told him to keep his mouth shut. Rondeau tugged open the door with his free hand, and Marla ran in—

—almost colliding with Dr. Leda Husch in the foyer. Husch's pale, classically beautiful face was soot-smudged, and she clutched one arm, which must have been injured, but she was *here,* and *whole,* and wasn't a few shreds of exsanguinated flesh scattered on the floor, as Marla had expected.

"Jarrow has been contained," Husch said.

Marla narrowed her eyes, looking for any telltale signs of mental domination. Husch had been director of the Institute for a long time, since its creation, but that didn't mean she was immune to the powers of her patients. But the woman's eyes were clear, and she had no microfacial tics, so she was *probably* clean.

"It's all right," Husch said. "Poe wrote on both."

Marla relaxed. She took off her cloak and draped it over her arm. No need to wear *that* any longer than necessary.

"Poe did what, now?" Rondeau said, flipping his knife closed.

"It's an answer to that Alice in Wonderland riddle, 'Why is a raven like a writing desk?'" Marla said.

"It's also our all-clear code phrase," Husch said. "So Marla knows I'm really me, and that I haven't been coerced or turned into a zombified slave or anything. Jarrow is in the reinforced bunker below the boiler room. It should hold, though I wouldn't mind if you refreshed the binding spirals before you leave."

Marla dropped the sense-nullifying stones into her pocket. She glanced at the still-crackling knife in her hand, then jammed the blade into a wax apple in a fruit bowl on a side table. The energy couldn't be dismissed—it had to be used—but who cared if a wax apple got paralyzed? It was an improvement, even—now the apple would never melt. "Okay. How did you stop Jarrow? When you called, you said she'd escaped her rooms, discorporated two orderlies, and was trying to find a way through the outer walls. We drove about ninety miles an hour down all those icy country roads to get here, and Rondeau's a shitty driver at half that speed. If I hadn't put a no-skid spell on the tires, we'd be upside down in a ditch somewhere. So, what, were things not as *bad* as you thought?"

"Oh, they were bad," Husch said, still clutching her arm. "But we found Jarrow unconscious in a third-floor hallway. Something knocked her out. One of our other patients *did* escape, though."

Marla braced herself. Was it Roger Vaughn, the mad sorcerer determined to sacrifice the world to a dark god that didn't actually exist? Norma Nilson, the nihilomancer, who had driven whole towns to suicide? Ayres, the necromancer with the Cotard delusion, who believed he *himself* was a corpse? None of the other patients in Blackwing was as dangerous as Elsie Jarrow, but they were all confined at the Institute for good reason. "Who got out?"

"Genevieve Kelley."

Marla frowned. "Who the hell's that?"

"One of my lesser-known patients. Not so much notorious as sad. Still, her escape . . . it's troubling. I'll tell you about her on the way to her room. But first,

Rondeau, would you be a dear and help me pop my dislocated shoulder back in?"

"Sure thing," he said.

"Wow," Marla said. "That's more action than he got the time you guys went out."

They both glared at her, but Marla just grinned. She'd expected a fight to the death when she left Felport, and hadn't been sure she'd ever see her city again, but now things weren't so bad. Marla had never heard of Genevieve Kelley, and even though the woman's tenure in the Blackwing Institute meant she was some kind of crazy and some flavor of magical, Genevieve couldn't be *too* dangerous if her name had never come up before. Marla made a point of educating herself on potential threats. It was all part of her job as Felport's protector, and head of the unruly tangle of sorcerers that lived there.

Rondeau wrenched Husch's arm back into place. The doctor grimaced, then relaxed, and looked up at Rondeau with a radiant smile.

"Okay, you're fixed," Marla said. "Tell me about the runaway, and show me the scene of the crime. I've got an appointment today and I need to get back to the city soon, country mouse."

Marla stood before the gaping hole in the southern wall of Genevieve Kelley's room, arms crossed against the cold, looking down at the snow-covered back lawn. There were no footprints or other marks of passage there, nothing marring the ground but a curved scatter of bricks which had, this morning, been part of the wall. It was too cold in here to talk comfortably, so Marla caressed the edges of the hole, whispering to the bricks and mortar, coaxing them into remembering the bricks that used to touch them, and after a moment a sort of shimmering gray ghost wall shuddered into existence, filling the hole, and the cold wind ceased ripping through the room. The patch wouldn't last for long, but it would do until the tireless orderlies—all homunculi created by the Blackwing Institute's original owner—could close it more permanently.

Marla stepped back and looked around the small room, with its single bed, bare walls, and plain wooden night table and dresser. "How long did Genevieve live here?"

"She's been a patient for fifteen years," Husch said, waiting by the door.

"She must not have much of a personality," Marla said. "Nothing on the walls, no personal effects, no knickknacks? Or did she take it all with her?"

"Genevieve has been catatonic for the duration of her stay. She was brought to me that way. I do have some of her personal items, in a box in the closet, but she was incapable of showing any interest in them."

"Rondeau?" Marla said.

"On it." He opened the closet door.

"Do you think Elsie Jarrow knocked the hole in the wall?" Marla said.

"Wouldn't have helped if she had," Husch said. "There are wards all around the building to keep her in, and they don't depend on physical walls. But she was prowling the building, looking for a weak spot in the binding spell, a crack she could slip through. It's a big building, and it's hard to keep up the protections on our budget." She looked pointedly at Marla, who was in charge of raising money from Felport's sorcerers to fund the Blackwing Institute—a task that was thankless in every direction. "But no, I don't think Jarrow would have bothered knocking over the wall. She can walk through walls."

"So maybe Genevieve did this?" Marla said. Rondeau put a shoebox on the bed—*kind of a small box to fit a life in*—and she began sifting through the contents. A blurry photograph, showing a smiling woman in a sundress with her arm around an older woman, probably her mother. "Is one of these her?"

"The younger," Husch said. "She hasn't aged a day."

Marla grunted. Lots of sorcerers didn't age when they were sleeping or comatose, or otherwise unconscious. It was one of the little tricks of extending your life, and one Marla had recently taken up herself. In her twenties, she'd felt invincible and eternal, and had scorned such magical life-extension as sops to vanity, but as her thirties unspooled and she took on more responsibility, she began to see the practical benefits. Of course, most nights she managed to sleep only four or five hours anyway, so it wouldn't help her as much as it did those who rested on a more regular schedule. "So she's been unconscious all this time? Why don't I see feeding tubes?"

Dr. Husch shrugged. "We used to try. But her state was almost one of suspended animation. Her body rejected sustenance. She never took in food, or voided her bowels."

"So was it some kind of a sleeping-beauty curse?" Marla sorted through the box. Not much to help her. There was a long yellow silk scarf, a hairbrush with a mother-of-pearl back, a couple of seashells, a book of Robin Hood stories, and that was it. Rondeau scooped up the book, sat down in a corner, and began flipping through it.

"By all accounts, Genevieve put herself to sleep," Husch said. "Though it wasn't voluntary. Fifteen years ago she was a promising psychic, apprenticed to an older sorcerer here in Felport, learning to use her powers. She had a great gift for creating illusions, I'm told. But in the first summer of her apprenticeship, she was attacked, physically assaulted on the street. She didn't know enough yet to protect herself magically, and though she fought back . . ." Husch shrugged. "He was bigger than her. You're a woman, Marla, and you haven't always been as strong as you are now. You know how it can be."

Marla nodded, then put the lid back on the box. Something like that had happened to her, too, when she was barely a teenager. Her brother—back when he was a good guy, or at least a bad guy who was on her side—had offered to kill the boy, but she'd asked him to teach her how to defend herself instead. She sometimes thought of that as the real beginning of her life; it had certainly placed her on a particular path. "Yeah. I do know. Did they catch the guy?"

Husch shook her head. "Genevieve was in no state to give a description. Her mind was already under a tremendous strain, as she was learning to use and control her psychic powers, and the trauma must have been even more horrible than usual. Can you imagine how much more terrible a rape would be if you could hear your rapist's thoughts, feel his feelings? If his senses became mixed up with your own?"

"Shit," Marla said. "I didn't even think about that." She sat down on the edge of the bed. "And after that, Genevieve just . . . shut down?"

Husch sighed.

"I see." But the Blackwing Institute wasn't a long-term-care facility or an old sorcerer's home. It was a prison for criminally insane sorcerers. "So what horrible thing did Genevieve do, to get locked up with the psycho killers and would-be world-destroyers you keep in here?"

"After her attack, she apparently wandered the streets in a daze until someone who recognized her guided her home. Her master—a reasonably accomplished old probability-shifter named St. John Austen—opened his door to her and brought her inside. And that was the last anyone saw of him. Or his house. Or the rest of that *block*. Sometime that night, Austen and his property vanished, replaced by an orange-tree grove. Genevieve was found sleeping in the branches of one of the trees, and one of Austen's associates brought her here, in terror the whole time that he and his car would be transformed into a piece of tropical fruit. Apparently the attack . . . tipped something over in Genevieve. Her power changed. In addition to creating illusions, she developed the power to reweave physical reality as well."

Marla whistled. Reweavers were rare as hell and more dangerous, and it was a blessing that most of them killed themselves by accident sooner rather than later. They could get right down to the atoms and move stuff around, change the face of the physical world, often with catastrophic unintended consequences. Some said the greatest reweavers were capable of changing even people's *memories*, but that was a tough hypothesis to prove, for obvious reasons. "Why an orange grove?"

Husch shrugged. "I don't know. There's an orange tree in that photo of her. Perhaps it represented a safe place. The orange trees died soon after anyway. The climate was all wrong for them. Genevieve never woke up. She retreated into herself, away from the trauma of the attack, perhaps, or from the enormity of the ability she found inside herself. I've kept her here because she's too dangerous to house elsewhere. I knew the binding spells wouldn't stop a determined reweaver, but, well . . . I didn't worry about Genevieve much. It's a bit like having a nuclear bomb tucked away in some corner of your house. Terrifying, yes, but over time, you get used to it. And she was asleep, after all."

"Something woke her up today," Marla said. "Probably Elsie Jarrow, shoving at every magical wall she could find, knocking down Genevieve's mental defenses in the process, freaking her out. But where the hell did she *go*? And why didn't she leave any footprints?"

"Ah," Husch said. "As to the latter, I have . . . a hypothesis. Come to my rooms. I want to show you some of the security tapes. They're frightfully boring, for the most part, as you'd expect from footage of a catatonic. But there are some interesting moments."

"Okay," Marla said. "Rondeau, bring the box. Some of that stuff might be useful."

Images flickered on the old television as Husch fast-forwarded through a few hours of surveillance tape. "We don't keep all the footage, of course. And we have to re-use the same tapes over and over, because we can't afford new ones every day, but I check them daily for warning signs. And I keep any recordings that seem noteworthy. Like this one." She stabbed the "Play" button.

Marla leaned in close. On-screen, grainy sunlight

streamed into the room from the windows in the southern wall—the wall Genevieve had blasted apart that morning. Genevieve herself lay sleeping in her narrow bed, hands at her sides, and then she was *gone*, like a jump-cut in the tape. Marla grunted, noting the time stamp, which rolled on at one second per second. The tape hadn't been spliced. Genevieve had just disappeared. "Does she—" Marla began, but then Genevieve reappeared, curled in the fetal position. A scatter of small objects appeared with her, drifting down from a spot midway up in the air, like torn pieces of paper, maybe, or—

"Are those flowers?" Marla said.

"Orange blossoms," Husch said.

"So, what, she sleep-teleported herself to an orange grove?"

"I don't think so," Husch said. "This tape was made last January. Where on Earth do orange trees bloom in January?"

"I'm sure there are places," Marla said, knowing she was being stubborn.

Husch sniffed. "I kept the flower petals in airtight jars afterward, but they disappeared in a few days. *Real* flower petals wouldn't do that, would they? I have a dozen tapes like this. Sometimes she reappears on the other side of the room. Sometimes she's wearing different clothes, though they disappear, too, in time. Once, Marla . . ." Husch bit her lip for a moment. "Once she came back bloodied, with a knife wound in her thigh. That *didn't* disappear. It scarred."

"Huh," Marla said. "So you said you have a theory. What's your theory?"

"Genevieve clearly has access to some other place, or dimension, or plane of existence. When Elsie Jarrow woke her, I think Genevieve psychically lashed out, knocking Elsie unconscious and smashing that hole in the wall. And then Genevieve just . . . went wherever she goes. At some point, she will reappear. Perhaps here. Perhaps elsewhere." She spread her hands. "I never claimed it was a *helpful* theory."

Marla nodded. Genevieve could have gone to . . . lots of places. There were plenty of folds in this world, and lots of other worlds entirely. Some of them didn't even exist until you entered them. Which didn't mean they were otherwise uninhabited.

"You have footage from this morning?"

Husch shook her head. "When Jarrow got free, she fried the cameras. I'll be sending you a bill for new equipment. Isn't it about time we went digital anyway?"

"I'll start passing the hat around," Marla said, sighing. It was tough getting the other sorcerers to give money to the Blackwing Institute. They all acknowledged the necessity of its existence, but none of them liked to be reminded that sometimes sorcerers went crazy. But she would try, and if they wouldn't pony up, she'd dip into her own coffers. Being chief sorcerer of Felport had a lot of benefits, and those benefits produced more revenue than she needed anyway. She sometimes thought about funding Husch entirely from her personal funds, but that would set a bad precedent, damn it—the other sorcerers needed to pay their share, too. It was only fair.

"Can you get Genevieve back?" Husch said. "I'm worried about her."

"I'm worried about everybody with her on the loose. Yeah, I'll see what I can do. We have the photo, and we have her scarf, and I know about the orange trees . . . that's probably enough to work with." She took Husch's arm, turned it over to look at the watch face under the woman's wrist, and grunted. "Rondeau!" He was poking through Husch's bookshelves, which included a rather impressive selection of erotica among the more staid volumes. "Let's go! We've got a meeting!" She actually had a while before the appointment, but she'd had enough of country life.

"Oh?" Husch said. "Who are you meeting?"

"New guy in town. I might hire him." She was reluctant to say more. Secrets were her habit anyway, and the existence of this particular prospective employee was more secret than usual. So far, none of the other sorcerers in the city knew the beautiful boy existed, and she wanted to keep it that way. Husch looked inclined to press—she was nosy by nature—but Rondeau spoke.

"Hey," he said, holding up a slim book with a red cover. "Can I borrow this?"

Husch raised an eyebrow. "That is a facsimile edition of the handwritten pornography Anaïs Nin produced for her patron. It is incalculably rare." She plucked it from his fingers. "No, you can't borrow it. Use the Internet. There should be enough pornography there even for you."

Rondeau grinned. "That time we went out, you told me I should be more intellectual. I'm just trying to improve myself."

"I believe I actually said, 'You're an idiot,'" Husch replied. "It's not quite the same thing."

"I've got high hopes for you crazy kids," Marla said. "Now let's go."

2

Rondeau drove back to Felport at a more sedate pace, seeming to take some delight in the wintry landscapes unrolling past them—the bare snowy fields, the icy ponds, the trees sparkling with frost. The main road back to the city was mostly plowed, with mountains of snow piled up on either side, much cleaner than the snow heaps that lined the streets in Marla's city—those were the ugly brown of car exhaust, when they weren't the black of a thousand tromping snow boots. God, she missed Felport, and she'd been gone only for the morning. Being out here under this open sky triggered Marla's agoraphobia. She missed the comfort of buildings and brick walls and chain-link fences. The morning hadn't been a waste of time, exactly, but it was *annoying*, and she had things to do. Better get her head back in the game.

"Rondeau, I need you to call Langford when we get back home. Maybe he can come up with a way to sniff out Genevieve."

"Why not call Gregor?" Rondeau said. "He's Mr. Omens-and-auguries, right? Couldn't he just swing a razor on a string over a map or something and find her?"

"Fuck Gregor. He hasn't returned my calls in a week. He's been a pain in my ass for years, and I don't want to owe him any favors. He's supposed to meet with me and the rest of the muckety-mucks about disbursing Susan Wellstone's property. If I ask him for help today, I might have to give him something good next week. I know he's had his eye on Susan's penthouse, and the apartment building under it." Susan had been one of Felport's most prominent sorcerers, but she'd relocated last month to take a leading role in San Francisco's magical underworld. She'd taken her personal possessions with her, but her property and business interests in the city were to be distributed among the other important sorcerers. And, as first among equals, Marla was in charge of doing the distributing, which meant she could have a *lot* of people owing her favors in a few days . . . and a lot of people seriously pissed about not getting what they wanted. Susan was probably laughing her ass off on the West Coast. She'd never liked Marla much.

"I'd look good in Susan's penthouse," Rondeau said.

Marla snorted. "The building's full of booby traps. I doubt she deactivated all of them, either. Leaving a few would be her idea of a joke. You'd wind up splattered on the ceiling. Besides, you're more in the way of a family retainer than a big bad sorcerer. I'd never hear the end of it if I gave you something prime."

Rondeau didn't seem to take offense, but then, he'd often said sidekicks got the best view of the action. "Okay, so you'll call Langford when you get back."

She sighed. "No, *you'll* call Langford, and then you'll drive me over to meet this new guy, Joshua Kindler—"

"No can do. The ladies' toilets in my club are all clogged, and I need to get them fixed before we open tonight."

"Rondeau. What's more important? Your toilets, or the fate of the world?"

He scowled. "Don't give me that. Every little thing you need doesn't involve the fate of the world. You tried that line on me last week when you needed your laundry done. You can catch a cab to see this Joshua guy, you know."

Marla slouched down in the passenger seat. She had been leaning on Rondeau a lot lately, sometimes for rather trivial shit. But she couldn't help it. This upcoming disbursement of Susan's property had taken a lot of her attention. Some of the sorcerers were resorting to sweet talk, while others were making subtle threats. They all knew Marla wasn't to be trifled with, but she'd been chief sorcerer of Felport for only three years, very much a late arrival to the corridors of power. Most of the other sorcerers had been squabbling among themselves and running things in Felport for decades. There were a lot of complicated relationships to consider, and handing out Susan's holdings without setting off feuds was going to be delicate. Marla had risen to her position through her willingness to do dirty jobs, her talent for making quick decisions, and her unrivaled ability to flatten those who opposed her—not because she was good at negotiating or making people happy. Diplomacy was alien to her, and though her consiglieri, Hamil, was trying to teach her, the lessons, combined with her usual responsibilities, didn't leave much time to deal with minor problems. "Fuck, Rondeau, what am I supposed to *do*? I forgot to eat yesterday, you know? I need help."

"You saying you're in over your head?"

"I can handle the important stuff. It's just . . ."

"The less important stuff. Laundry. Phone calls. Making sure you eat. Right?"

"Right."

"You need a personal assistant," Rondeau said. "Why waste a man of my talents on things like that?"

"Huh." She'd never considered hiring a p.a., but it wasn't like she couldn't afford to pay someone to keep her shit straight. Money wasn't an issue these days, but she'd spent too many years sleeping rough and living cheap to remember that. "That's not a bad idea. We just have to find somebody. And quick. I'm only going to get busier in the next few days."

Rondeau scratched his chin. "There's some loose apprentices rolling around who haven't joined up with the Honeyed Knots or the Four Tree Gang. I could ask—"

"No, I don't want some little cantrip-throwing climber who wants to improve his own status by standing next to me. Constantly bugging me for pointers and trying to steal my magical talismans, which he'll refuse to believe I don't even *use*. I need somebody who doesn't care about this business at all."

Rondeau groaned. "You want an *ordinary*? And how do we explain it to her when, like, blood starts dripping from the ceiling, or some out-of-towner crackling with eldritch energies comes around looking for trouble?"

Marla shrugged. "It's not like that stuff happens daily. We'll deal with it when it happens. You'd rather have a wannabe sorcerer in your club, who knows just enough to be dangerous? The place could wind up a smoking crater in the ground because some ex-apprentice tried to light a cigarette with magic instead of a match."

"Fine, okay, hire an ordinary. But don't expect me to nurse her through her rude awakening when she realizes the world is full of mysterious horrors and et cetera."

"Great. Line up some interviews."

Rondeau swore. "I thought this was supposed to make *less* work for me. What, do I just put a notice in the classifieds? Take out an ad on Craigslist?"

"Yeah, whatever," Marla said.

"Maybe an ad that says something like 'Attractive eighteen- to twenty-two-year-old woman sought for demanding position—'"

"*No,*" Marla said. "Get a man. I don't need you sexually harassing my assistant." She paused. "Better make it an *ugly* man. I know you."

"You just took all the fun out of this."

She grinned. "At least this way you can concentrate on unclogging your toilet instead of doing my laundry."

"You do have a way of putting things in perspective."

An hour later they reached the outskirts of Felport, its ungainly skyline filling the horizon. Marla relaxed, tension in her shoulders bleeding away. This was her city. She was bound to it, sworn to protect it, and leaving it even for a morning made her antsy. Her trip to San Francisco the month before on life-or-death business had only intensified her desire to stay close to home. She'd found her life's purpose in the decaying rust-belt grandeur of Felport, and she loved every dank alley and dirty rooftop of the place.

"Maybe *you* forget to eat, but I could go for a burger," Rondeau said. "Want to stop by Smitty's for a bite before we head back in?"

Marla glanced skyward. It was a bright clear cold day, and the sun stood just past noon. She had a little time before she was supposed to meet the beautiful boy Hamil had found. "Sure."

Rondeau pulled into the parking lot at Smitty's, an old-school diner that had once served a busy railroad crowd, back when Felport was more of a hub for trains. Now the tracks were mostly torn up, and only old-timers came to Smitty's. Marla took her leather shoulder bag with her. She hated lugging the thing, but it contained her cloak, her dagger of office, the sense-annihilating stones, and miscellaneous bits of personal ordnance. Not stuff she could leave in the Bentley. Any thieves who tried to boost the car would have an unpleasant experience ahead of them, but better safe, especially in this part of town.

Marla and Rondeau sat at the worn counter and ordered from the surprisingly sprightly waitress, who kept the coffee coming without prompting. By the end of the meal Marla was almost content. Sure, there was a crazy psychic fugitive on the loose, but Marla could track her down. She'd recruit the beautiful boy, who would help with delicate negotiations, and hire a personal assistant to ease some of the pressure on her. Things would work out.

When they returned to the mostly empty parking lot, Marla eased into the passenger side of the Bentley. The door had already clicked closed by the time she realized there was someone sitting in the backseat. Before she could turn, she felt the prick of a blade at the back of her neck, just below the base of her skull. "Crap," she said. "And I was having such a good day." She cut her eyes to the left, and saw Rondeau sitting stiffly, hands on the wheel, eyes wide. Probably a knife at his neck, too, which meant the guy in the backseat—how had she not *seen* him?—was sitting awkwardly, with both arms outstretched. If she could signal Rondeau, and time it right—

"Do not move. My name is Albertus Kardec. I am a slow assassin."

Marla exhaled. No point trying to surprise this guy. If he was telling the truth, she was dead already. Slow assassins didn't fail. But . . . the whole point of a slow assassin was to create dread in the victim, and make their last days—or months or years—haunted and miserable. If the victim didn't know there was a slow assassin after them, they wouldn't be looking over their shoulder constantly, wondering when the inevitable strike would come, trying fruitlessly to escape their fate. Nobody had ever let Marla know she was marked. "You aren't here for me," she said. "What, then, for Rondeau? Are you shitting me? I can't believe he's ever pissed off anyone who could afford to hire *you.*"

Kardec chuckled. "I am not here for either of you. We have received . . . inquiries . . . about you, Ms.

Mason, but the price we set has so far been too high for any would-be clients to accept."

Marla didn't know whether to be flattered that the most accomplished group of hired killers in the world apparently had such respect for her, or annoyed that more than one person had contacted them about putting a hit out on her. Actually, that was kind of flattering, too. "So if you aren't here for murder most foul, what do you want?"

The knife withdrew. He'd made his point, she supposed. She turned in her seat to face him. Kardec was a mild-looking man of middle years, with thinning hair, dressed all in black. She expected the residue of a look-away spell to sparkle around his edges, but there was nothing. He'd avoided being seen just by sitting very still and being one with the shadows. Any doubt Marla had about his identity dissolved. You had to be pretty badass to do a trick like that without magic, and it was the kind of thing the slow assassins taught. "I am the outreach coordinator for my organization," Kardec said. "I've come to you, in your capacity as a civic leader, to inform you of some activity in your city. I am here with a few of my colleagues to apprehend a criminal."

"Since when do you guys do law enforcement?"

He smiled, showing small, perfect teeth. "We enforce the laws of our organization, of course."

The light dawned. "Ohhh. You've got a deserter, huh?" She'd heard stories of men and women who went into the slow assassins, learned some tricks of the trade, and then tried to freelance. Marla had never heard of a deserter living more than a few months. The slow assassins didn't bother drawing things out when settling such internal . . . *disagreements.*

"Yes. He calls himself Zealand."

Marla frowned. "I've heard of him. He's been working as a freelance hitter for a long time, Mr. Kardec. He's one of yours?"

"Oh, yes," Kardec said. "He is not some initiate who broke under the stress of the patience we require. He completed our whole course with great aplomb, and took a twenty-year contract as his first."

Marla whistled. The slow assassins would stalk their victims for as long as the customer wanted, though of course the victim never knew how long they had. Six-month contracts weren't too expensive—more than a normal contract killing, but nothing mortgaging a nice house wouldn't cover—but the longer the term, the pricier it got. She couldn't imagine how much money it would take to hire a slow assassin to stalk a victim for twenty *years*. Even she probably couldn't afford it.

"At first," Kardec went on, "we thought he was engaged in his duty. He introduced himself to his victim, and pursued at a reasonable pace as the victim attempted to flee. But at some point Zealand . . . got bored. He began taking other contracts, secretly. Simple murders and assassinations. We don't approve of such moonlighting. Eventually his actions came to light, and we sent a crew to apprehend him." He frowned. "They were all killed. At that point, some dozen years ago, Zealand went completely rogue, abandoning his first target." Kardec shook his head. "If we'd started him on something easier, a two-year contract, perhaps . . . but who knows. Zealand likes killing, and has made a nice living doing so. We've been after him for years, but he is a hard man to catch, and, of course, he is very familiar with our techniques. But we have finally had some good fortune. He was seen here in Felport by one of our operatives, an assassin who studied with him years ago. We don't know what he's doing, who his target is, or who has employed him, but we'll find out."

"You want me to get in touch if I hear anything?"

Kardec produced a business card and handed it over. "My cell number. Please do. But don't spread the word too far—we don't want to spook Zealand. I was more concerned with you . . . overreacting . . . if you noticed the presence of several dangerous individuals in your city." He smiled thinly. "It is true that we value contracts above all other considerations, but we don't wish to cause any unnecessary trouble."

"Understood," Marla said. "Thanks for the heads-up. And next time you try to touch me, with a knife or anything else, you'll have a spurting stump where your hand used to be. And I'm not speaking metaphorically."

Kardec slipped out of the Bentley, walking swiftly away to disappear among the derelict train cars.

"This has been a crappy morning," Rondeau said, starting the car. "It's not fair that I've got a clogged toilet in my future and you've got a beautiful man in yours."

Marla snorted. "I'm not going to see Joshua because he's pretty, Rondeau."

"Oh? I thought being pretty was the only thing he had to offer."

"Touché."

3

Marla mistrusted cabdrivers—they all reported to *somebody,* even if they didn't realize it—so she waited for a bus on the corner near Rondeau's club. He owned the place, having inherited it from the previous owner, a troubled pharmacomancer named Juliana, but Marla kept an office upstairs in a spare bedroom of Rondeau's apartment, and did a lot of business there.

The bus arrived almost twenty minutes late. It was mid-afternoon on a weekday, so there weren't many people on board, aside from a few street people trying to keep warm, most of whom she recognized. One, in the very back, was an unfamiliar face—middle-aged, slumped, glassy-eyed, wrapped in a beaten camouflage coat. Marla wasn't dressed all that differently, having changed in her office, trading her cloak for an old brown overcoat. The cloak and her dagger of office were locked up in a secure safe, protected by all sorts of nasty anti-personnel magic. Marla had a special fondness for martial magic in all forms, and collected destructive spells whenever she could. She dropped into a seat near the stranger, curious. There was the briefest of pauses before she glanced at the guy and commented, "You smell."

He cocked his head and smiled, showing coffee-stained teeth. There was whiskey on his breath. He'd probably been handsome once, but now his face was lined and he looked exhausted. Marla expected a perfunctory "Fuck you," but instead he said, "I can take a shower and get the stink off, but you'll still be a bitch."

Marla wrinkled her nose. "I've never smelled you on this bus before. You new in town?"

"Been here a few days. What're you, the world's rudest social worker?"

She shrugged. "None of my business if you freeze to death. Not many people come to Felport in the winter. There are nicer places to sit out the end of the year."

"There are colder places, too. Some places, they make Felport look like a tropical paradise in comparison."

"So, what, you used to stink up Siberia or something?"

"Been everywhere, done everything, don't need to explain myself to *you*."

"Amen to that," Marla said amiably. She always enjoyed a little impromptu back-and-forth. The slight bristle of hostility reaffirmed her faith in human nature. "Got a place to stay?"

"I'll get by."

"I bet you will."

"Why, you offering to share your bed?"

"There's not enough soap in the world, Stinky. You might check out the Marlo Street underpass though, down by the docks. Some good people there, they won't steal your shit, and there's enough of them all together to keep the punks and crackheads on good behavior."

"I'll take that under advisement."

They rode for several stops in silence. Marla made a point of meeting the long-term denizens of Felport's streets and alleys. They saw things nobody else did, and many of them were happy to spill secrets in exchange for cash, which kept her better informed than the other sorcerers, in their high towers and libraries and laboratories. After forty minutes or so Marla pulled the cord to request a stop. Hamil's place was a few blocks away, but she wanted to walk a little.

This part of town was nicer than the neighborhood where Rondeau's club and her office were, with apartment buildings overlooking Fludd Park, lots of bike paths, and plenty of little shops, coffeehouses, and restaurants nearby. Some of the professors and administrators at Adler College lived in the area, though the cheap student housing was mostly on the other side of the campus.

Snow flurries began as Marla strolled along the salted sidewalks. It was February, and winter wasn't through with Felport yet. Marla turned a corner, three blocks from Hamil's building, and saw a woman sprawled out in the snow near the base of an apartment house. The woman's thick caramel-colored hair obscured her face. She wasn't dressed for the weather in jeans and a pale yellow blouse, and wore only a black wool scarf as a concession to the elements. Her cheeks were rosy, and her dingy white tennis shoes had no laces. The woman's arms were extended in a Y over her head, and her legs were spread apart, as if she'd passed out in the midst of making a snow angel. But there was no snow around her body, just dead grass, as if all the snow had melted around her.

Marla knelt and touched the ground. Warm, but not hot. She studied the woman, watching her chest rise and fall and her eyelids flicker. Not dead, only dreaming. Could a fever be hot enough to melt snow and ice? If so, Marla should have felt the heat radiating from the woman, and she didn't. Was she some kind of pyromancer, then? Or hag-ridden by a now hibernating fire demon? Marla consulted her mental clock and chewed her lip. She should look into this, have the woman checked out, but she didn't have time to do it herself. No one else in town knew about Joshua Kindler and his valuable power, but the longer he hung around unrecruited, the greater the chance Gregor or Ernesto or some other sorcerer would discover his presence and make him an offer. She'd send Hamil to check out the woman after she got to his apartment.

"Sleep well," she said, rising. And then stopped. "Holy shit." Marla tried to remember what the woman in the photograph at the Blackwing Institute had looked like. It had been a lousy picture, blurry, but this woman was petite, she had that mass of hair, it *might* be her. "Hey," Marla said. "Is your name Genevieve Kelley? Are you . . . lost, hon?"

The woman moaned, a sound of deep distress, and Marla knelt again. "You okay?" She touched the woman's cheek.

The street tilted, and the sides of the surrounding buildings bulged out like the bodies of huge creatures taking deep breaths. Marla ducked her head and tried to grab the pavement, vertigo upending her sense of gravity. This was like falling through space, but the only movement was inside her head.

The woman opened her eyes—they were violet, the color of crushed flowers—and clenched Marla's hand. "His mouth," she said, her breath a hot wind on Marla's face. "His reeking mouth."

Marla fell backward, breaking contact with the woman and sitting hard in the snow. She looked around, bewildered, head pounding.

What happened? Why was she on the ground? Had she fainted? She looked at the homeless woman lying on the grass. *I didn't even see her. Did I trip over her?* She stood and brushed snow from her coat. The woman before her shifted a little, her fingers fluttering as if grasping for something. Marla felt a twinge of pity mixed with disgust. A thin layer of snow had started to form on the woman's face. She'd be buried within an hour if she didn't move. Marla nudged her in the side with her booted foot, but the woman didn't respond. Sleeping off a drunk, probably. Marla sighed, took off her long coat, and put it over the woman's sleeping form. That would keep her from freezing to death at least, and Marla had other ways of dealing with the cold. She'd walk back this way when she left Hamil's place, and if the woman was still there, Marla would call someone from a shelter to pick her up. She stepped around the woman and went on her way.

Z watched Marla from the shadows of an alleyway across the street. He couldn't believe she'd actually spoken to him on the bus! He'd been riding to the nightclub where Marla spent most of her time, to continue his stakeout, and had been astonished when she boarded the bus herself at that stop. He'd been in disguise all week, assuming the invisibility of the homeless. Instead, Marla had seemed to notice him more readily in his down-and-out disguise than she would have if he'd dressed in a suit and pretended to be a businessman. After she departed, he'd stopped at the next corner and circled back to observe her.

Z could have put a knife into her ribs while they were sitting on the bus, and he'd been sorely tempted, but his employer wanted him to cut out Marla's heart and deliver it to him—something about preventing magical resurrection, Z gathered—and that demanded a more private location and a stretch of uninterrupted time. He would keep stalking her, pin down her routines, and kill her during some dark empty hours when she wouldn't be missed for a while.

He watched as she knelt to examine a woman sprawled on the ground. Suddenly, Marla fell backward in the snow, landing hard on her ass. She sat still, chin on her chest, eyes closed, for almost a full minute. Z inhaled and exhaled seven times while Marla sat unmoving. Very interesting. Was she narcoleptic? No one had mentioned that. A woman who fell unconscious on the street would not be difficult to kill, he thought.

Then she jerked, lifted her head, and looked around, confused. Z didn't breathe—the puffs of his exhalations made small clouds of mist, and she might see them when she looked his way. Marla rose to her feet, draped her coat over the still-unconscious woman, and walked on purposefully.

When Marla turned a corner, the assassin slipped

out of the doorway silently and padded after her. As he passed, the sleeping woman stirred and sat up. She yawned and stretched, as if waking in her own warm bed, Marla's coat sliding down her body to puddle in her lap. She looked at him, frowned, and said, "You remind me of someone. No. Wait. I remind *you* of someone."

And she did, though he wasn't sure who, exactly. There was something about her hair, triggering some fond association. . . . He shook his head. No reason to call attention to himself. Would he be more memorable if he helped her, or if he walked away? He extended his gloved hand. She grasped it, and he pulled her to her feet. But then the world spun around him, the sky swapping places with the ground, and a strong, horrible smell—old meat, and halitosis, and mold, and rotten spinach—filled his head.

Z recovered his senses and realized he was sprawled half on the sidewalk, half in the street, the curb cold and uncomfortable under the small of his back. He sat up, wondering if he'd been shot or hit on the back of the head with a blackjack, but he could find no evidence of injury. Had he simply . . . blacked out? Did he have some undiscovered neurological condition? The idea of such a loss of control terrified him utterly. He rose to his feet and looked around. Hadn't there been a woman in the grass here, sleeping? There was something about her . . . but the memory melted from his mind, the way a memory of a dream sometimes did upon waking. The woman was gone now. How long had he been unconscious? He hurried down the street, hoping he hadn't been down too long, that he hadn't lost track of Marla, that he wasn't going to fall again and die twitching in the street.

Hamil greeted Marla at the door of his vast apartment, his bulk filling the entryway. Beads of perspiration glistened on the dark skin of his shaved head. He smiled broadly. Hamil was her consiglieri, her chief advisor and closest ally among Felport's secret magical elite. Without his support, she would have been assassinated during her first year as chief sorcerer, though since then, she'd solidified her position by saving the city from destruction once or twice. He still helped smooth over the inevitable interpersonal conflicts, though. The powerful sorcerers in Felport were used to deference and respect, and Marla was lousy at faking such things. "You're sweating," Marla said as he stepped aside to let her in. She gasped as the heat of the apartment hit her. "It's sweltering in here, Hamil! God, doesn't all the fat on you keep you warm enough?"

"It's only eighty degrees here," Hamil said, shutting the door. "You just feel hotter because you've been outside in the cold."

Marla shook her head. "Eighty degrees? Why so warm?"

He shrugged. "I'm growing orchids. They like it hot during the day." He led her across the gleaming tile floor toward a long, low table that took up most of a wall, with about twenty evenly spaced pots, each bearing a single flower, all different colors and shapes.

"I guess they're pretty enough," Marla said. "But you won't see me taking orders from a bunch of damn flowers. I'm the boss of my thermostat." She squinted. "But . . . ah. Sympathetic magic, right?"

Hamil nodded, gesturing for Marla to sit. She settled herself on his black leather couch and he lowered himself into a big club chair specially made to accommodate his weight. His apartment was sleek, modern, and spare, everything her own place was *not*, which was why Marla preferred to take her meetings here.

"Growing orchids is very delicate, but the result is a beautiful flowering. I am involved in some, ah, other delicate negotiations, as you know, and by caring for the flowers, I've created a field of sympathetic resonance. As the flowers prosper, so will my other endeavors."

Marla laughed. Hamil looked like a giant bruiser, a movie version of gangster street muscle, but in reality he was a master of delicate sympathetic magics. Marla could work a few sympathetic magic spells—burning effigies to create bad luck for her enemies, that sort of thing—but Hamil was an artist of the technique. Specialization had its benefits, though Marla preferred her own hodgepodge approach to magic, using a little bit of everything. She'd been called a brute-force-o-mancer, and a foul-rag-and-bone-shop sorceress, and though both terms were usually meant as insults, she supposed they were accurate enough. She preferred broad adaptability to niche expertise.

"You can meet with Mr. Kindler in my office, if you like," Hamil said. "The heat there is less oppressive. He should be along shortly. He called to say he was running late."

Marla grunted. "He'd better learn to be punctual if he wants to work for me."

"Oh, yes, I'm sure you'll be very stern with him," Hamil said. "It's not as if he has some supernatural power that makes people fall in love with him—oh, wait, he *does*. He's a Ganconer, Marla. I doubt even *you* would find it possible to speak sharply to a lovetalker."

"Whatever. You'll see. Besides, he's not a Ganconer, a Ganconer's a kind of *fairy*, and I'm not even convinced those things are real, despite what your crazy-ass friend Tom O'Bedbug says. Joshua Kindler was born of man and woman. He's no elf."

Hamil rolled his eyes. "But we call his kind lovetalkers and Ganconers for convenience, though they do more than seduce. When I was young we called them Charismatics, but since the '50s that word has too many religious associations." He glanced at his watch. "I hear from one of my street urchins that you rushed out to the countryside this morning. Any problems?"

Marla grunted. "Your little orphans have eyes everywhere, huh? Yeah, I went out to Blackwing. Dr. Husch has a runaway."

Hamil's eyes widened. "Not Jarrow? No, of course not, you wouldn't be sitting here so calmly if that were the case. Who, then?"

"Genevieve Kelley. She's a psychic, *maybe* a reweaver. She's been catatonic for a long time, but Jarrow woke her up while *trying* to escape, and now it's Genevieve who's gone wandering. I'm going to track her down before she gets hurt, or hurts anyone else."

"Do we have a description? I can put the word out among my children."

Marla shrugged. "White lady, light brown hair, petite. Wearing a yellow blouse and a black scarf . . .

Wait." She frowned. "Strike that last. We don't know what she's wearing. Probably a nightgown. I don't know why I thought . . . huh. Funny. I have this mental picture of her in yellow and black." She shook her head. "I'll have Rondeau send the picture over."

"I'll expect it to arrive in six to eight weeks, then," Hamil said dryly.

Marla grinned. Rondeau was not the most reliable courier. "*And* I met a slow assassin this morning. There are a bunch of them in town looking for one of their wayward brothers."

She recounted her conversation with Kardec, and Hamil clucked his tongue. "An eventful morning. I hope this Zealand isn't in town to eliminate anyone we know. Well, unless it's Gregor. I wouldn't shed any tears over him." His phone rang, and Hamil answered. "Yes? Ah, Mr. Kindler, I'll buzz you in." He closed the phone. "Your beautiful boy is downstairs. Don't be too rough on him. I'm sure he's very delicate."

"Yeah, a precious flower who's always gotten his own way. A little jolt will do him good." She cracked her knuckles.

A few moments later the doorbell rang, and Hamil opened the door. "Do come in," he said, and Joshua Kindler entered.

Once she saw him, Marla couldn't stop looking. His slim hips, his pale eyes, his dark, long eyelashes, his sweet lips, his copper-colored tousled hair, his beautiful hands, the entirety of him. Looking at him was like sipping brandy, like snuggling into down comforters, like soaking in a warm bath. Just the sight of him was sensual. The thought of touching him—it was enough to make her a little dizzy.

Fucking pheromones. Or aura manipulation, or empathic projection, or however the hell it works. "Mr. Kindler," she said, putting a lot of steel and razor wire into her voice. "If you're going to work for me, you're going to have to learn to be *on time.*"

Kindler still stood in the open doorway. He looked shocked, and in his shock, he was beautiful. Marla wondered if she was the first person to ever see that expression on his face, or even the first to cause it.

"I haven't agreed to work for you yet," he said cautiously, "Ms. Mason. I've just come to hear you out."

Marla shrugged. "So come into Hamil's office, and we'll talk."

"If you don't mind, Marla, I'm going to make a few calls," Hamil said. He couldn't take his eyes off Joshua, either.

Marla gave her assent, and beckoned for Joshua to follow her. He moved like a cloud, and for the first time she noticed his clothes, perfectly white coat over an immaculate shirt and slacks. Most lovetalkers didn't bother to make themselves look good, trusting their magical attractiveness to win over anyone they encountered. Marla had met a few who were disgusting slobs, who took pleasure in their ability to seduce people even while picking their noses or sucking on foul, cheap cigars. Joshua was different, special, more wonderful than the rest—

Ah, shit. His power was *strong.* Marla shut the door to the study and pointed to a chair in front of Hamil's desk. She plopped down in Hamil's huge executive chair, grateful to have the desk between them, and squelched the mental voice that lamented her choice of clothes, that wished she'd worn something more feminine than loose pants and a baggy shirt—after all, her breasts were still pretty good; she'd been a topless waitress once upon a time; early thirties wasn't too old for him—a whole annoying line of insecure bullshit.

Joshua sat down, gentle as fog settling over the city.

"Let me get right to the point," Marla said.

"Please," he murmured, looking at her from beneath his long lashes, eyes fixed on hers. Marla thought of pictures she'd seen of Persian harem boys, bronze-skinned and slim with girlish lips, and thought, *I'd like to kiss him all over.*

She leaned forward in her chair, counteracting her urge to lean back and stretch, catlike. "Occasionally I require certain services." He raised an eyebrow and smiled, and Marla blushed, much to her irritation. "Not the kind of services dried-up rich women cruising in Cadillacs ask you for, Joshua. I think you know that."

"I would never suggest such a thing," he said, quirking an amused smile. The look didn't even piss her off, and her failure to get angry *made* her angry. That whole emotional tangle only served to fluster her further.

She gritted her teeth for a moment, then spoke. "You're charming. Unusually so. People like you, *everybody* likes you, even I like you, and I don't like anybody. I've been told that I can be a little abrasive, and I don't have a lot of patience for bullshit. My job sometimes requires a lot of diplomacy, and frankly, I don't have the skills for it. You do, and your skills could be very useful to me."

"I'm sure." He looked into her eyes. Marla wanted to pour wine down his chest and lick it off. "But I have to ask . . . why should I work for you when I can get anything I want just by asking for it?"

"Because if you're not bored with that kind of life already, you will be soon. I think you're too smart to enjoy drifting through life, getting everything handed to you on a silver platter. You came here to meet with me because it seemed like it could be interesting, right? I can promise you interesting times, Joshua."

He chewed thoughtfully on his thumbnail, a gesture Marla found unspeakably endearing. "I'm intrigued," he said. "All this is new to me, understand, sorcerers, mysterious societies, underworlds within underworlds . . . I used to think I was just very lucky, and likable. I believed no more in magic than anyone does. Your associate, Mr. Hamil, has shown me things I can't explain, and so I have no choice but to believe there is a whole side to the world I never imagined before. He tells me you are the most able guide to that world I am likely to encounter."

"So that's a yes?"

He frowned. "I have . . . one concern. Mr. Hamil is often accompanied by small children. Forgive me if this is indelicate, but . . . is he a pedophile? If so, I'm afraid I can't work for anyone who would condone such a thing. When I was a child . . . Well, let's just say I've *always* been very attractive, and there were those who tried to take advantage when I was young."

Marla shook her head. "No, you've got him all wrong. Hamil . . . no. It's not like that. He's organized the street kids of this city into a small army. He keeps them fed, makes sure they stay healthy, and when they get old enough, he helps get them off the street. It's not about sex. I'm not saying his motives are totally pure, but they're motivated by healthy self-interest, not any perverted shit. Nobody pays much attention to street kids. Nobody thinks they notice much, or that they care if they *do* see things. The kids get everywhere, and they're *nosy.* They're perfect spies. That's why Hamil stays so *fat*—because he's got so many mouths to feed."

Joshua frowned. "I don't understand. What does his weight have to do with it?"

"Sympathetic magic, Joshua. Hamil keeps himself fat, and his kids never go hungry. They're all connected to him. It's like . . . you've heard of the Fisher King? A king connected to the land? If he's sick, the crops fail, and if he's healthy, everything thrives? Hamil's like that, on a small scale. He's sated, and so are his kids. Plus, fat is an indication of wealth, magically speaking, and by *appearing* prosperous, Hamil *stays* prosperous."

"There are many fat people who are not prosperous," Joshua said. "It is an American epidemic."

Marla shrugged. "Those people aren't *sorcerers,* Joshua. Hamil is. And he's not a pedophile. Sorcerers can be morally flexible, but I've got a few limits, things I won't do and won't let my people do, even if they can be magically potent. Any kind of rape. Permanent mental domination. Nonconsensual human sacrifice. Things like that."

Joshua's eyes widened. "But . . . *consensual* human sacrifice?"

"It's not my thing—I think it's sad and creepy—but I can't think of a good reason why people shouldn't be able to end their lives if they want to, and if they choose to do it in some magical ritual, hell, whatever. I'd rather they donate their organs to medicine, but it's not my place to say."

"I see," Joshua said. "Yes. I think this could all be very interesting."

"Great," Marla said. She wanted to take him in her arms and welcome him into her family. "Come to the nightclub, tonight, midnight. Hamil will give you directions. I've got a little meeting you could help me with. Nothing major, so it won't be the end of the world if you fuck it up, but if you do okay, we'll see about keeping you around."

"A test of my abilities?" He looked amused.

"I don't doubt your abilities. I do doubt your punctuality, your seriousness, your commitment, your loyalty, your willingness to follow orders, and your general stick-to-it-iveness. That's what I want to test."

"Fair enough." He rose and extended his hand. Marla hesitated. Could she take his hand without dropping to her knees and sucking his fingers? Fuck yes, she could. She'd once kicked a hound from the underworld across a room. She'd killed Somerset, one of the most infamous sorcerers of all time. She'd apprehended the Belly Killer, and outsmarted *both* Roger Vaughs. She could control herself around a pretty boy.

Marla shook his hand, firmly. "Remember, midnight. And don't be late, or the deal's off the table. You're not the only beautiful boy in the world." She came around the desk and left the room without giving him another glance.

Hamil sat reading in his chair, and looked up when she emerged. "That was quick," he said. "Did you charm him?"

"He's in. Tell him how to get to the club. And do you have a coat I can borrow?"

4

Marla walked briskly through the streets, away from Hamil's apartment, clear sky making a sunlit dazzle of the snow, though the brightness didn't lessen the cold. She was deep in her head, far more so than usual, all because of that *boy*. Even knowing Joshua's loveliness was supernatural, that her attraction to him was a brain-hijack based on pheromones or psychic invasion or something, didn't change her feelings. She wanted to eat him with a dessert spoon. How was she supposed to work with him? Maybe she'd make Hamil give him all his instructions. Her consiglieri was the most heterosexual person she knew, so he probably saw Joshua as a long-lost son or something, and wouldn't lose his head around him the way Marla feared she might.

She walked past a thin man huddled on a grate, paused, and turned back to him. "Hey," she said. "You're sitting on Dutch Mulligan's grate."

The man looked up at her, squinting. He wasn't very old—mid-forties, maybe, and the wings of white in his brown hair at the temples made him seem distinguished.

He didn't have a coat, and even in the heat of the grate, he shivered. "What?" he said. "I'm sorry?"

Marla crouched before him. "You're sitting on Dutch Mulligan's grate. He's probably out buying a bottle or something, but he'll be back here, and if he finds you on his grate . . . well, Dutch will fuck you up." She shrugged. "Maybe you're looking to get fucked up, I don't know, but if not, you'd better move along."

The man struggled to his feet. "I didn't realize I was . . . trespassing. Thank you." He was trying for dignity, and almost achieving it, despite his stained pants and the sweet reek of his body odor.

"How long have you been on the streets?" Marla asked, rising.

"A few weeks. It wasn't so bad, until the weather turned."

Marla nodded. The winter had been almost mild until a few days ago, when a blizzard came pounding down on them. February was the worst. The city was still digging itself out. "What's your name?"

"Ted." He extended his hand in an automatic gesture that he clearly regretted. He started to pull back his hand, but Marla gripped it and gave it a shake.

"You've got a good handshake, Ted. Tell me something. What kind of drugs are you on?"

"None. Do I look like I'm on drugs?" He didn't. He looked offended.

She shrugged. "If you're not, you really haven't been on the streets for long. Would you describe yourself as a detail-oriented person, Ted?"

"I . . . why do you ask? Who are you?"

"I'm the person interviewing you for a job. I'm looking for a personal assistant. You're my first applicant."

"Please leave me alone," he said, sad and resigned. "You're mocking me."

"Ted. I'm really not. Listen, I'm a busy woman, but if you don't want the job, I'll find someone who does."

"Nobody hires a . . . a *street person.*"

Marla snorted. "I'm not asking you to be a brain surgeon. I need somebody to fetch coffee, file things, take phone calls, and make sure I don't forget anything important. Do you want the gig or don't you? If it turns out you *are* drunk or stupid or strung out or something, I'll fire you, of course."

"Ah . . . I'm not interested in being an indentured servant. What does it pay?"

"It pays more than you're making out here on Dutch Mulligan's grate. You can discuss the details with my human resources representative. Look, here's a card and some cab fare. The address is a nightclub called Juliana's. Go over there and knock on the door. My associate Rondeau owns the place, and when he answers, tell him I sent you, and that you're my new personal assistant. He'll get you set up. But if he tries to make you unclog his toilet, *don't do it.* You work for me, not him. You can tell him I said that, too."

"All right," Ted said, taking the card and frowning. "Will you be there?"

"Yeah, pretty soon. We'll talk more then. I'm Marla Mason. You can call me Marla." Poor guy probably thought she was planning to drug him and steal his organs or something. Well, who could blame him? People weren't trained to expect good things to drop on them from out of nowhere. But Marla had a lot of bad karma to burn off, and the occasional spontaneous outbreak of kindness was called for. Besides, Ted couldn't be any worse than the people Rondeau would line up for her to interview. "See you later," she said, and set off. She went the long way around Fludd Park, having no desire to walk on paths through bare trees, past a frozen duck pond, in *nature*. She'd seen enough nature this morning from the passenger seat of her Bentley. She should call Rondeau, tell him to expect Ted—

Her vision blurred, her head pounded, dizziness overwhelmed her—and the city changed.

She stepped down two inches, hard enough to make her teeth click together. The sidewalk beneath her feet had vanished. Instead of icy concrete, she stood swaying on broad cobblestones in the center of a wide avenue that curved away in both directions. The air smelled of orange blossoms, like Cordoba in spring. The buildings around her were no longer constructed of brick and stone, but of fluttering canvas with doors and windows painted on, like theater backdrops. A gust of wind blew through the street, and the sides of the buildings bulged like sails as air slipped into the cracks near the ground. Her vertigo faded as quickly as it had come. She wished for her cloak, or her dagger of office, something to make her more dangerous than endangered.

Her impeccable sense of direction was gone, and she couldn't remember when she'd been more disoriented. She knew her city, and this wasn't it. Had she been teleported somewhere? But, no, that wasn't possible, being teleported was a far more traumatic experience than *this*, and she didn't sense any breaks in her consciousness. She was just . . . someplace else. Marla turned and turned about, checking her sight lines, looking for threats, and breathing slowly to calm the spike of adrenaline that caused her heart to hammer. No snow fell, and the warm, humid air already made her want to shrug out of her borrowed coat.

Never one to wait when movement was an option, Marla hurried along the cobblestones, past the buildings, which sighed and billowed. The road curved and then dead-ended at a grassy square surrounded by leafy trees with branches full of bright yellow fruit. A woman sat on a stone bench in the center of the square.

Approach, or observe? Before Marla could choose a course, the woman turned around and beckoned her. She had caramel-colored flyaway hair, and she wore pale yellow, except for a black scarf draped around her neck. She looked familiar, but vague, like the memory of a dream.

"What's your name?" the woman asked once Marla came within hailing distance.

Marla ignored her, looking into the treetops and making sure no one waited to ambush her.

"I'm Genevieve. Are you lost?"

Genevieve? Shit. This was Husch's fugitive, and this . . . place . . . was hers, somehow. A little scooped-out pocket in the universe, a pinched-off piece of Dreamtime, a hallucination made real . . . or else, Genevieve was a reweaver, and she'd transformed Felport into this place of cobbles and oranges.

"I guess I am lost," Marla said, looking Genevieve up and down. Late twenties, early thirties, probably a bit younger than Marla herself—except, of course, she had to be older—with a pleasant smile and startling violet eyes. Not exactly pretty, except for the eyes.

"You'll be safe here," Genevieve said. She patted the bench beside her.

Marla remained standing. "I didn't realize I was in danger."

The woman cocked her head as though listening to something far away, and for a moment Marla thought she heard the distant strains of some pop song on a tinny radio, but then the wind snatched it away. "He's passing by now, but you should probably wait a while."

"Who's passing by?"

"He . . . he's dangerous," she said. "He'll hurt you. He likes that. Hurting women. You aren't safe. I don't mind giving you refuge. I owe you, after all; without you, I—" She broke off abruptly, touching her forehead in a chillingly familiar gesture. Marla's mother had suffered from migraines, and she had touched her own forehead that way just before the bad ones started. "You helped me?" the woman said, more a question than a statement, more to herself than to Marla.

"I don't think so," Marla said, but then a memory rose up, the sort of drifting blurry remembrance she associated with dreams. "Did I see you lying in the snow, just a little while ago?"

"It never snows around me," she said, still rubbing her forehead. "I don't like snow. Bad things happen in the snow."

"Bad things happen everywhere." Marla took off her coat and hung it over her arm. The heat here, gods! Like being back in Indiana at the height of humid summer, what her mother had called three-shower weather, because you needed to take at least that many showers a day just to feel clean.

"You should go now, before I have a nightmare," Genevieve said. "The danger's past, you'll live to see nightfall. You have to live, to help me, or . . . I'm not sure . . . it's uncertain. . . ." She shook her head. "This is going to be a bad one," she said apologetically.

The wind picked up, howling through the square, and this time it came cold, chilling the perspiration on her skin. Marla started to put her coat back on, but the wind tore it from her grasp and sent it flying into a tree. Genevieve held her hands up, as if to ward off something, her hair blowing across her face and hiding her features. Marla's own hair, cropped short, gave her no such problems. She squinted into the wind, until all the leaves were torn from the fruit trees, whirling through the square, striking Marla in the face. She crouched, sitting on her heels and covering her face with her hands, until the leaves had all blown away. When she looked again, the canvas-covered buildings were rippling. Long tears appeared in the painted fabric, swelling slits that revealed blackness. The canvas shredded into tatters, streamers blowing out to reveal the frameworks underneath. These weren't buildings at all, just skeletal constructions. . . .

Literally skeletal, Marla saw, and that chilled her more than anything else she'd seen in this place. Instead of steel girders or wooden beams, the buildings were made of bones, like macabre box kites. With the canvas torn aside, the white length of gigantic femurs and spines were exposed underneath, with bits of flesh clinging to the knobby ends. These buildings were built from the bones of giants and leviathans.

Except they aren't built from anything. *They're just manifestations of a poor sick woman's mind.* Marla shouted, though her words were torn away by the violence in the air, "Genevieve! I can help you! Come with me, I'll take you somewhere safe, back to your room—"

Genevieve wailed into the still-rising wind.

Marla looked beyond the square and saw a black tower in the center of the street, which had been empty before. The spire's height disappeared into the heavens, and it cast a long shadow—a shadow that seemed to have as much substance as the building itself.

Someone emerged from the shadow. He wore a long, shiny black coat that flared from the waist—the sort of coat goth posers might like—and it whipped around him as he approached. His bald head looked mushroom-soft and white, but at this distance Marla couldn't make out his features. She stepped into the wind, the air itself pushing hard against her, and shouted, "Hey, you! Piss off!"

When the man was about fifteen feet away, a pair of long knives slid from his sleeves, hilts dropping neatly into his hands. He didn't change his pace, and his close-set, narrow black eyes looked beyond Marla, focused on Genevieve. The canvas tatters blowing on the bone frames made her think of banners flying over medieval castles, or battle-flags on grisly standards. Marla set her legs shoulder-length apart, taking a defensive stance. Fighting weaponless against a man armed with knives could be tricky, especially with the wind trying to push her over, but Marla wasn't going to stand by and watch Genevieve get carved up—maybe it was a knee-jerk reaction, but she tended to favor unarmed women over knife-wielding trench-coated thugs who dressed like they'd seen too many action movies.

Several long strips of canvas tore loose from the buildings and whirled toward her. One struck her in the face, stinging her eyes and driving her back a step. Blind and in danger of suffocation, she tore at the fabric.

As she pulled the canvas away from her face, the wind died. Marla stood holding the shred of rough fabric, then almost tumbled forward as the earth tilted beneath her.

Everything changed again. No square, no skeleton

buildings, no leafless trees, certainly no black-clad mushroom men or wailing psychic fugitives. She was back in her own icy city, standing next to a monolithic bank on a deserted street. But she still had the bit of fabric, heavy and painted to look like red brick, in her hand. She'd lost her coat, too, and she shivered.

Marla dropped the fabric to the sidewalk and took deep breaths. She reoriented herself and realized she was not far from Rondeau's club. Two dozen blocks away from the place where she'd first shifted into the orange-scented nightmare, a distance she'd somehow traveled without crossing the intervening space.

Or maybe in that other place, the distances were shorter. When things got hyperspatial, Marla sometimes became disoriented. She didn't like folded space, and found scallops in the fabric of reality unnerving. All that space had to come from *somewhere.* There were consequences to screwing around with reality so blatantly. That's why reweavers were so dangerous. They were like genies with limitless wishes, but every wish had unforeseen consequences. The ripples could take years to show themselves, like earthquake compression waves that started out small but had the potential to become enormous and destructive over time and distance.

She hurried on to the club, her mind already spinning through contingencies. She had to put a lid on this Genevieve situation. It was more dire than she'd realized. Having a crazy psychic on the loose was not an acceptable situation, especially when Marla had to meet with the assembled sorcerers of Felport in a few days. She'd call Langford, and they'd track down the poor lady. Maybe get him to scry for Zealand while he was at it. And if Langford's arts couldn't cut it, she'd grit her teeth and ask Gregor for help. Nobody was better than him when it came to nailing down the flapping gauze of future possibilities and identifying the clearest likelihoods—and if that talent made him into an arrogant bastard who always acted like he knew more than anybody else, well, that didn't mean Marla couldn't use him. He did owe his fealty to her, whether he liked it or not—she ran Felport, and if he didn't like dealing with her, he was welcome to leave town, or try to overthrow her. The latter wasn't likely. Gregor was a seer, not a fighter. He'd gotten very rich off divination—futures trading was a snap when you could *predict the future,* even somewhat imperfectly—and most of the heavy hitters in town owed him favors because of information he'd provided over the years. Gregor was a lurker in shadows, basically Marla's polar opposite. They couldn't stand each other, but she'd use him if he was the right tool for the job.

She flipped open her cell phone and dialed. "Rondeau! I sent a guy over to the nightclub. His name's Ted. He's my new personal assistant. Get him set up with the Rolodex."

"The Rolodex," Rondeau said. "What century do you think it is exactly? We keep all that stuff on computers. Or we *should.* In practice, you just have a big pile of notes and business cards all over your desk."

"Whatever," Marla said. "Just show him where everything is, all right?" She flipped the phone shut. The wind gusted, and she looked up at the buildings around her, half expecting them to flutter in the wind. But, for now, everything was solid, metal and glass and cold concrete, just as it should be. "Fucking reweavers." She lowered her head and hurried on. "Like dealing with the world as it *is* isn't hard enough."

5

Unless you have Marla's heart in your coat pocket," Gregor said, "I'm very disappointed to see you." He sat in a deep wingback chair behind an ultramodern glass-and-metal desk, its surface as smooth and flawless as Gregor himself. Nicolette sat off to one side, loudly smacking a wad of chewing gum and smirking.

Z stood, hands clasped behind his back, reminding himself this was only a job, just a job. He imagined tossing Gregor out one of the floor-to-ceiling windows to fall screaming thirteen floors to the pavement below, letting some dirty city air into this sterile and climate-controlled space. Everything in Gregor's presence was simply too neat. Except for Nicolette, who was messy, and—as Z's mother might have said—no better than she seemed to be.

"Well?" Gregor said. "You used to be a slow assassin—I didn't realize the word 'slow' referred to your mental faculties, or your power of speech. Why are you here?"

Those who knew Z treated him with respect, and

those who did not know him could still sense that Zealand was not the sort of person who tolerated rudeness. That was part of the problem with sorcerers—they thought they were better than everyone else. But there was no point in getting worked up over Gregor. This was just a job. "I'm afraid Marla disappeared while I was tracking her. You asked me to come to you in person if anything unusual happened while I watched her." He shrugged. "I thought vanishing qualified."

Nicolette snapped her gum, and Gregor winced. Zealand smiled, but only on the inside. She said, "You sure you didn't just lose track of her? You checked to see if your shoelace was undone, and when you looked up, she was gone? Like that?"

Zealand wasn't sure what Nicolette's role was exactly—whether she was Gregor's bodyguard, private secretary, lover, or something else. She was petite, a little birdlike, with fine bone structure, but that didn't mean she wasn't dangerous; you could never judge a sorcerer's capabilities by looking. Her whole personality, and her messy bleached-white hair—festooned with ribbons, tiny plastic monkeys, rubber scorpions, feathers, and other things—injected a wide streak of chaos into Gregor's domain. Gregor wouldn't tolerate such disorder if she didn't have *something* to offer. Zealand thought it best to tread lightly.

"No," he said, addressing Gregor. "I did not lose track of her. I followed her to Hamil's apartment, and waited until she emerged. I trailed her for a few blocks, and then she vanished."

"You must have spooked her," Gregor said, dark eyebrows drawn down. "She *can* fly."

"She didn't fly. I was *watching* her. I would have noticed flight."

Gregor waved his hand. "Invisibility, then. She probably followed *you*. She might have followed you here." He drummed his fingers on the top of his desk. "Nicolette, we'll need to go downstairs later, and see . . . what repercussions this has caused. If the prognosis has changed."

"Yep," Nicolette said. "We'll see how bad Mr. Z here has fucked us."

"I was *not* followed," Zealand said, through clenched teeth. "I am a professional. It is possible she saw me—Marla is a professional, too, after all—but she will not connect me with you." In truth, Zealand didn't think she'd noticed him at all. Marla's footprints in the slush on the sidewalk had ended abruptly, so she hadn't simply turned invisible. Unless she'd turned invisible *and* flown away, which seemed like a lot of unnecessary effort. Such behavior didn't suit what he'd observed of Marla's personality, either. If she thought someone was following her, she'd confront them. But Gregor was a skulker and deceiver by nature—hence his hiring of Zealand to secretly assassinate Marla—so it made sense he'd assume the same of others. "I only told you about Marla's disappearance because you insisted I notify you of any irregularities. I am accustomed to more autonomy. You're paying me for my skills—why don't you try trusting them? Killing people is what I *do*."

"He did kill Archibald Grace," Nicolette said, kicking her heels against her stool. "I mean, that old guy was *twice* the badass Marla is."

"Yes," Gregor said, and then fell silent. After a

moment, he sighed. "All right. Do proceed. I apologize for my . . . what do you call it, Nicolette?"

"Being a tight-assed control freak?" Nicolette said. She winked at Zealand, a friendly gesture which, coming from her, he found repellant. "Gregor's heavily into precision, and that works for him, most of the time. But messy things have value, too." She shook her mane of clinking, clattering hair. "So when are you going to take Marla out?"

"Tonight. Or tomorrow. Or two days from now. Better if no one knows for sure, not even me. You predict probable futures—surely you know the value of discretion."

"Sooner is better," Gregor said.

"It's best if I know her patterns and routines, when she's alone, when she's at her most unguarded. She isn't an ordinary target, after all. I don't intend to become a victim myself. I've only been watching her for a week, but fear not, she seems remarkably consistent so far."

"I've heard a rumor," Gregor said. "Some of your old associates are in town looking for you?"

"Yes," Zealand said. "It won't interfere with our business."

"See that it doesn't." Gregor dismissed him with a gesture.

Zealand left the office, scanning the hallway in both directions before hurrying to the elevators. Gregor's security was formidable, but nothing a slow assassin couldn't overcome. That was another reason to get this assignment over with quickly. The slow assassins were closing in on him. They'd been tacitly ignoring Zealand for years, but some recent business in Dublin had stirred them up again. He'd killed one of their operatives, and even though the murder had occurred in the course of other business, they were furious, and now he had to be more vigilant than usual.

As he rode down in the elevator, he wondered if he'd chosen to kill one of the slow assassins because, on some level, he *liked* having them on his trail, for the excitement. He was getting older, after all, and his life and work increasingly failed to entertain him. Zealand chose not to examine his motivations too closely. A man needed some secrets, even from himself.

Nicolette sat down on the edge of Gregor's desk. "Think we should have killed him?"

Gregor sighed. "I feel like a man in a shark cage, Nicolette. I'm afraid to reach my arms outside for fear they'll be bitten off. I thought perhaps I could undercut the probability of the Giggler's predictions by having Marla killed, but it's all gone wrong."

"Zealand is supposed to be the best. Maybe he'll kill her tonight, or tomorrow."

"If Marla thinks she's being followed, she'll change her patterns." He put his elbows on the desk and held his head in his hands. "I was perfectly happy with my position. What do I care if Marla runs the city? I don't want to be a kingslayer."

"Fate leads him who will, and him who won't it drags. You were always destined for greater things." She smacked her gum, and Gregor shuddered. He liked Nicolette. He'd guided her from her days as a street child, and helped nurture her great talent. He just wished she hadn't shown such an aptitude for chaos magic. It was so *messy*.

Gregor sighed. "There's no such thing as fate. Just likelihoods, and situations where there's no right move, only moves of varying degrees of wrongness. It's a case of zugzwang."

"Zugzwang? Is that a dirty word for something interesting?"

"It's a term from game theory," Gregor said. Most games involved matters of probability, and scrying probability was the closest you could come to telling the future, which was Gregor's specialty. "'Zugzwang' means being put in a position where you have to make a bad move. It would be better to stay still, because any move exposes some weakness or creates disadvantage, but staying still is made impossible by the rules of the game."

"That about sums it up," Nicolette said. "But, hey, boss—there are paths out of this that don't wind up . . . you know . . ."

"With me dead in the snow? Oh, I know. But walking those paths will not be pleasant. Sometimes I think it would be better *not* to know what's coming."

Nicolette was silent for a moment. Then she said, "No you don't. I know you. You'd *always* rather know."

"Hmm. I suppose you're right. Let's go see the Giggler."

Nicolette groaned. "You're not gonna get all pissed off again, are you?"

"No promises."

After a short walk down a broad, climate-controlled hallway, Gregor and Nicolette boarded the elevator and descended wordlessly to the basement. On the seldom-visited bottom floor, after the doors had whuffed open and then closed again without either of them getting out, Gregor fitted his penthouse key into the appropriate slot. He turned it and pressed the "B" button again, twice.

Nicolette took a handkerchief from a pocket of her paint-spattered cargo pants and handed it to Gregor on the way down. Gregor nodded thanks and pressed the cloth to his nose before the doors opened.

Nicolette had tried scenting the cloth with different things—expensive colognes, rubbing alcohol, juniper extract—but nothing worked as well as industrial antiseptic. It didn't disguise the odor as well as some of the other substances did, but it soothed Gregor in the same way his clean building did, even if the fumes did make his head spin a little.

Nicolette showed no reaction to the stink when the doors opened, except perhaps a slight flaring around the nostrils. Nicolette didn't get bothered by the same things Gregor did. That's why it was good to have an assistant, to be strong where you were weak.

"He's broken the lights again," Gregor said. The dim concrete hallway before them should have been lit by halogen bulbs in cages on the ceiling, but the Giggler didn't like such brightness.

Nicolette took a penlight from her pocket and shined it into the darkness, sweeping it across the floor. The Giggler wouldn't attack them, but sometimes he left things before the doors, like a worshipper offering sacrifices at a temple gate, or a pet bringing kills to the door. Gregor had stepped in a dead cat once, and been forced to return upstairs in his stocking feet. He couldn't bear to wear the shoes after that, and Nicolette had burned them.

"All clear," Nicolette said, and led the way. Gregor followed, and the elevator whispered shut behind them. "He's quiet tonight."

"As long as he isn't dead," Gregor said.

"Nah, he'll live forever." Nicolette seemed amused by the idea. "He told us so himself, right?" She pushed open the flimsy door at the end of the corridor with her foot. It squeaked on its hinges. Gregor winced. "Hey, laughing boy! Chow time!"

Gregor looked at her questioningly.

"He likes those oatmeal cookies," Nicolette said, patting yet another pocket. "I got him a couple."

"I didn't realize you two were so close," Gregor said.

"I had a dog for a while, when I was on the street. The Giggler reminds me of that dog—dumb, but kind of loyal, you know? My dog wasn't as creepy, of course."

"Of course." Gregor inhaled from the handkerchief deeply, then stepped into the dark room to confront the Giggler. They'd tried locking him up, keeping him in cells or in bare white rooms where he couldn't make a mess or a stink, but the measures always failed. The Giggler couldn't be held. He had resources Gregor didn't understand, capabilities beyond anything Gregor had studied. They would lock him away, only to find him outside the cell the next morning, drawing cartoon animals with his feces, using frothy spittle for the highlights, the door still locked behind him. Giggling, of course. Surveillance equipment malfunctioned when trained on him, and guards fell asleep when assigned his watch. Some strange power had touched the Giggler, and while that touch had damaged and twisted him, it had given him talents as well.

The Giggler *had* to live in the midst of mess and profusion. His previous owner had understood that, and after a time, Gregor had accepted it, too. The Giggler needed disorder for his fragile mental well-being, and more important, he needed it for his work. Where Gregor saw clutter, the Giggler saw the secret traceries of the universe.

Nicolette flipped a switch, and cold fluorescent light flooded the room. "He didn't break this light yet, at least." The Giggler's living quarters were revealed, a pile of blankets, a jug of water, and a bag of salty pretzels beside the pillow. The Giggler himself was nowhere in evidence.

Gregor had inherited the Giggler from the city's former chief sorcerer, Sauvage, although "stolen" might have been a more accurate word. But Sauvage had been past caring, and the Giggler didn't care where he went, as long as he got pillows to sit on and food to eat and things to play with. Little animals to disembowel. Tea leaves to stir with his finger. Yarrow stalks. Ancient coins. Small bones, from the feet of children and the limbs of lizards. He even possessed a dirty, well-thumbed deck of Tarot cards, though he never laid them out in any pattern Gregor had heard of. He kept big sheets of posterboard to wipe his boogers on, and often propped the sheets against the wall and gestured to them when talking to Gregor, like a marketing executive noting pertinent points on a graph at a meeting. Gregor stood in the middle of the room, away from the moldering cat pelt nailed to the wall, away from the shelves with their algae-infested aquariums, away from the wooden boxes full of different kinds of mushrooms, some of which the Giggler ingested, some of which he studied for omens.

The frayed black drape at the back of the room fluttered and parted, and the Giggler emerged, pulling his stained corduroy pants up. He wore a surprisingly clean white undershirt with round eyes drawn all over it with a black laundry marker. He tugged the drawstring in his pants tight and smirked at his visitors. His black hair was greasy as always, and his clogged pores looked big enough to drive trucks through. Wiping his perpetually runny nose with one hand, he waved shyly at Nicolette with the other. "Feed me."

Nicolette tossed him a cookie, and the Giggler caught it one-handed, still rubbing away at his nose. He tore the plastic wrapper open with his teeth and ate the cookie in two bites. He smiled, belched, and sank to the floor, sitting cross-legged.

Then he tittered, an eerie high-pitched sound, like a schoolgirl's ghost might make.

"What have you divined this day, oh Seer?" Gregor asked formally.

The Giggler touched the eyes on his undershirt, caressing them and the skin beneath. He reached for a plastic bag and dumped out a pile of bottle-caps and pop-tabs from aluminum cans, fingering them. "There's a man in black," the Giggler said, staring at the bits of metal. "He'll help you, for a price."

"You mean Zealand?" Gregor asked, frowning. The assassin had been wearing black, this last time.

"No, no, not an assassin. This man is mean. He has a mushroom head. White like a snake belly, skin like something growing under an old log."

"You're one to talk," Nicolette said. Gregor glared at her, and Nicolette shrugged.

"Not the assassin, then. Someone else."

"The enemy of your friend is your enemy, yes?" the Seer said.

Gregor digested that. "Possibly."

"You've got another enemy, then, if you make the mushroom man in black your friend. His enemy."

"Do you think he'd be less obscure if we shot him in the kneecap?" Gregor mused.

"Pain is a great clarifier," Nicolette said.

The Giggler just giggled. "Do you ever dream when you're awake?"

"I barely dream when I'm asleep," Gregor said. Once upon a time that had been true, though it wasn't anymore, not lately.

The Giggler nodded. "The woman who saved my life is still your downfall," he said. "Many things have changed, but not that."

The Giggler meant Marla. Once upon a time, she'd held the Giggler's life in her hands, and she'd chosen to spare it. He always spoke of her in faintly awestruck tones, which annoyed Gregor. Marla had stumbled into a position far above her proper place. She was qualified to be muscle, absolutely, perhaps even a minister of war, but running the city? It didn't suit her. Not that Gregor wanted the job, either. It was thankless, and the advantages wouldn't outweigh the inconveniences. "But she can only hurt me if I go outside," Gregor prompted. "I'm safe from Marla as long as I stay here, inside the building, correct?"

"I want a puppy," the Giggler said, smiling, showing mossy teeth.

"That hasn't changed, has it, in light of these other developments?" Gregor insisted. "You said if I stayed out of the weather, I'd be fine, that she couldn't kill me. That if I didn't go into the elements, I'd weather the storm." He took a step forward, no longer bothering with the handkerchief, intent on the Giggler.

"Sometimes it snows in her dreams," the Giggler said. "Or the wind blows, or it rains. Those are always the bad ones, when the weather starts."

"Who? When who dreams?"

"The enemy of the friend you haven't met. The man in black's enemy," the Giggler said. "The woman who dreams and weaves the world around her. The woman in yellow with violet eyes. *Her.*"

"This is different," Nicolette said. "The last few times it's been the same, once you strained out the craziness. This is new, though."

"Bring me a puppy," the Giggler said. "A stupid, loyal one." He grinned at Nicolette and cut an enormous fart. Nicolette flinched, startled by the noise or by the echo of her earlier statement, Gregor wasn't sure which.

"One last question, and you can have anything you want," Gregor said. "When will I meet this man, my new friend?"

"Why? You planning on going somewhere?" The Giggler laughed again, throwing his head back and wrapping his arms around his belly. Bouts of humor like that usually lasted half the night with him.

Gregor walked away, Nicolette following. "Should I watch the door for surprise visitors, boss?"

"I don't know," Gregor said, getting into the elevator. "I don't know if I even believe him."

"He's never been wrong before," Nicolette said. "Confusing, sure, but we've always made sense of it eventually."

"Maybe those oatmeal cookies are interfering with his vision."

They returned to his office. Someone stood in front of the windows, hands clasped behind his back, looking out at the freezing rain and the city lights below. Nicolette whipped a chain of paperclips out of her pocket, a miniature scourge with a diamond-tipped pin wired onto the end, but Gregor put a hand on her forearm before she could ripple any nasty magic across the room. The person at the window wore a black coat made of vinyl or plastic, bunched tight at the waist and flaring out around his legs. His bald head was albino-white and looked soft as an uncooked biscuit. Or a mushroom. He turned and nodded to Gregor. His eyes were the yellow of jaundiced skin. "Hello," he said. "My name is Reave."

"I've been expecting you," Gregor said. "I think we're meant to be friends."

6

Marla almost knocked on the door to her own office, but thought better of it at the last moment, and just barged in. She wasn't sure what to expect—Ted slumped behind her desk with a needle in his arm, or asleep on the beat-up old couch, or practicing forging her signature in the checkbook. Instead she found . . . much less than she was expecting. "What happened to my mountains of crap?"

Ted turned from a row of filing cabinets along one wall. "I filed them."

Marla mulled that. "Those file cabinets were filled with old carpet samples and comic strips cut out of fifty-year-old newspapers."

He nodded. "I put those away in some banker's boxes Mr. Rondeau found for me. I wasn't sure if you wanted to keep them or not, but—"

She waved her hand. "No, no, they were left by the woman who used to run this club, I just hadn't gotten around to cleaning them." Marla had to admit she'd found the clutter and detritus somewhat comfortable. While she wasn't the sort of magician who directly thrived on chaos, clutter, and rubbish—that was more Ernesto's specialty, or that girl who ran with Gregor—she did prefer unpredictable, messy environments from a purely aesthetic standpoint. But having a wrecked office was ultimately more annoying than comforting, and if she wanted the soothing comforts of junk and decay, she could always just go home to her apartment.

"I'll toss them out in the Dumpster, then," Ted said. "I hope you don't mind, I cleared off the rolltop desk in the corner there, and hooked up a spare phone, so I'd have a place to work."

Marla crossed the room and looked at the desk. "Huh. There was a desk under all that, uh . . . what used to be here?"

"Fabric remnants, mostly," Ted said. "I put them—"

"In banker's boxes, right." She looked around. The office wasn't exactly spotless—the shelves were still crowded with hunks of exotic rock, tinted glass bottles, hand-bound books, and the traditional mummified alligator, though hers wore a little straw hat emblazoned with the word "Orlando." Most of it looked suitably occultish, though it was all left over from Juliana's tenure as owner of the club. But the dust was cleared, the piles were organized, and the top of her desk was actually visible. "This is good, Ted. You might work out. Do you drive?"

"I—of course."

"Good to hear it. Top drawer, there's a set of keys. I need you to drive me across town. I've had enough of tromping through the goddamn snow today. And grab that shoebox."

Ted retrieved the keys and picked up the shoebox

containing Genevieve Kelley's worldly possessions. "I talked to Mr. Rondeau," Ted said. "He let me take a shower in his apartment upstairs, which was wonderful. But when I asked him about my wages, and benefits, and hours, and . . . he wasn't very helpful. He said he was on call 24 hours a day, and that the last time you let him take a vacation he was nearly killed."

"That wasn't a vacation. It was a business trip. Come on, we'll talk on the way. Oh, wait." She knelt by the small safe behind her desk, spun the dial a few times for the look of the thing, and then subvocalized the *real* command that opened the lock. She reached into the safe for a banded wad of cash, turned, and tossed it to Ted, who managed to catch it with minimal fumbling even with the keys and shoebox in his hands. "You're a consultant, so we don't do any of that tax withholding crap. You're responsible for reporting your own income to the government. Or not. Though I'm sort of a government myself, and I encourage people to be community-minded and pay up."

"You're . . . a government?" Ted said, still staring at the wad of cash in his hands. It was probably a lot of money, Marla supposed, though it was just the take from one slow evening at one betting parlor down by the bay. Marla ran a lot of rackets.

"It's complex, Ted," she said, shutting the safe. "Stick the money in your pocket or something and let's go." She led him through the club, pausing briefly to smile at the sound of Rondeau cursing in the bathroom. "Rondeau!" she shouted. "Ted's driving me to Langford's, so I can talk to him about that thing!"

"How nice for you!" Rondeau said. "I'll just be here wrestling the Skatouioannis!"

"I trust you mean that metaphorically?"

"Go away! I need some alone time!"

"Skatouioannis?" Ted said as they got on the freight elevator.

"Greek word. Means 'Shitty John.' It's like a demon made out of crap." Marla stabbed the button for the parking garage, a real subterranean bat cave sort of place, with a tunnel that came out of a garage a few blocks away. "I've never actually *encountered* one, don't even know if they exist, but Rondeau read a story about one once, and now he's convinced that's the reason the toilets are always backing up."

Ted quirked an eyebrow. "This is a very odd workplace."

The elevator doors opened, and the silver Bentley gleamed before them, sleek and seemingly long as a yacht. Even after a morning's hard drive over salted roads, it was spotless—just a little enchantment laid on the car by its former owner. It was probably the world's only all-terrain Bentley. Marla wasn't particularly into cars, but she could appreciate fine workmanship, and this car was an unsurpassed blend of engineering and magic. It couldn't actually fly, but riding in it, you got the feeling it *wanted* to. "Yeah, it's a weird place to work," Marla said. "But there are perks. For instance, you get to drive a car like *that*."

Ted drove safely and sedately out of the city center, which pleased Marla, even though she was in a hurry. The Bentley was nigh indestructible, but she was glad to see him treat it with care. "Do you mind if I ask where we're going?" Ted said.

"To see a consultant who does some work for me. Guy named Langford. He has a lab uptown."

"Ah," Ted said. "I'm still not clear, exactly, on what business you do."

"I'm not into organized crime, if that's what you're worried about," Marla said. Which wasn't exactly true—she'd inherited a few not-strictly-legal businesses from her predecessor, Sauvage, including several betting parlors and some drug trade, though limited strictly to gentler substances, like hallucinogens and pot. Those could be abused, sure, but they weren't a debilitating cancer on a city the way crack or meth or heroin could be. But she wasn't involved with the mafia or any of those hard-core types, which was what Ted was probably worried about. "I own a lot of real estate and some local businesses, and I'm heavily into civic pride. I deal with important people in city government and do my best to protect the best interests of Felport. There's not really a name for the job I do." There *was*—chief sorcerer and protector of the city—but it was a little early to get into all that with Ted. "I need somebody to help me deal with the mundane shit, drive me around, keep things organized, make calls, etc. You can crash at the office for a couple of days, then we'll get you set up in an apartment in the building where I live. You can stay right next door to me, I just need to get some of the junk cleaned out of the rooms. It's not fancy, but it's better accommodations than Dutch Mulligan's grate. Your salary won't be huge—what I gave you today, every week or so—but your housing will be taken care of."

"What about time off?"

Marla stared at him. He glanced away from the road at her, then back to the road, then back at her. "What?" he said.

"Haven't you had enough time off lately, Ted? If you need a few hours here and there to deal with personal shit, yeah, we can talk about it. I'm not inflexible. But this isn't a 9-to-5 job. It's an *all the time* job. I sleep about four hours a day. I can teach you some techniques so you can get by on that little sleep, too. You'll need it. If you don't like the gig, you can go back to your life of leisure."

"I'll give it a try," Ted said, though whether he was thinking of the wad of cash in his pocket or the cold months of winter that still stretched ahead, Marla wasn't sure.

"I don't mean to be harsh," Marla said. "But I don't want there to be any misunderstandings. I need you to *lighten* my load, not complicate things."

"Is there any possibility for, ah, advancement in this position?"

You're the personal assistant for the most powerful sorcerer in Felport. How much more advanced do you want to get? "Let's not get ahead of ourselves. We'll see how you handle this. If you last a month, we can think about your future."

Ted parked on the curb in front of Langford's lab, a low, unassuming building that blended in nicely with the various doctors' offices on the same street. Langford was a doctor, too, sort of.

Marla buzzed the door, and it clicked open. She was surprised—Langford had a bunch of insects with their senses jacked into his own consciousness that he used for surveillance, but Marla had expected the cold to keep the bugs inside. Then she noticed the glass lens set in the wall. An ordinary camera. Trust Langford to build in redundancies. She went in, followed by Ted, who carried the shoebox holding Genevieve Kelley's effects.

The inside of the building was one large, cluttered room, all the interior walls knocked down. Metal shelves stood on all sides, and various long workbenches and lab tables were arrayed at seemingly random intervals throughout the room. The back wall was covered in stacked cages, from Chihuahua-sized to one that could have held a couple of mountain gorillas, though all but one were empty. A yellow-eyed coyote paced the length of the cage, and Marla wondered if it was a skinchanger or just an ordinary animal. Langford sat at a stool before a workbench scattered with shiny metal components, soldering something and humming to himself. He might have been sitting that way for hours. He liked to work, and as far as Marla could tell, he didn't like doing much else. He was a weird guy, with a tendency to stare at people like he was thinking about dissecting them, but he was fast and effective, and Marla counted on him. He was probably as powerful as any of the city's most prominent sorcerers, but as far as she knew his interests didn't run toward city management, big business, or organized crime, so he didn't take a hand in governing.

"That's not Rondeau," Langford said, not looking up. "New apprentice?"

"He's Ted, my personal assistant," Marla said. "Listen, I need a rush job."

"You always need a rush job," Langford said. "Your personal assistant knows not to *touch* anything, right? I know Rondeau had to learn that the hard way."

Rondeau had nearly lost a finger to one of

Langford's experiments, an experience that had finally stopped him from poking around the lab's shelves.

"Ted's solid," Marla said. She walked over to Langford and snapped her fingers in front of his face. "Hey, there's a human being talking to you now. Can I get some attention?"

"I can pay attention to many things at once," Langford said. He looked up at Marla, though, and today his eyes were silver. Langford had a vast array of colored contacts, each pair magically altered to enhance his senses in a different way. She wondered what silver did, but asking Langford would just lead to a long lecture on the subject, and she didn't have time. "What's today's emergency?" he asked.

Marla glanced toward Ted, who stood holding the shoebox and staring at the coyote. "Hey, Ted, leave the box here, and go wait in the car, okay?"

He nodded and slipped out of the room.

"Here," Langford said, rising and walking over to a silver refrigerator. He took out a small vial of clear liquid. "Put this into Ted's food. He's got prostate cancer, and without this, he'll die. But this should clear it up."

Marla blinked at him. "Say *what*?" But she took the vial.

Langford tapped the spot between his eyes. "These are diagnostic lenses. They scan for unusual masses and inconsistent densities, among other things. Cancer is easy to see with them."

"No, I figured that part; I mean, you have a *cancer* cure? What the fuck, Langford? Why isn't this in every drugstore in America?"

Langford shrugged. "It's not science. Or, it's only partly science. It reprograms the cancer tissue and convinces it to be more community-minded, gives the chaos a plan, but it's mostly magical, so I can't exactly get FDA approval."

"Still, you could dump some in the municipal water supply, at least!"

"It's not easy to make in quantity, Marla. Even that vial is dear, but you're my main patron, so I'm willing to part with some of the substance to keep your assistant alive, and, I trust, earn some personal gratitude?"

Marla nodded slowly. She'd follow up about this another time. Langford had weird priorities sometimes, and curing cancer might not be high on his to-do list if he had some other, more interesting project on his table. "Do you think Ted knows he has cancer?"

"He's probably shitting blood by now, so I suspect he's worried, but perhaps too afraid to go to a doctor."

Or too poor. Or he just figures shitting blood is the sort of thing that happens when you eat out of garbage cans and live in alleys. "Right," Marla said. "Thanks, Langford."

"Yes, yes. What do you need? I *am* working on something."

"A woman escaped from the Blackwing Institute this morning. Her name's Genevieve Kelley. She's—"

"I know who she is," Langford said. "Dr. Husch has me in periodically to make sure the homunculi on her staff are functioning properly, and we sometimes consult on other cases, if Husch thinks there might be a physiological component. Kelley's case has always interested me. She *escaped*? Fascinating."

Marla snorted. "You could call it that. The thing is, I *saw* her today. I was walking in the city, when everything around me changed. I went . . . someplace else.

But it wasn't anywhere on this Earth." She described the strange buildings, the groves of trees, the cobblestones, the wind, the black tower. "Genevieve was *there*. I think it was her place."

Langford nodded, then stared at the ceiling for a moment. Marla waited. She was used to this. "She disappears, sometimes, in her sleep," Langford said at last. "I've hypothesized that she has access to some sort of conditional universe, a little bit of pinched-off reality furnished by her subconscious, filled with comforts and monsters. Or possibly a place created by *stretching* reality, the way you can press your finger into a sheet and create a little cone of extra volume by straining the fabric."

"And what happens if you poke too hard?" Marla said.

"What you would expect," Langford said. "You poke a hole in the fabric."

"That's what I figured."

"I wonder how many other people have been pulled into her world since she escaped?" Langford said.

Marla sat down on a bench. "Shit. I didn't even *think* about that. But why should it just be me? Gods, are people just popping into her world at random?"

"It may not be totally random. There could be some sort of vector. A particular place that gives entrance to her world, or a touch—did you have any contact with her before you found yourself in her world?"

"No, I never—" Marla paused. That same hazy image, like a picture from a dream, came to her. There was a woman, laying in the snow, and Marla had draped her coat over her. But now, thinking back, the woman was *familiar,* she was—"Hell," Marla said. "Yes. I saw her in the snow. I bet I even touched her. Why didn't I *recognize* her?"

"You probably did. You probably just don't *remember* that you did. Dreams are hard to remember, Marla—they go into short-term memory, and unless you make a special effort to remember them, they disappear from your mind. I've always suspected her power is linked to dreams. The place Genevieve took you sounds like a dream world, something beyond her control, something she experiences as reality. But it's a dream she can pull other people into. If she's a reweaver, as Dr. Husch believes, it may be a dream she can bring into *this* world."

"It was a *nightmare,* Langford. At least the last part was."

Langford nodded. "I am, actually, reassured to hear that she touched you. That could be the vector of contagion."

"So you think if she touches people, they get sucked into her dream world?"

Langford shrugged. "It's just a hypothesis, but it's possible. You haven't received widespread reports of people popping into her world, which means you may be an isolated case, and since you had direct contact with Genevieve, it seems reasonable to assume, for now, that direct contact is a prerequisite. Of course, the question then is whether it's black plague or bird flu."

"Beg your pardon?"

"Contagion models," Langford said. "People initially catch black plague from rat fleas, but once they've caught the plague, it can pass from human to human. With bird flu—at least, the unmutated strain—

you can only catch the disease directly from a bird. A human with bird flu can't pass the disease on to other humans. The question is, can you catch this dream-sickness from Genevieve alone, or can it be caught from another person who is already infected?"

"Like . . . me," Marla said. "Shit."

"Who have you touched since this happened?"

Marla thought. She'd touched Hamil's shoulder. She'd shaken Joshua Kindler's hand. She *hadn't* touched Rondeau. She *had* touched Ted. She hadn't touched Langford. "A few people."

Langford nodded. "Observe them. If they have . . . experiences . . . you can assume you are contagious. Until then, limit your contact with new people. As for people you've already touched . . . well, it's probably too late for them. And if she's a reweaver, and her world starts intruding into *our* reality, any random passerby in the vicinity could be swept up into her world, too, I suppose."

"Great. Do you think my trip to dreamland was a onetime thing, or will I get sucked back in again?"

"I have no idea," Langford said. "I assume you'd like me to help you find our patient zero?"

Marla pushed the shoebox of Genevieve's things toward him. "Here are a few of her belongings. Can you use them to get a fix on her?"

"Certainly," Langford said. "I'll call you. But it could take a couple of days, if she's popping in and out of our reality."

Marla scowled. "Can't you just, like, dangle a weight over a map or something?"

"I'm not a *dowser,* Marla," Langford said, affronted. "I'm a *scientist*. I have some techniques that might work to connect these items to their owner, using spooky action at a distance and principles of quantum entanglement—"

"Don't care," Marla said, holding up her hands. "Just get it done. And call me as soon as you know anything. The sooner we get Genevieve settled back in Blackwing, the happier I'll be."

"She's awake now, Marla, at least sometimes. She may not be willing to go to sleep again."

Marla smiled. "That's what sedatives are for."

Ted drove Marla back to the club, where Rondeau was talking to the bouncer and the bartender, getting ready for the evening ahead. His club, Juliana's, was currently pretty popular with kids from Adler College looking to dance all night, and Marla's operation was making good money selling them tabs of ecstasy, though she'd nixed Rondeau's plan to charge dehydrated customers $10 each for bottled water. She sent Ted upstairs with instructions to call in an order for lemon chicken and some egg rolls, then beckoned Rondeau over to the DJ booth to talk privately. "So, this Genevieve Kelley we're looking for, if you see her, don't let her touch you. She's contagious. If you touch her, there's a good chance you'll get pulled into a fucked-up dream world full of buildings made of bones and bald guys with daggers."

"Sometimes I hate my job," Rondeau said. "I assume you contracted this little malady? But didn't manage to catch the lady in question?"

"Yeah. And it's possible I'm contagious, too, since

she touched me. So keep your hands to yourself, all right? I haven't touched you since then."

"But you've touched Ted?" Rondeau said.

Marla nodded.

"And I touched *him*, when he got here. I shook his hand. So . . ."

Marla sighed. "Good point. At least if you find yourself in a place that smells like oranges, you'll know what's going on. Just hunker down and wait it out. I didn't stay in the dream world for long."

"That's a comfort." He rolled his eyes. "But for now, I should get back to work. The DJ's late, and we open in an hour."

Marla shooed him away and went upstairs. There wasn't much she could do now—wandering the city aimlessly looking for Genevieve wouldn't do much good. If Langford got a fix on her, Marla would call Dr. Husch and they'd figure out a containment plan. Maybe something as simple as shooting Genevieve with a tranquilizer dart, maybe some kind of big constrictive magic, whatever seemed warranted. She paused on the stairs and called Hamil to fill him in on the potential for contagion, and he groaned. "Shall I let Joshua know? I assume you did touch him?"

Marla hesitated, then sighed. "Hell. Yeah. Go ahead. I hope he doesn't get pissed off and quit." She hung up. She thought about telling Ted, but how could she explain to an ordinary that he might get sucked into a surreal dream world? She *couldn't,* not yet. She'd just have to keep him close, and hope for the best.

She went into the office. Ted was looking at her antique chess set, with its inlaid board and weird pieces carved from stone. "You like it?" Marla said.

"It's a chatrang board," he said. "It's remarkable."

"That's a chess set, Ted."

He shook his head. "Chatrang is a precursor to chess. The pieces must be very old, though the board is newer."

"Huh," Marla said. "I got the set from an old friend. I don't know its history. I just thought it was chess with funny pieces, you know, like the boards that have Civil War soldiers or whatever instead of normal chessmen." She'd inherited the board, along with most of her other worldly possessions, from Sauvage, her predecessor as chief sorcerer. Her possessions would, in turn, pass on to the next sorcerer to take over Felport, though if she retired, she'd get to keep enough money to be comfortable. Retirement was unlikely, though. Most chief sorcerers didn't retire to anyplace but the grave.

"You can play it like chess," Ted said, setting up the pieces. "The chariots are rooks, the elephants are bishops, the vizier is a queen, the soldiers are pawns, the horses are knights. The rules of chatrang are different, but not as much fun, honestly. Would you like to play?"

"I do like the game," Marla admitted. "But I'm not very good. I don't get to practice much." Rondeau didn't have the attention span to play without getting bored and wandering off halfway through, and Hamil refused to play chess. His powers of sympathetic magic made it dangerous for him to play games. If he started to lose at a chess game, his real-life fortunes might fall in tandem. Marla's old mentor, Artie Mann, had taught her the game, but he hadn't been very good, either. He used to tell Marla it didn't matter—"Even Napoleon

Bonaparte was a lousy chess player!" he'd exclaim each time she toppled his king, as if by losing at chess he was practically imperial himself.

"I used to teach chess club at a high school before my . . . fortunes fell," Ted said. "But a lot of the kids were better than me, so don't worry."

"All right, we can play while we wait for the food to get here," Marla said. Why not? Maybe it would distract her from thoughts of Genevieve. And the impending division of Susan Wellstone's property. And her inappropriate and magically motivated attraction to Joshua Kindler. And rogue slow assassins wandering her city. And all the other bullshit.

Marla played white, in her usual aggressive, hack-and-slash style, but before long she found herself pinned down across the board by a fence of Ted's pawns, all backed up with other pieces and limiting her movements, pushing her into a corner of the board, sniping at her pieces and whittling down her defense steadily. As they played, Ted told her a little about the history of the game; annoyingly, his little history lesson didn't seem to impede him when it came to kicking her ass. He checkmated her, and she scowled. "Another game," she said, and he agreed. This time she started killing his pawns right away, and when the food came, Marla paid the delivery guy impatiently.

She was so into the game that she almost forgot about the vial Langford had given her. She took a moment to open up the boxes and pour the cancer cure into Ted's food, knocking a few drops into her own as well—it couldn't hurt. Then she hurried back to the board, eating while Ted concentrated on his moves. He didn't seem to notice any odd taste in his own food, which was good. No need to tell him he was sick. It would require too much effort to explain at this point—better if he just started to feel better, and never knew why.

Marla was concentrating on setting up a sweet fork with her knight, hoping to make Ted sacrifice his rook to save his queen, but somehow he wiggled a bishop down the far side of the board and got her in check. In two more moves she was doomed. She tipped her king over to concede defeat and started in on an egg roll. "You're good at this, Ted."

"You're a very romantic player."

She lifted her eyebrow. "I've been called a lot of things, Ted, but 'romantic' isn't usually one of them."

"I mean the romantic school of chess. The earliest grandmasters played in the romantic style. They set traps, used pieces cleverly in combination to attack, and made bold sacrifices to gain advantage. They valued beautiful moves over winning. If you were playing in the nineteenth century, you'd be considered very good, I think. But that style was supplanted by positional chess, where control of the board is more important. It's a slower, less dramatic way to play, but a positional player can almost always beat a romantic. That's the only reason I won. I don't claim to have a deep understanding of the game, but I've read enough to know a few techniques." He shrugged. "Romantic players have good tactics, but tactics are no defense against strategy."

"I don't know about *that*," Marla said, spearing a chunk of lemon chicken. "I've always defined strategy as a long-term plan that goes wrong at some point. It's too easy to lose track of today when you're focused on your five-year plan or whatever."

"Tactics are fine for the short term," Ted said. "But they're vulnerable in the long term."

"Life is nothing but a series of short terms. One short term after another. And if you can control each of those short terms, you can keep control for a long time."

"Well," Ted said, glancing down at the chessboard, where Marla's king lay on its side. "I guess life and chess aren't the same, though you can learn something about each from the other, I think."

Marla opened her mouth to argue—after all, she considered herself a skilled tactician, and Ted was implicitly criticizing the way she lived her life, ran her businesses, and defeated her enemies—but then someone knocked at her door. She narrowed her eyes. It wasn't Rondeau—he would've just barged in—and it always paid to be wary of surprises. "Who's there?" she called.

"Joshua," a beautiful voice replied, and Marla's heart fluttered a little.

7

Crap, Marla thought. "Hey, Ted, you like booze?"

"Sometimes," Ted said. "I—"

"So go downstairs, get a drink, start to form a bond of manly friendship with Rondeau. Okay?"

"Whatever you say," Ted said slowly, rising from his seat.

"You can send Joshua in." Marla resisted the urge to touch her hair. She kept it cut short so she didn't have to worry about it, damn it. She scowled, and Ted hurried away, opening the door.

"Hello," he said. "I'm Ms. Mason's assistant. She says you can go in."

"Thank you," Joshua said, entering. He moved like a snowflake falls, and wore white to match. Ted lingered in the doorway for a moment, looking after Joshua, his lips slightly parted, until Marla said, "Shut the door on your way out, Ted." Her assistant shook his head rapidly, then pulled the door closed.

Joshua stood in the center of the room, the focal point of Marla's attention shifting to him instantly. He looked around, a half smile on his lips, then cocked his head at Marla.

Marla found herself trying to sit up straight and keep her legs crossed, and very consciously leaned back in her chair and put her feet up on the low table that held the chessboard. "I said come at midnight. You're early. That's almost as bad as being late. I'm not a big fan of the drop-in." Of course, in truth, she was intensely happy to see him. His magic made him the most desirable thing in any situation. "Call first in the future. You *do* work for me now, right?"

"I suppose," Joshua said, taking Ted's chair and looking thoughtfully at the chessboard. "I've never liked this game."

"Ted was telling me that some people say chess is all about free will and independence, a game where luck has no bearing. You win or lose entirely on your own merits. According to some legends, the creator of chess intended it as a refutation of the idea of destiny. His rival created a dice game, where the winner was determined by chance and fate. You like dice better, Joshua?"

"I like video games. Especially car racing games. Though I like driving real fast cars better."

Marla started to say something about her Bentley—*Ooh, we'll have to go for a drive sometime, you'd* love *my car,* and clamped down on the impulse. "Well, to each his own. What can I do for you, Josh?"

"Hamil told me there's a chance I might . . . disappear?"

"I doubt he told you *that*. You might possibly get sucked into the dream world of an escaped mental patient. Though to an outside observer it could look like you disappeared, I guess." She grinned. "Hell, I promised you excitement, didn't I?"

"Is this dream world dangerous?"

"Anything can be dangerous."

"You know, I *could* stop working for you. I haven't even properly started." He picked up a pawn and began tossing it from one hand to the other. "It's not as if you've placed me under a geas. If associating with you proves too dangerous, I might have to consider such action."

Marla shrugged. "Lovetalkers aren't exactly common, but I can find another one. Besides, you wouldn't be any *safer* if you quit. Did you come here to threaten me? Because that's the sort of thing you can do in a phone call from now on, or even a postcard. I won't be offended, I promise, and you'll save both of us some time."

"No, that's not . . . no. I was just worried. I told you, I'm new to all this. Magic."

His vulnerability and uncertainty were adorable. "Sure, I get that. But magical sleeping sickness? That's *nothing*. You have to embrace the weird shit, Joshua. It only gets weirder. If you can't roll with it, you'd better not hang around." She checked the clock on her desk. She *wanted* to ask Joshua if he felt like making out for a couple of hours, but that wouldn't do. Pretty or not, magically attractive or not, he was a stranger. What if he was a flake, a coward, a boor? She didn't believe in being coy, but it was too soon to act on her attraction. Though after she got to know him . . . "Look, go downstairs, enjoy the club, come back up here at midnight, like I told you. Or don't come back, and I'll know you can't hack it."

"I'll see you at midnight," he said, rising with the grace of a plume of pale smoke.

"I'm not sure I should park here," Joshua said, peering out the windshield of the Bentley at the dark shadows of warehouses all around. Off in the distance, a car alarm wailed. "It doesn't seem safe."

"Magic, Joshua, remember?" Marla opened the passenger door, letting in a draft of frigid post-midnight winter. "I'll cast a look-away spell on the car, and ordinary thieves won't even *see* it. And any thieves who can sense magic should know better than to touch my car." She got out, and Joshua followed, buttoning up his long pale overcoat. "This way." She kicked empty plastic bottles and the eviscerated remains of old newspapers out of the way and headed down the sidewalk. "We're going to broker a peace between the Four Tree Gang and the Honeyed Knots. They've been scuffling over this territory for weeks, and the ordinaries are starting to notice. I'm here to put a stop to it. The leaders of both gangs are waiting up ahead in a warehouse."

"These are . . . magical street gangs?"

Marla nodded and cut down an alleyway between two buildings. "Mostly made up of apprentices who washed out, or who pissed off their masters, or who got orphaned when their masters died. Quite a few of those last, actually, and they form the cores of the two gangs. A few years ago there was a serial killer hunting down the city's most prominent sorcerers. He even killed my old teacher, Artie Mann. A lot of apprentices were left at loose ends after that, and when they couldn't find other placements, they went feral."

Unable to resist bragging a little, Marla said, "I stopped the killer, by the way."

"Impressive. But you let these gangs remain?"

Marla shrugged. "They aren't especially loyal, but they can be bought. It's handy having a mercenary force with some magical ability at my disposal when shit gets out of hand. We even give their leaders non-voting seats in our councils, so they can feel like they're part of the process. Sort of like they're Puerto Rico. Keeps them from going totally rogue. Best of all, they're territorial, so they keep ordinary street gangs from getting out of control. This area, down by the docks, is a pretty shitty part of town, and without the gangs doing a little de facto police work, things would be a lot worse."

"You can't just clean up the area?"

"Every city has places like this, Joshua. Places where you can get drugs, or stolen goods, or your baser desires satisfied. Try to suppress such things completely, and pressure builds up in other parts of the city. Better to keep it contained here, though I do keep a lid on the worst of it, and try to keep the predators from preying on innocents. I don't much care if the wolves eat one another."

"Not exactly utopian, is it?"

"I'm practical," Marla said. "If you know nothing else about me, you should know that."

"So why the conflict between the two gangs? Philosophical differences?"

"Eh. The Honeyed Knots are more badass, much more exclusive. They also like face tattoos and body piercings and crap like that. The Four Tree Gang outnumbers them by about three to one, but they're mostly wannabes and never-weres. If they didn't have the numbers advantage, they'd get splattered. I'd rather keep some parity between them, though. Letting them scuffle with each other keeps them from bothering *me*. The Four Tree Gang is encroaching on Honeyed Knot territory lately, hence the increased hostilities. Hamil's been spreading the word that you're my new apprentice, so no one should suspect you're a lovetalker. You'll be charming and get them to chill the hell out—"

"Evening," drawled a voice from the shadows. Marla had her night-eyes on, and she could see the man standing there, holding a gun, perfectly well. "Be nice, and nobody will get hurt."

"Oh, dear," Joshua said, and the man in the shadows stood a little straighter and peered at him, mouth hanging open. Joshua had that effect on people.

"Well, not *nobody*," Marla said. "I mean, *you'll* get hurt." She was glad of the opportunity to show off. She'd have to be careful not to kill the guy, just disarm him and make him beg for mercy a little.

"It's impolite to startle people," Joshua said. "And a gun? Very tacky."

"I—ah—"

"Say you're sorry," Joshua said firmly.

"Sorry," the mugger said. "Really, sorry. I didn't know—I mean, if I'd seen . . ." He trailed off. Joshua stepped forward, took the gun from him, and tossed it over his shoulder, a move he executed with such great grace and panache that Marla wanted to applaud. "Move along, now," Joshua said, putting a hand on the man's shoulder.

"Maybe I'll see you later?" the mugger said hopefully, staring at Joshua wide-eyed.

"If you're good, perhaps."

The mugger nodded and hurried away, looking back over his shoulder at Joshua as he went.

"Very smooth," Marla said. "I'm impressed."

"Strangely, Marla, I find myself eager to impress you. I'm not sure why."

"Maybe because I'm not easily impressed. By the way, next time you throw a gun over your shoulder, you should make sure it's not loaded. Or at least that the safety's on. It could have gone off when it hit the ground, and getting killed by a richochet would have spoiled the effect." She found it hard to criticize him, but forced herself to do so. He deserved it. His charms were tremendous, but she was aware of them, and surely that gave her some power to resist?

"Of course. You're right. I don't have much experience with guns."

"Let's go talk to the gangs, shall we? Follow my lead, nod and smile when I signal you, and smooth things over if they start to bitch and snarl, okay?"

"I am yours to command," he murmured.

Zealand followed the Bentley from a fair distance, troubled by the break in Marla's routine. She usually worked all night in her office, going to her flophouse apartment in the wee hours, presumably to sleep. But now she was out, with a stranger, headed who-knows-where. When they parked and headed into the warren of warehouses he decided to sit and wait. He wouldn't be able to follow unobtrusively on foot, and they'd come back for the car eventually, when they finished whatever business they had here.

He cursed. The Bentley shimmered and vanished. More magic. Probably just a theft deterrent, but he hated the uncertainty of dealing with sorcerers.

About twenty minutes later, a tree appeared in the center of the street, not fifteen feet from Zealand's car, showering blossoms to the pavement. Something long, dark, and oddly jointed slithered down from the branches and paused on the ground, lifting an angular head and looking at the car. Zealand turned on his headlights, and the thing scurried away into the shadows before he could get a good look, though there was something horribly asymmetrical about its movements. The tree's branches waved, as if in a wind, and then, abruptly, the tree disappeared.

"Magic," Zealand muttered. He doused his headlights and checked to make sure all his doors were locked.

"Not bad," Marla said after the meeting broke up. She and Joshua were alone in the big, drafty warehouse, sitting side by side on some splintered wooden pallets. Marla resisted the urge to scoot even closer to him. He smelled amazing, like honey and vanilla and sweat. "You played them like cheap violins." The Four Tree Gang had agreed to withdraw to the limits of their old territory, in exchange for right of free passage through certain areas controlled by the Honeyed Knots. Marla could have forced them to make the agreement with threats and verbal bludgeoning, but the peace would never have held. Under Joshua's influence, though, the gang leaders had actually shaken hands before leaving, something unheard of in Marla's experience.

"I'm happy to have helped. So I passed the test?"

Marla laughed. "These guys were kittens. Pretty soon you'll be dealing with tigers. The leading sorcerers are cranky, egotistical, and a little bit psychopathic. All necessary qualities in a top-notch sorcerer, of course, but it does make them hard to wrangle. Those negotiations are going to be a bitch. But, yeah, you did well enough that I'm willing to toss you in the tiger pit and see how you fare."

Joshua yawned, and Marla wanted to kiss his mouth. "Are we done for the night, then?"

"Need your beauty sleep?"

"This face doesn't happen by accident," Joshua said dryly.

"Come on, then. I've got a few hours of work left in me, but I'll give you a lift back to the club and send you on your way." She wanted to invite him up to her office for a nightcap, but it wouldn't do to look too eager. If *he* asked *her* if he could stay, though, maybe she'd allow herself to grudgingly consent. . . .

They stepped out of the warehouse, into the alleyway, and Marla stumbled, her sense of balance deserting her entirely. She fell into Joshua, who exclaimed in surprise and then caught her—but a moment later he disappeared, and she completed her fall, sprawling on—

The cobblestones? "Oh, hell," she said, rising, the ringing in her ears subsiding. She was back in Genevieve's world, sunlit and warm, surrounded by dozens of orange trees heavy with fruit, a whole orchard growing unaccountably up from rounded cobblestones. The branches rustled, though there was no wind, and something like an ambulatory spinal column with too many legs and a head like a wedge dropped from a branch and hissed at her. Marla drew her dagger of office—she always went armed to gang situations—and crouched. "Come on, then, you slithery bastard." Abruptly, the light vanished, and it was suddenly *cold.*

"Marla!" Joshua said. "Where did these trees come from?"

She was back in Felport, among the warehouses. But the trees—and the slithery thing—from Genevieve's dream world had come *with* her. This was bad. Getting infected with Genevieve's dreamsickness was trouble enough, but now the woman's nightmares were popping up in Felport spontaneously?

The slithering thing ran back up the tree, apparently as freaked out as Marla was by the change of venue. Joshua hurried to her side, and she opened her mouth to warn him away, but it was too late. Sunlight reappeared. "What's happening?" Joshua said, bewildered, and Marla felt an overwhelming desire to protect him. "You just vanished, and now . . . ?"

"I think we just accidentally hopped on a freight elevator to dreamland."

"Does this mean—I'm infected? Like you were afraid would happen?"

"Well . . ." She gestured. "Not necessarily. Look at all the bits of trash scattered among the trees. I think anything that happened to be in the vicinity when the trees transitioned back to the dream world got swept up with them. Langford warned me that might happen."

"We'll go *back,* though, right?" He shrugged out of his coat, and Marla followed suit.

"I'll get us back," she said firmly. The trees began to

shiver again, all of them, and Marla wondered how many segmented nasty things lived in this grove. "Better to move on, though. There's stuff here that won't succumb to your charms, I don't think. Unless you've got a special rapport with monsters?"

"Only people. Dogs don't even like me."

"Come on," Marla said, grabbing his hand—thrilled at the excuse to touch him—and pulled him away from the trees, toward cobblestoned hills.

"Where are we going?"

"Higher ground, so we can see . . . anything there is to see." They went up the hill. Marla glanced nervously back at the grove, but whatever lived there seemed content to stay. "All right," she said when they reached the hilltop, trying to figure out what the hell to do next.

A decision that became even more complicated when she looked down the other side of the hill and saw a dozen ordinaries clutching one another, terrified. Men, women, and children, from the well dressed to the ragged, sat in a huddled mass beneath the burned remnants of a gazebo. "Oh, fuck," Marla said, and one of the people—a woman in a nurse's uniform—approached her, coming warily up the hill.

"Who are you? I don't remember you from the hospital."

"Hospital?" Marla said. None of the people down there looked particularly ill or hurt, just scared.

The nurse frowned. "Yes, Felport General. That's where we were."

Marla nodded slowly. "Did you, ah, happen to see a woman with light brown hair, kind of weird violet eyes . . ."

The nurse began nodding. "She came into the

waiting room, talking to herself, bothering people, grabbing their hands, and I went to talk to her . . . I think I fainted. I woke up here, and these others . . . they were all in the waiting room, too. What's happening? Can you help us?"

Marla wasn't sure what to say. These were *ordinaries*. How could she begin to explain?

Then Joshua stepped forward, and the nurse only had eyes for him. "It's all right, dear," he said gently. "We'll help. Why don't you introduce me to everyone?"

"Joshua," Marla said, questioningly.

"I'll keep them calm," he said. "And you'll figure out how to get us home. Yes?"

Marla couldn't disappoint him. "Of course."

Joshua went down among the people, and they all turned their faces toward him like flowers toward the sun. He was gentle, he was kind, he soothed them, he told them everything would be all right. In a few moments he had them laughing, telling their stories, smiling, convinced this was something like an adventure. Religions formed around people like him. He glanced up the hill at Marla, and she jumped a little, startled by the directness of his gaze. If she wasn't careful, she'd become a worshipper, too. "I'll be back," she called, and went back down toward the orange grove.

Escaping this dream world—let alone leading innocents back to Felport—wasn't in Marla's power, but she couldn't let Joshua down, not after he'd proven himself. Now that she wasn't in his immediate presence, his supernatural attractiveness was lessened, but she still *liked* him, he was brave and good-hearted, and from disarming muggers to helping refugees he'd proven himself tonight. This morning, she'd expected to meet a callow selfish spoiled brat, but Joshua was more than that. She wanted him to like her. She wanted him to *admire* her. Which meant fixing this mess.

She skirted the orange grove and walked on, finding an iron park bench. If this place really *was* made from Genevieve's mind, she probably wasn't far off.

Marla sat on the bench. "Genevieve," she said. "Could I have a word?"

"You've been here before," Genevieve said, appearing on the other end of the bench. "Haven't you?"

"There are some scared people over there," Marla said. "They don't belong here. Can you take them back?"

"Back? People? What?"

"You know what it's like to be afraid," Marla said. "Do you want to make other people afraid?"

Genevieve began humming to herself.

"Will you walk with me?" Marla said.

Genevieve frowned at her. "I will walk," she said, rising, and set off toward the orange grove. Marla hurried after her. "Nasty things there," Genevieve said, gesturing at the trees. "Used to be pretty, but ugly things get in everywhere, everywhere."

"There are some people I want you to see," Marla said, not touching Genevieve, but guiding her with gestures to the top of the hill. "See? Those people don't belong here." None of the people below looked up, all of them enthralled with Joshua, who seemed to be telling a story.

"I'm tired," Genevieve said.

"Damn it, don't you understand me?" Marla said.

"Those people. They need to get back to Felport. Do you understand me?"

"Is it cold?" Genevieve said. "Are you cold?"

"It's not cold, it's—"

But then it *was* cold, bitterly, and the hill was gone. Marla fell several feet to the sidewalk, barely managing to land in a crouch that made her ankles pop but, fortunately, didn't do anything worse than jar her bones. They were on the snow-covered quad of Adler College, about a mile from the hospital where these people had started out.

"It's okay!" Joshua shouted above the general hubbub. "Everyone, come to me, it's okay, we're back now! I told you we'd be safe!"

For the moment, Marla thought. Genevieve was gone, but she'd touched these people, and that meant they might vanish back into her dream world at any time. Marla wished she could believe she'd convinced Genevieve to bring them all back, but talking to her had been like talking to a river. If the woman wasn't stopped, somehow contained, Marla could have a serious state of emergency on her hands. She opened her cell and called Hamil, who answered sleepily.

"Send four or five cars," she said. "And a few doses of that special forget-me-lots potion. I've got some short-term memories to blur here."

"Is this about Genevieve?" Hamil said.

"The lady gets around," Marla agreed, and told him where they were.

"You were pretty good back there," Marla said, when she and Joshua were alone again in the back of a car driven by one of Hamil's employees. The refugees had been sent back to the hospital with confused memories, already filling in their harrowing experience with plausible inventions—low blood sugar, fainting spells, sleepwalking. Ordinaries were good at covering over the cracks in reality.

Marla wanted to snuggle up to Joshua, but she kept herself on her side of the car with an effort. It had been easier to resist his charms when she thought he was probably a bastard, but he'd come through tonight, and now the magical attraction was joined by genuine admiration. The whole point of lovetalkers was that they *made* you love them, but Marla now thought Joshua was probably *worthy* of love.

"You were wonderful, too," he said. "You brought us back from that place. I'm not ashamed to say I was frightened."

"I did promise you working for me would be interesting."

"I can't say you lied."

"Want to get breakfast with me tomorrow?" Marla said, keeping her tone businesslike. "We can go over the game plan for the big negotiations."

"I'd be delighted to dine with you. But . . . don't you have to deal with the strange woman and her plague of dreams?"

Marla shrugged. "I've got people working on it. A crazy wandering sorcerer isn't a *good* thing, but she's not actively malevolent. I'll handle it. I've had worse problems."

Joshua shook his head. "I don't know how you can stay so calm."

"All part of the job," she said. The driver stopped in

front of the club. "Sleep well, Joshua. I'll see you tomorrow." *And I'm sure I'll see you in my dreams before then.*

Two days later, Hamil dropped by the office to see her. "My spies have further reports of strange manifestations. Orange trees, mostly, where they shouldn't be. Is Langford any closer to finding Genevieve?"

"I called him yesterday, he said he's working on it. Don't worry. Mysteriously appearing orange trees aren't the end of the world." Marla watched the clock on her desk. In half an hour, she was having lunch with Joshua. They'd had breakfast, lunch, and dinner together the day before, and the more time she spent with him, the more fun she had. He had a wealth of amazing stories, and he'd traveled all over the world, seen so many things, met so many people. No doors were closed to him, of course, and Marla could see why. Even if he *hadn't* been a lovetalker, he would have still been charming, beautiful, funny—

"Marla, are you listening to me?" Hamil said.

She frowned. The clock said two minutes had passed. Had she really just spent two minutes staring into space thinking about Joshua? Well, so what if she had? Was there anything *better* to think about? Didn't she deserve some *happy* thoughts? "Of course I'm listening," she snapped.

Hamil scowled. "You were supposed to have lunch with the Chamberlain yesterday, and she told me you canceled. And you missed the afternoon meeting with Granger, about planting trees inhabited by dryads in the freeway medians to help combat car emissions. And I note the pile of expense reports on your desk is still there, untouched. Then there's the matter of Viscarro's unauthorized tunneling toward the park—"

Marla held up her hand. "Enough. You don't have to tell me my job. I just got busy."

"So busy you had lunch with Joshua at the Green Apple yesterday?"

Marla drew herself up. "You spying on *me* now? I think you're confused about the nature of our relationship."

"Hardly spying. I *do* own the restaurant, you know, Marla, and the maître d' knows you by sight. He said you looked like a woman in love."

"Bullshit. It was just lunch. Joshua's a new employee. We have a lot to talk about."

"I'm a bit worried about all the time you're spending with him. Being near a Ganconer is like being near plutonium. You . . . soak up the radiation. The effects become more and more powerful, and they stay with you. The more time you spend with a lovetalker, the more susceptible you become to his charms, until you don't even need to be in his *presence* to fall under his sway."

"Please. He *works* for me. He only charms the people I tell him to. Anyway, he's a stand-up guy. I told you how well he handled himself at the gang meeting, and how he helped out with the little reality breakdown afterward."

"I'm glad he's working out. I just don't want your . . . association . . . with him to interfere with your other responsibilities. I understand you and Joshua went on a date last night?"

"It wasn't a date, it was a *business* dinner. But even if it was a date, so what? I don't answer to you, Hamil." Sure, she'd put off a few things, but nothing *vital*. The responsibilities that she'd felt so buried by all week seemed less pressing now. Her priorities had shifted, somehow. She was almost *happy,* and she couldn't remember the last time she'd felt that way when she wasn't actually beating someone up or making an enemy miserable.

"I'm your consiglieri. It's my job to worry. With Genevieve loose, and slow assassins in the city, it just seems like an inopportune time to start a romantic relationship. And if you sleep with a lovetalker . . . well, their power is supposed to become even greater then. It's not your fault, it's just impossible to be rational when you're under the sway of—"

"I haven't fucked him, Hamil."

"I'm just afraid that—"

"Your concerns are duly noted," Marla said coolly. "Now get lost. I've got places to be."

Hamil levered himself up from chair, opened his mouth, then apparently thought better of it, giving her a curt nod and leaving the room.

Marla scowled. So maybe she was spending a lot of time with Joshua. Was it so bad, that she should enjoy herself a little? You'd think he'd be *happy* for her. Hamil was always telling her she worked too hard, that she should take a break every once in a while. But as soon as she did, he got pissed!

Ted knocked on the door. "Marla, your lunch date is here."

"Great." She almost asked him if she looked okay, but bit her tongue in time to stop herself. "Send him in."

Zealand, dressed in a fine suit, glanced over his newspaper to watch Marla laughing and flirting with the same companion she'd been with for the past few days. She never had come back for the Bentley the other night—Rondeau and Marla's new personal assistant had retrieved the car after dawn. Marla's relatively regular daytime patterns had changed, and now she seemed to spend all her time with this man, who was reputedly her new apprentice. Though she still went home, alone, late each night. Zealand decided he should strike soon, before that pattern, too, changed. Tonight, then. It would be good to finish. The other slow assassins were still looking for him. It was time to kill Marla and leave Felport behind. He went back to his newspaper, and across the room, Marla Mason laughed at something her companion said.

8

After dinner at one of the city's finest restaurants, Joshua and Marla went back to her office, ostensibly to continue going over the dossiers on the city's leading sorcerers. Marla thought he'd already learned enough about the major players in the city to handle the negotiations regarding Susan Wellstone's estate, but it was a good excuse to remain in his company without letting him know how much she enjoyed him.

"If I have to read another word about Viscarro and his vaults, I think I'll scream," Joshua said, tossing the folder into the middle of her desk.

"All right, fine. I guess I've worked you hard enough for tonight."

Joshua leaned forward, looking into her eyes, and Marla felt something inside her melt. Gods, he was pretty. "I was hoping . . ."

"Yeah?"

"That you might agree to come back to my hotel room tonight."

"Oh?" she said, leaning back, playing it cool. "Why's that?"

"So I can do my best to seduce you," he said matter-of-factly. "There's something about you, Marla. You're not like other women. Or men, for that matter. These past few days have been eye-opening. You fascinate me."

"You really think it's a good idea to try to fuck your boss, Joshua?" Marla wasn't sure. Her head thought it was a bad idea. The rest of her thought it was a very good idea. And part of her couldn't figure out why he'd *want* to, when he could have his pick of the most beautiful women and men in Felport, serially or simultaneously, as he desired. Marla thought she had a pretty good sense of her own looks—her features were more strong than pretty, and though she was in great shape, she had more than her share of scars. Some men found her attractive, certainly, but they were mostly people who were attracted to strength and power, and nobody in the *world* had any power over Joshua. . . .

Oh. Despite her growing attraction, Marla had never stopped talking shit to him. She was snarky, brusque, condescending, and impatient, all very conscious behaviors born from her annoyance at being so fucking *smitten* with him. She was mean to him because to do otherwise would mean admitting she was in his power, and she wasn't *about* to do that. *And I'm probably the only woman who's* ever *talked to him this way*. Most straight girls probably just dropped their panties as soon as he smiled at them. Marla must seem like an impossible thing—a *challenge*.

"I don't know if it's a good idea or not, but I think you'd have a very pleasant time," Joshua said. "Are you interested?"

Marla yawned. "It's been a while since I've indulged. I'm usually too busy for that sort of thing. In all honesty, I'm *currently* too busy for that sort of thing."

"It doesn't have to be a *relationship,*" he said. "Though, if that's what develops . . . Do you find me attractive?"

Marla laughed out loud. Most guys were more sophisticated than *that*. But why would Joshua have ever needed to learn techniques of seduction? "Of course I do, Joshua. You could weigh four hundred pounds and have two heads and I'd find you attractive. The whole reason you're valuable to my organization is because *everyone* finds you attractive. So what? Maybe I'm looking for more." In truth, Marla wasn't looking for anything, not romantically. She had plenty of other things to keep her occupied, and like she'd told Ted, she wasn't much of a romantic.

He bowed his head. "I'm sorry. I thought, perhaps . . . I'll go."

Marla had to bite her tongue, literally, to keep from speaking right away. She waited until he was halfway to the door before saying, "Wait. It's been a long week, and a romp wouldn't be out of the question. Sure, let's do it. But we'll go to my place."

"Whatever you want," Joshua said. "I have a limousine waiting downstairs. Hamil was kind enough to provide it."

"Good," Marla said, rising. She decided, since she'd come this far, that she could afford to flirt a little. "His limo has nice leather seats. We can get started on the way to my place. I'm curious to see if your talent lives up to the hype."

"I will endeavor to give satisfaction," he said, with a smile that made her feel light-headed.

When Zealand was about a block from Marla's apartment, the world changed. A sudden wave of dizziness overtook him, and he fell toward the side of a building, barely catching himself, and dropping his heavy leather tool-bag. A moment later he was facedown, sprawled inelegantly, his nose pressed against the freezing concrete, with no memory of actually hitting the ground. He sat up, groaning, but the vertigo was fading. There was a trick in hand-to-hand fighting of slapping your opponent against the ear to upset their equilibrium, leaving them to lurch out of balance. He felt like *that*. He closed his eyes and took deep breaths until he felt level again. When he opened his eyes, he saw a massive palace in the center of the street. Made of opalescent stone, it disappeared into the sky, an upthrusting construction that baffled the assassin's sense of scale. Silver rods protruded from the tower at regular intervals, and yellow banners flapped at the ends of the poles. Arched windows of different sizes dotted the tower, and a few rounded balconies protruded from the sides. It was a beautiful, impossible thing.

Zealand closed his eyes again and did a slow count to ten. Gradually, the sound of the flapping flags diminished, then ceased. He looked, and saw only the icy street and a passing yellow cab, rolling slowly in the evening gloom. No palace.

He rose, picked up his bag, and continued toward Marla's apartment. Zealand depended on his senses to survive, and a hallucination or loss of equilibrium at the wrong moment could spell death. He'd been working too long among these magicians, with their rituals and mysteries. He didn't want their indefinite, ever-shifting world to become his own. He'd kill Marla and go elsewhere, maybe back home to the West Coast.

Marla lived in a five-story former flophouse, a squat broad building of crumbling brick with an elaborate sign that read "Hotel Felport" sagging on the roof. It had probably been home to drunks and failed door-to-door salesmen once upon a time, but now Marla lived there alone, on the top floor.

A pair of chipped stone lions, draped in piled snow, guarded the front steps. Cardboard filled the holes in several windows, while the wind whistled through others, though all the windows on the first two stories were barred. A battered wrought-iron gate protected the garbage cans, and a fat tabby crouched beside a disconnected bicycle wheel chained to the gate. Icicles completely choked the gutters, frozen cascades of spikes, and more glistened like teeth from the roof's overhang. As always he wondered why Marla, Queen of Felport's Underworld, chose to live in such tawdry quarters.

The front door was well secured, but he found a side door that gave way under the proper application of leverage from his crowbar. Once inside, he headed up the stairs, mistrusting the look of the old-style elevator with its sliding grate. Half the lightbulbs were broken, and trash lay piled on the stairs. The lobby smelled like urine, and the second-floor landing like vomit, while the third floor reeked of pine-scented disinfectant. The fourth floor smelled like mold and motor oil. The fifth floor smelled like dust and nothing much else at all. He went to Marla's door—501—and frowned at the crudely hacked designs around the doorjamb. They resembled a blend of Arabic and Cyrillic characters, sometimes flowing gracefully, sometimes jagged and angular. Nothing as simple or familiar as a pentagram or a spiral. Zealand took a long, flexible metal rod from his inner coat pocket. He used it to break into cars, sometimes. He extended the rod toward the door slowly, his eyes widening when the hacked runes began to glow with a pale blue light. The end of the rod reddened, and he pulled it back, then spat on the metal. His spittle sizzled where it struck.

Hmm. A problem, but not an unexpected one. Gregor had warned him that Marla might have defenses like this, and they had discussed strategies. Zealand knew the floor plans for these apartments. He went to the next apartment and knocked imperiously at the door. No one responded. Zealand's surveillance indicated that Marla lived alone here, but guests were always a possibility. The assassin picked the lock laboriously. He could kill in a thousand different ways, from the subtle to the extreme, but he'd never been much good at picking locks. He could have broken the door open, but he didn't want to leave any warnings for Marla.

He finally opened the lock and went into the apartment. A little light came in through the window from the one working streetlight outside, and he used a flashlight for the rest. Boxes were piled everywhere, and a cursory examination revealed old clothes, paperback books, mismatched dishes, and other detritus. Marla probably used this apartment for storage.

He went into the bedroom, noting the scurry of

mice. He opened the closet door, and found the space beyond empty. Why use the closet when the whole apartment was her closet? He rapped his knuckles on the wall and smiled. Cheap apartments, thin walls. He drew a hammer, chisel, and miniature hacksaw from his bag, then placed the chisel against the wall and tapped it lightly. The chisel punched right through the wall. Working quickly, listening for the sound of Marla's door opening, he cut a large rectangular hole near the bottom of the closet. Once he had a hole big enough to squeeze through, he pulled out the dirty cotton-candy-like insulation. He tugged on the few wires in his way experimentally and decided they would spread apart without breaking when he wriggled through.

Using the saw and the chisel, he carefully cut a corresponding section from Marla's wall. He would enter her apartment, a mirror-image of this one, through her bedroom closet. He eased out the chunk of drywall and shone his light into the space beyond.

Hanging clothes, various shoes and boots, and the closed door. He wriggled through into Marla's closet, then reached up and tried the doorknob. It turned, and he pushed the door open incrementally, his ears straining for any sound. Nothing, not even the creak of the closet door. Good. He wouldn't have to bother oiling the hinges.

He stood and stepped into her dark bedroom, shining his flashlight. The room was messy, dominated by an unmade king-sized bed with a heavy iron frame. A large mirror with elaborate scrollwork hung on the wall, but it needed to be cleaned, and clothes lay piled on the floor and on top of a cheap wooden dresser with its drawers half-open. The nightstand by the bed held several heavy tomes, a dusty glass of water, and a blue vibrator. The only beautiful object in the room was a large wooden wardrobe, intricately carved with snakes and vines, standing against the far wall, next to the door. He went closer, intrigued, and saw runes similar to those outside cut into the wood near the door handles. He didn't bother to reach for them, but he wondered what sort of treasures lay within. Probably nothing he'd know how to use anyway. Sorcerer things.

He went into the living room, surprised to find it almost completely bare. A cheap plywood shelf dominated one wall, covered with leatherbound books, but there was no other furniture, and the floor had been stripped of carpet. He stepped into the bathroom. Cracked porcelain and a water-stained basin—about what he'd come to expect. The bedroom provided the best hiding place, the closet especially. He would lie in wait there. Perhaps he'd even be able to kill Marla while she slept.

He returned to the bedroom, careful not to disturb the piles of clothing and old magazines, and got back into the closet, sitting behind the hanging clothes. He opened his bag and withdrew one of the few high-tech devices he liked, a tiny fiber-optic camera with a wide-angle lens that he snaked under the crack beneath the closet door. The camera cable plugged into a little handheld monitor, giving him a sharp, high-contrast image of Marla's dim bedroom. He'd be able to watch and wait for the optimal moment to strike. Now, though, it was just waiting. Marla's work hours varied wildly, and with his luck, this would be the night she decided to stay out until 4 A.M. Ah, well. Gregor was paying him well for his patience. Zealand settled in.

Kissing Joshua in the back of the limo was the most sensually pleasurable thing Marla had ever done, better than the first taste of caterpillar rolls from her favorite sushi restaurant, better than a soak in the hot tub after a hard workout, better than fifteen minutes alone in bed with some well-thumbed porn and a Hitachi magic wand. Kissing him was like the way she'd imagined kissing boys would be back in junior high, a delicious act of transformational wonder.

She managed to break the kiss—she was in danger of melting against Joshua with a long low moan of pleasure, and once she did *that*, she'd be like everyone else who'd ever been trapped in his spell, and why would she interest him then? She saw the irony, of course. She'd started out being mean to Joshua to show him that she wouldn't fall victim to his lovetalker's charms, and now that he seemed attracted to her indifference, she was using that to try to seduce *him*. Marla wasn't sure how exactly she'd tumbled into this tangled relationship, but it felt good, and for the moment, she was willing to roll with it.

"You're a hell of a kisser, Joshua Kindler," she said, touching his cheek for a moment, then leaning back against the seat of the limo. Being in such close quarters with him was increasingly intoxicating. The limo moved slowly down the icy streets, so it would be a few minutes before they reached her building. Would she be able to keep herself from climbing on top of him in the meantime? She opened the window a crack, letting in a stream of cold, refreshing air. Did it clear her head a little? Maybe his powers *were* based on pheromones. "Most lovetalkers just stick their tongues down your throat and have done with it, I've heard. You actually seem to care about your technique."

"You seem to be constantly surprised that I'm not a beast. I haven't met anyone else with my power. Hamil tells me we tend not to get along, perhaps for the same reason queen bees can't stand the presence of another queen—not that I'm a queen, mind you, as I hope you'll find out soon—but I'm sad to hear most of them are so indifferent in their manners. I was raised better, I suppose."

"Sorry, Joshua. You seem like a good guy, but then, you *would,* wouldn't you? The very fact that I like and trust you gives me grounds to dislike and mistrust you, you know?"

He sighed and shifted a little in the seat, and it was, somehow, like watching a perfect statue settle itself into an even more perfect pose. "I cannot help what I am, Marla. I didn't go to the crossroads at midnight and make a deal with the devil. But I am more than a lovetalker. I am a man. And I am often bored. You're the first interesting thing to come along in ages."

"People who get whatever they want for the asking are often bored. Having something that challenges you a bit is more interesting. Maybe you should play more games. Though people would probably just lose on purpose to make you happy."

"I don't think *you* would lose just to please me," Joshua said, smiling.

"When I play, I play just as hard as I can," she agreed.

"Are you playing with me now?" Joshua asked, as if the question was very serious.

"I'm not exactly what you'd call a hedonist, Joshua, but I'm not indifferent to pleasure, and, well . . . I've made love to a few men, and a couple of women, and even an incubus—that's a story for another time—but they say sex with a lovetalker is an experience unlike any other."

"According to the old stories, it ruins you for all other love," Joshua said. "Those seduced by the Ganconer pine away unto death when their lovers leave them. But you don't strike me as the pining type."

"Guys who fall for me tend to get their hearts not so much broken as disintegrated into their component molecules. So watch *yourself*, Joshua." *Was that too presumptuous? Am I giving myself too much credit?* He was a lovetalker. He could have anyone. Really, why would she assume she was anything more than a passing fancy for him?

But he only nodded, still serious, and said, "Duly noted. You know the way very wealthy people often worry whether anyone loves them for *themselves*, or if all who profess adoration for them are merely pretending love to disguise greed?"

"Sure," Marla said, seeing where this was going, a little uneasy about how to respond.

"Well. You can imagine how it must be for me. I can never tell if anyone likes me for myself. Most people are wholly unaware of my 'self.' I am just . . . a projection to them. A smell, a taste, a touch, a fantasy, something they adore because it is my nature to be adored, and they do not look at me as a human being. But I *am* a person, Marla, and it can be very lonely to be universally loved. Sometimes, I wonder if it might be possible to rid myself of this power, and live the way other people do." He paused. "But then I remember how much I enjoy oral sex and caviar on demand, and I resign myself to my lot."

Marla laughed. "Joshua, I believe you just made a *joke.*"

He raised one eyebrow. "Sometimes I surprise even myself."

The limo pulled up in front of her building, and Marla activated the intercom to speak to the driver. "We'll let ourselves out. No need for you to go into the cold." She opened her door and stepped onto the sidewalk, and Joshua scooted over to let himself out after her.

The limo drove away, a black shadow swallowed by the cold night, and Joshua looked up at Marla's building. She saw it with fresh eyes, the way he surely did, as a battered old flophouse that probably warranted demolition. But she loved the place, and she pointed, saying, "See the gargoyles up there, on the corners by the roof? They're replicas of famous gargoyles, from Notre Dame and Duke University, and other places. There's only one that's original, that one there on the left that looks like a lizard with a rooster comb. The gargoyles were the first thing that attracted me to this place. I've looked at the old building plans, and there's no mention of that kind of architectural flourish. Somebody added them after the fact, and I don't know who—the construction site boss, the first owner, who knows? They're totally ornamental, not even real waterspouts."

"Are they . . . magical?" Joshua said, clearly trying

to understand the appeal. "Do they watch the street for you, or come to life, or anything like that?"

"Nah," Marla said. "They're just statues. I could make them come to life, but they wouldn't move too gracefully, and they probably wouldn't be inclined to hang out on my building anymore. Come on up. My place isn't much to look at, but it's private, and warm." She led him through the dusty lobby to the elevator, slid open the grate, and gestured for him to enter. They rode up to the fifth floor in silence, and when they stepped out into her hallway, Joshua said, "You know, if you weren't the undisputed ruler of the supernatural side of Felport, I would feel like I was slumming."

"Yeah, well, I like to keep people guessing. Besides, compared to how I grew up, this is palatial. There's a magical ward on the place to keep the roaches out, it's likewise magically climate-controlled, the roof doesn't leak, and best of all, I've got the *whole* building to myself." Which wasn't strictly true. The cantankerous ghost of a pensioner who'd died here in the flophouse days lived on the third floor, but he was only manifest two or three times a month. "I used to have magical wards set up to keep out intruders, but a couple of street kids got hurt when they tried to break in last winter, so now the nasty spells are limited to the doors and windows of my apartment. I don't care if the occasional homeless guy seeks shelter in the lobby."

Marla touched certain runes hacked into the frame around her door, blocking her movements from Joshua's view with her body, not because she distrusted him necessarily, but out of simple secret-keeping habit. The runes flared blue for a moment, then went dark, and she pushed open the door and gestured for Joshua to enter.

She showed him where to find the bathroom when he asked, tried briefly to tidy up a bit, then quit, annoyed at herself for even making the effort.

When Joshua rejoined her in the living room, she pointed him toward the futon, currently folded to look more or less like a couch. He sank onto it with that persistent look of cognitive dissonance on his face. Marla could understand it—Hamil was her consiglieri, lower in the city's hierarchy than herself, and his apartments were modern and comfortable. Marla resisted the urge to spout some justification about the state of her living space, something about the magical potential of relative squalor, but the truth was she just couldn't be bothered to work on the place. It wasn't like she spent much time at home, and she couldn't remember the last time she'd actually entertained a guest.

"Want a drink?" she asked instead, trying to wrest control of the situation back; letting Joshua take charge would be too much like letting water run downhill, so easy and obvious it felt like a law of nature. She crossed to her liquor cabinet—really just an old desk she'd liberated from a street corner. Marla very seldom drank, but she kept a few things on hand for when Hamil or Rondeau came over.

"Brandy?"

"Yeah, I think Hamil finally broke down and brought a bottle to keep here."

Joshua stretched out his arms along the back of the futon, which suited him like a throne. Marla took a pair of slightly dusty shot glasses from a drawer, wiped them clean, and tipped out a measure of brandy. "No snifters. Around here, you have to improvise." She handed him a drink.

"I'm good at improvisation. Cheers." Joshua raised his glass.

Marla clinked hers against his and tossed her drink back, which wasn't the right way to drink brandy, but whatever. It hit her stomach fast and fiery, and, if only psychologically, helped her relax a bit. She thought about Joshua, how pretty he was, how unknown, how brave he'd been when they fell down the rabbit hole into Genevieve's world. Before that, he'd been merely tasty. Now, after seeing him deal with a crisis, she was beginning to think of him as a *prospect*. Marla had not hoped for love since she was a teenager. Romance was for other people. She believed romance was *real,* but that she was no more likely to succumb to it than she was to develop male pattern baldness or die from spontaneous human combustion. Now, with Joshua, she dared to hope, and even though she *knew* he had magics to win her heart and mind, she couldn't help hoping there was something genuine underneath, a core of true connection. Maybe she was fooling herself. But then, he did choose to be with her tonight, when he could have had anyone. So screw it. Even if there was nothing more to this than a romp, didn't she deserve a romp?

He leaned in toward her, cupping her chin in his hands, and murmured some compliment. They kissed, curling together, the taste of brandy on his mouth, on her lips; underneath, the taste of him, the delicious mouth of a lovetalker. After a while, she pulled away, and looked at him searchingly. His expression was open, inviting, up for anything. "Bedroom," she said, tugging him up by the hand and leading him toward her room, a slow process as they paused along the way to pull each other's clothes off. They tumbled onto the bed, their hands reaching everywhere, trying to touch each other all over at once.

"I want—" Joshua said, and Marla had the presence of mind to slip a finger into his mouth to keep him quiet. He *was* a lovetalker, after all, impossible to resist, and Marla knew she'd be lost if he started giving her instructions. She wouldn't be able to disobey, and then she'd be just another of his many conquests, an eager submissive desperate to please him, and whatever mystique she'd covered herself in by being a forceful dominant woman would disintegrate.

"I've got an idea," she said, grinning, and managed to tear herself away long enough to get off the bed and kneel by a cabinet. She slid open a drawer and pawed through until she found what she was looking for, a bundle of black silk scarves. Joshua was spread out on her flannel sheets, eyes half-closed. Gods, he was luscious. She climbed into bed and draped a silk scarf over his belly, making him laugh. Maybe this was too kinky for him—her last relationship had been with an incubus, and that kind of involvement tended to skew one's sense of propriety.

She held up a scarf. "Feeling playful?"

"Of course."

"Open your mouth."

"Yes, ma'am," he said, and she told him to sit up. She gave him a deep kiss, then pulled away, balled up the scarf, and tucked it into his still-open mouth. She used another scarf, tied around his head, to hold in the gag. "Too tight?" she asked, and he shook his head. She took Joshua's wrist and bound it swiftly to the headboard with a scarf, not too tightly, then straddled his chest and bound the other wrist. She looked down at him. He was heavenly in the lamplight, his skin golden and unblemished (she thought fleetingly of her own many scars, and wanted him to kiss every one), the black scarves a gorgeous contrast to his flesh. And those eyes, begging her for pleasure, acknowledging her control over that pleasure; oh, yes, this was the essence of good sex. He was just as beautiful and supernaturally charismatic without his voice, but with him silenced, she could keep herself from fulfilling his every whim, and instead fulfill some of her own.

"My beautiful boy," she murmured, and leaned down to kiss his neck. She reached down, touched him, guided him in, and began to move gently on his body. She was about to whisper something in his ear when she heard the rattle of coat hangers and a soft footstep from the closet.

Why now? She moaned inwardly, not with pleasure but with frustration, then rolled herself off Joshua so she could do whatever proved necessary.

9

Zealand was first surprised, and then annoyed, when he heard a man's voice coming from the living room along with Marla's. He would almost certainly have to kill the man, too, and he hated killing people for free. He kept his eyes on the screen of his surveillance device, wishing he'd thought to bug the living room for audio—he hadn't expected there to be conversation to overhear. He preferred knowing what to expect, but whatever happened, he'd deal with it—in his line of work, improvisation was often necessary.

Then Marla and the man—the beautiful, beautiful man, whom he'd never seen up close before—rushed naked into the bedroom and tumbled into bed. Zealand grunted. He hadn't expected *this*. He'd gotten more of a warrior ascetic vibe from Marla, and Gregor had said that, as far as he knew, she had no lovers at the moment. Watching the lovemaking itself bored him, but this man was so incredibly *captivating*. Zealand's own taste in men was broad and wide-ranging, but this was the most beautiful human being he'd ever seen. The slim hips, the artfully mussed hair, the skin . . . Zealand noticed himself beginning to breathe heavily and forced himself to look away from the screen until his exhalations were under control. He could still see the man in his mind, though, stretching languidly on the bed . . . and he had to be fucking *Marla*. Had to be a breeder. What a waste. Still, perhaps Zealand could eliminate Marla and keep the beautiful man alive, take him to Gregor, and exchange his fee for some sort of love spell . . . it wasn't a terribly *practical* idea, but oh, it was appealing.

He looked back at the screen in time to see Marla gagging the man. Zealand could think of *much* better uses for such a mouth. Then Marla bound the boy to the bed with scarves and straddled him. Zealand wasn't terribly kinky, himself, though he could see the appeal of power and control, and it didn't surprise him to discover that Marla liked tying knots and being on top. And now that she *was* on top . . .

Ah. There was a possibility here. Zealand's adjusted plan had been to wait for Marla and the man to fuck themselves into exhaustion, then creep out of the closet and put a knife through Marla's eye, into her brain. But now the man was tied down—effectively neutralizing him as a threat—and Marla's back was turned. She was gasping, and the man was moaning around his gag, and they both seemed utterly absorbed. What better time to strike than now?

Zealand set his surveillance screen aside and eased open the closet door, slowly, slowly, so as not to create any breeze against Marla's bare back. He took a garrote from his pocket—the easiest strike from here would be to loop the wire around Marla's throat from behind and jerk her backward off the man.

Then Marla leaned forward, laying her body on top of her lover, and Zealand stifled a sigh. He placed the garrote on the floor and unsheathed a hunting knife. He would creep a few steps closer, then leap onto the bed, landing his weight on Marla's back and driving the blade through her back and into her heart, if his aim was good. And even if it wasn't, well, he could just pull the knife out and plunge it in again. Marla was strong, but Zealand weighed about 240 pounds, and she wasn't *that* strong. She'd have a hard time using magic on him with a knife ripping into her back, too.

He took a step—and then the vertigo that had assailed him on the street before hit him again, making him stumble. His shoulder touched a coat hanger, which clattered into *another* hanger, and for a moment the whole room flickered, replaced by a vast plain of yellowed ivory, dotted by a pool of green that might have been an algae-covered lake in the middle distance and mountains far beyond. He squeezed his eyes shut for a moment, opened them, and was relieved to see the room had returned to normal. His balance seemed mostly restored, too, the vertigo more a breaker than a tidal wave this time.

He was rather less relieved to see Marla roll off her lover and fall to the floor in a crouch. She spun to face him, then reached under the dresser and came out with a knife of her own—well, of course, she was the type to have weapons secreted around her room, wasn't she? Zealand cursed. This wasn't an assassination anymore. This was *combat,* and he was much less comfortable with that, though he could manage in a pinch. Marla's lover was bleating through his gag and jerking around on the bed, trying to get out of his bonds, but for now, he was still irrelevant to the situation. Zealand hesitated for a moment over the choice of weapons—he had a pistol holstered under his arm and a stun gun hanging from his belt—and by then Marla had *launched* herself at him. He rolled out of the way, pulling the stun gun loose, and when she came at him again he brought the flat black device up, hitting her firmly in the breastbone, and pulled the trigger. Light pulsed from the weapon. There was a chance a stun gun to the heart could kill her, but she just cried out and fell to the ground, twitching and writhing. Only when she fell away did Zealand notice the bloody knife on the floor and register the pain in his arm—her knife-strike had hit his shoulder, the blade sliding across and gashing him. She'd been aiming for his neck, probably.

The beautiful man on the bed moaned.

Zealand took a moment to look at his body. "We'll talk later. And maybe do more than talk. But first . . ." He glanced down at Marla, who was staring up at him, her body twisted at the foot of the bed. He reached for the pistol under his arm.

Fucking stun gun. Marla had been hit with one before, and it had taken her a couple of minutes to get her power of movement back then. She didn't have a couple of minutes here. The knots holding Joshua weren't all that tight, but even if he did free himself, he was a lover, not a fighter. And since he was gagged, he couldn't even sweet-talk this man into laying down his arms.

The attacker was a stranger to Marla—he was tall and broad, dressed casually, dark hair, face lined and middle-aged. He was clearly skilled, a pro, so—shit. "Zealand," she slurred.

He looked at her, surprised, his pistol half drawn from its holster. She was gratified to see blood running down his arm. Made her wish she'd poisoned her knife, though having poisoned knives hidden around the place was a bad idea for obvious reasons. Then he nodded. "Ms. Mason. Nice to meet you. Sorry about all this. Just business."

He *was* the renegade slow assassin, then, here in town for a job—and she was apparently the job. Who'd hired him? She didn't bother asking. He wouldn't answer willingly, and she didn't have the leverage to force him.

It occurred to Marla that she was about to die with an assassin's bullet in her head, and she wouldn't even know who to blame.

She couldn't work magic—she was too paralyzed for gestural spells, and purely vocal spells were beyond her ability at the moment, too. Incantatory magic tended to be complex, and she couldn't manage much more than muttering curse words—

Or maybe even Curse words. Rondeau was teaching her to swear the way he did, misshapen syllables of creation that rippled reality. You could never be sure what the effects would be, but she was about to be killed, and it wasn't likely to be worse than *that.*

So she Cursed, a string of guttural syllables that felt as if they tore her throat coming out.

The ornate mirror on the wall *jumped,* glass breaking as it moved, and slammed into Zealand's back. He spun, looking behind him, and she Cursed again. The lamp on her bedside table exploded with a noise like a gunshot, and the iron bed-frame groaned as if it were bending, bringing a sound of alarm from the still-bound Joshua. Zealand looked around wildly, and Marla Cursed again. The room jolted as if in an earthquake, her night table fell over, and car alarms began going off in the street. Marla still couldn't move, and by now Zealand had realized she was doing this, somehow. He pointed his gun at her.

Desperate, she Cursed once more.

The lights in the apartment brightened, the vibrator by the bed came on with a buzz, her clock radio began blaring industrial music at earsplitting volume, and the stun gun hanging from Zealand's belt pulsed brightly. He fell like a bag of sand, and Marla managed to grin. A quarter second of contact from a stun gun was enough to repel someone, and a couple of seconds was enough to put them in the state Marla was in now. The stun gun had buzzed against Zealand's body for five or six seconds before the effects of the Curse dwindled and the weapon turned off, along with the radio and the vibrator.

The bed creaked, and Joshua sat up, having finally managed to free his arms. He pulled the gag off and tossed it aside. "Are you all right, Marla?"

"Ngh," Marla said. All that Cursing had tired her out. She was beginning to feel some measure of muscle control returning, but she couldn't get up yet. "Yes," she managed.

"Who *is* that man?"

"Killer," she said. "Help."

"I was afraid he'd murdered you." Joshua crawled

across the bed and looked down at her. His face above her was lovely, his expression one of infinite concern and tenderness.

"Tie . . . up. Him," she said.

"Ah," Joshua said, and went to get the scarves from the headboard. He returned, kneeling by Zealand. Marla managed to sit up, finally, though she still felt all jangly and stretched out.

"Lousy date," she said. "Sorry 'bout that."

"Still interesting, though."

Marla prodded Zealand with her foot. He groaned. "I won't kill you if you give me an alternative," she said. "But I am going to need to know who sent you. I know, code of killers, yadda yadda, but you bailed on the slow assassins, so I know you don't have *that* much honor."

"I . . . feel . . . dizzy," Zealand said. Joshua was tying his wrists together quickly and efficiently.

"I'd think so," Marla said. "I sure as shit did when you hit me with that stunner."

"No . . . this . . . different," he said. And then he disappeared.

Joshua sat, holding the silk scarves in his hands. They were still knotted, but the wrists they'd been tied around had disappeared. "Magic," he said.

Marla groaned. "Damn it. *That's* a good trick. Wish I'd invested in some teleportation of my own. Shit." She glanced around. "At least I've got some of his *stuff*, though. He dropped a garrote and a knife along with the gun, and he's got a whole bag back in the closet, it looks like. I can get Langford to track him using that, assuming they're possessions he's owned for a while. We can keep him from flitting away again, and then I'll find out who wants me dead *this* week. I—"

Joshua reached out and put a hand on her knee. She stopped talking and looked at him, captivated by his regard. "I'm hungry," he said. "Let's order Chinese food."

Marla stared at him for a minute, then started laughing. "I had Chinese earlier. How do you feel about Thai?"

"I feel pretty good about it."

Zealand lay staring at the ceiling as that beautiful, beautiful man tied him up, wishing desperately that their positions were reversed. He was a big man, with a strong constitution, but he didn't think he'd recover from the effects of the stun gun for several minutes, and by then Marla would be in a position to make him talk. Or worse. She knew his name, which meant she'd probably spoken to one of the other slow assassins, maybe even Kardec himself. Marla might be willing to let him live if he cooperated, but his former brothers and sisters would not. They were patient, though. They'd let him die *slowly.* He resolved to tell Marla whatever she wanted to know in exchange for freedom. After he left town, he'd return the advance portion of his payment to Gregor. He rather doubted Gregor would be alive to receive it, of course—not after he told Marla that Gregor was the one who'd paid for her death—but Zealand was an honest man when it came to his business dealings.

Then, abruptly, with another wave of vertigo, the eggshell-white ceiling was gone, replaced by a sky so blue it made his eyes water. The floor beneath him was no longer ancient carpet but something hard and smooth, marble or another polished stone. There was no sun in evidence, but the place was bright all the same, and the smell was utterly different from that of Marla's musty apartment—there was a whiff of something green, and something more acrid and even faintly poisonous, like a strip-mined hillside after a hard rain. *What now?* Was this some sort of extra-dimensional holding cell Marla had sent him to?

He tried to move, and to his surprise, discovered that he could. Everything still felt jangled in the wake of the stun gun's jolt, but he was in control of his movements again. He stood up and kicked the ground. It was yellowish-white, the same plain he'd glimpsed when the vertigo hit him in Marla's closet. Maybe this place didn't have anything to do with her. There was nothing on the horizon but faraway mountains and a swath of bright green, so in the absence of other options, he began walking toward the green. He did an inventory as he walked, and the situation was not good. He had his cell phone, but it didn't get any reception here, of course. The only weapons he had left were a pair of brass knuckles in his inner jacket pocket and the stun gun at his belt, which he was tempted to hurl away.

Maybe there would be water in the green place. He was very thirsty, though it wasn't particularly hot here. Perhaps there'd be a convenient portal back to the reality he knew as well. He resolved not to panic. Yes, he was in a strange place, perhaps not even an earthly place, but Zealand was a pragmatist. He would cope.

After perhaps half an hour of walking—time was

hard to judge here—he reached the green place. It was vaster than he had supposed, an irregular blob the size of several football fields, faintly glistening. It didn't look like living plant matter so much as a carpet of old vegetables, and it smelled like . . . spinach. He knelt at the edge of the blob and reached down, tugging at the green, to see if it was somehow rooted in this stony ground, but no, it was just lying there, like the world's biggest compost heap. He brushed the green stuff off his hands, wishing for something to wipe them on beside his pants.

"I remember his breath," someone said behind him, and Zealand whirled, hand going for his stun gun.

The woman standing before him—and where had she *come* from? He had sight lines endlessly in all directions!—was familiar. Wild, caramel-colored hair. Violet eyes. A yellow dress, a black scarf. He'd seen her lying in the snow, hadn't he? Marla had draped her coat over this woman. "What is this place? What have you done to me?"

She didn't look at him, but at the green. "His breath was hot, and smelled like spinach. He had a cavity in one of his teeth, I could *see* it, a little black crater. His teeth were straight but yellowed. His mouth hung before my eyes, his breath on my face." She shuddered.

"Tell me who you are."

Now she looked at him. "I'm Genevieve. I couldn't let you die, be captured, not there, not then. I need your help."

Zealand laughed. "My help is quite expensive, though I suppose if you snatched me from Marla's clutches, that counts as a down payment. And letting me leave this place might convince me to lower my rates still further."

She took a step toward him. "Will you be my protector? My knight?" Something like a smile touched her lips. "My . . . green knight, protecting his lady?"

"I'm no knight, and I'm not even remotely interested in ladies."

"I know that. It makes me feel safer." Now she looked to the horizon. "He'll come for me soon. He'll storm my castle. Do you see? My castle?"

Suspecting a trick, he turned his head, and saw a tower of opalescent stone, with arched windows, and yellow banners flying from silver poles. The same vision he'd seen on the way to Marla's apartment. "That's . . . your castle?"

"My stronghold," she said. "It moves, just like *his*. But his moves faster. And he is closing in."

"Who?"

"Reave. He lives in the black tower. He marshals nightmares. He hurts me forever and ever and over and over."

"If you take me back to Felport—and promise other compensations—I'll kill him for you," Zealand said. He stared at the palace. It did not look made. It looked as if it had grown, like a conch shell or a crystal.

"He'll come for me," she said, as if she hadn't heard him. "And you will protect me."

"If I can," Zealand said. He tore his eyes away from the glimmering palace. "Assuming I'll be rewarded."

"I can give you things," she said simply.

"I like things." His gaze slipped back to the palace.

"Beautiful things. When do you think he'll come for you?"

"Yesterday, and tomorrow, and forever," she said, sadly, then sighed. "Good-bye, green knight."

"What do you—" Everything tilted, and Zealand gasped as cold ripped through him. He'd left his coat in the other apartment, the one where he'd cut through the wall, and now he was outside, in the ice and snow. He groaned and sat up, looking around, seeing only barred storefronts and empty sidewalks. He didn't know where he was, but then he saw the glowing tip of the Whitcroft-Ivory building, the tallest skyscraper in Felport, and his mental map of the city oriented itself accordingly. He hugged himself and limped in the direction of the hotel where he was staying.

Who was that woman? Genevieve? What did she have to do with . . . anything? She was a sorcerer, and she was trying to involve him in her business. He shouldn't have been interested—he should only be interested in getting out of Felport before Marla could track him down. But that palace of hers had been so lovely, almost as beautiful in its way as Marla's lover, and he wanted to pass through its doors, see its walls. If this other man, Reave, wanted to storm that castle, Zealand wanted to defend it.

He wondered, briefly, if he'd been ensorcelled. Possibly. But he wasn't sure what he could do about it.

The cell phone in his pocket vibrated. He'd had it turned off in Marla's apartment, of course, but he'd turned it on in that . . . other place . . . and hadn't thought to deactivate it again. Zealand sighed and looked at the readout. It was Nicolette, calling to see how things were progressing, no doubt. It wasn't a call he *wanted* to take, but he was a businessman, so he did.

"It's all fucked," he said. "Marla fought me off. I escaped, and didn't give her any information, but she knows who I am, she said my name. The element of surprise is lost. I'm sure she'll be on her guard against further attacks now."

"You just fed me a big shit sandwich, Zealand," she said. "The boss man isn't going to be happy about this at *all*. But, hell, I figured something went wrong, I had a fishbowl full of 'chanted guppies swimming around, and every single one of them floated belly-up about thirty minutes ago. Gregor's gonna want to talk to you."

"I'm sure," Zealand said, grimacing. "Can you send a car?" He gave her the address of the nearest corner.

"Sure," Nicolette said. "But you're gonna have to reimburse us for mileage. I've got a feeling you're off the payroll."

"A shame. I did so enjoy this job." He flipped the phone closed. Gregor would bawl him out, possibly even try to kill him, though Zealand doubted it—Gregor was a cautious man. He'd want to know *exactly* what happened, how the assassination attempt went wrong. And what would Zealand tell him? The truth? Maybe. Gregor knew many things, and he might have some idea who this woman Genevieve was. Sorcerers were always poking into one another's business.

The back of his hand itched a little. He scratched it and felt something strange. Peering closer, he saw a little speck of green. He tried to rub it away, but it didn't come off, and his hands were cold, so he shoved them in his pockets. He'd shower later. Dirty hands were the least of his problems now.

He stood stomping his feet until the car came, driven by a surly kid who looked like he'd been kicked roughly out of bed. Zealand rode up front with him; he figured it was *possible* the boy was supposed to drive him to the waterfront, kill him, and dump his body there, and Zealand was opposed to that. Instead the boy just yawned hugely every few minutes and without speaking drove toward Gregor's high-rise. He parked in the garage underneath, pointed Zealand toward the elevator, then walked off on his own.

Zealand rode the elevator up, up, up. Nicolette waited for him in the gleaming hallway, chewing on her fingernails, which were painted in a rainbow of colors. "Marla's people haven't called," she said. "So *that's* good. But shit is crazy here, so don't fuck around, okay? Just tell the boss what happened. And ignore the new guy. He's been hanging around the past couple of days, but it's nothing to do with you." She beckoned and led Zealand into Gregor's office. A man stood by the window, looking out over the city, his bald head weirdly soft-looking, his black shiny coat like something from a noir sci-fi movie.

"Gregor," Zealand said, nodding to the sorcerer, who sat behind his desk massaging his temples. "Who's the new guy?"

Nicolette kicked him in the ankle, but the stranger turned from the window and looked Zealand up and down. "My name is Reave."

Zealand kept his face still. The spot on the back of

his hand began to itch more furiously. "Pleasure to meet you."

"I understand you failed to kill a *woman,*" Reave said, and sniffed. "I can hardly say it's a pleasure to meet *you.*"

Zealand wondered if he could kill Reave right now. If the windows were breakable, he could hit the man and drive him out, but that would kill them *both,* and if Zealand died, he would never see the inside of that opalescent castle or receive the rewards Genevieve could offer. Better to bide his time. "These things happen," Zealand said. He turned to Gregor. "I'll return the funds you paid me, of course. And if you're willing to wait some time, I can try to kill her again. She'll be on her guard for a while, I'm sure, but she'll grow impatient with caution, I suspect."

"I should have known it wouldn't be so simple," Gregor said. "The divinations were inconclusive—it seemed *possible* you might succeed. But Marla has more lives than an alley cat. You gave her no information? Didn't mention my name, or Nicolette's?"

"I am, at least, that much of a professional," Zealand said. "No, I did not mention your name. I'm willing to leave the city, of course."

"No," Gregor said. "You left things behind, didn't you?"

Zealand considered lying, but doubted he would be able to hide the truth. "A few things. Weapons. No fingerprints, of course, but—"

"She doesn't need fingerprints. If you owned those items for more than a few days, there will be . . . psychic associations. If you leave, she *will* be able to track you. While you're inside this building, however, she can't trace you. I have defenses against that sort of peering-in. Even if you leave Felport, it won't deter her. She might be reluctant to leave the city personally, but she wouldn't hesitate to send Rondeau or Hamil or one of her employees after you. And she *could* extract information from you. I can't let her discover I was involved in this."

"Ah. So I'm to be your . . . guest here?"

Nicolette snorted. "We won't put you in a dungeon, but you'll be a prisoner, no doubt."

"For how long?"

Gregor shrugged. "Until Marla is dead. Or I am. Or seven years, by which time every cell of your body will be new, and she won't be able to track you anymore." He leaned back in his chair. "Arguments?"

Zealand shrugged. "I could use a vacation. Provide me with some books, decent food, and other amenities, and I'm content to stay for a while."

Gregor gestured. "Get him set up in one of the visitor apartments, Nicolette. I have to discuss things with Reave."

Nicolette gestured, and Zealand followed. When they were in the elevator, he said, "The new fellow seems very unpleasant."

"He won't even talk to me," she said. "Because I don't have a dick, apparently. You hear the way he sneered when he said 'woman'? That's a man with *issues*. But Gregor thinks he's worth working with, so . . ." She shrugged.

"Seven years," Zealand mused. "That's a long vacation."

"Shit," Nicolette said. "You won't be stuck here that long. Things are in motion. Something's going to break, and soon. Marla, or, gods forbid, Gregor. Or, hell, everything else. My boss's auguries are all fucked up, but I don't care. Chaos is in the air, possible futures multiplying, and me and chaos, we get along just fine. I don't expect the next days or weeks to be peaceful ones."

"And yet I'll somehow content myself with reading and relaxing," Zealand said. And if he had the chance, he would kill Reave. He'd had enough of working for men like Gregor, of running from slow assassins, of doing dark deeds for money and entertainment. This world, and his work, bored him more and more, and the sight of Genevieve's castle had been a glimpse of another kind of world, another kind of life, something sweet and transcendent.

Zealand scratched idly at the spot of green on the back of his hand.

10

Marla dropped a sack of bagels on the battered table in Rondeau's kitchenette, just outside her office, and said, "Morning, Rondeau. I brought breakfast."

Rondeau slowly lowered his racing form, showing the sleeves of his seersucker suit. Rondeau was never one to heed the dictates of fashion, even seasonal ones. "Marla. You never bring breakfast. What's wrong?"

She rolled her eyes, sloughing off her coat and dropping it on the back of a chair. "Nothing's wrong. I went past the bagel shop, it smelled good, I stopped in and got a dozen. We've got a busy day ahead of us, so I figured breakfast would be a good thing."

Rondeau leaned forward, unrolled the bagel bag, stuck his face in, and inhaled. "Garlic, tomato and basil, jalapeño, and, um, everything." He looked up at Marla. "You have a really weird energy this morning, Marla."

"'Weird energy'? What, are you seeing Lorelei again? She's a bad influence on you. Next thing, you'll be using crystals for deodorant."

"Lorelei is a very spiritual person." He removed a bagel and a plastic knife, and began sawing ineffectually at an onion bagel, bits of mauled bread flying. "You slept with Joshua last night, didn't you?"

"I'm sorry, are you asking me about my personal life? Don't we have a rule against that?" Marla took a tomato basil bagel from the bag and slipped one of her daggers from its wrist sheath to neatly halve it. She felt vaguely guilty for using a weapon as a utensil, but she wasn't about to hack away with plastic like Rondeau was doing; style counted for something.

"No, there's no rule." Rondeau had given up on cutting the bagel, and was now tearing it into bite-sized chunks and dipping them in a container of garlic cream cheese. "You've told me you don't want to hear about *my* personal life, but you never said I shouldn't ask about yours. Of course, you never *had* a personal life before, except for the incubus, and no offense, but that's practically masturbating. And, wait, you still don't have a personal life, because Joshua *work*s for you, so I guess this is a business thing? Isn't that sexual harassment or something?"

"I never said I slept with him."

"It's so weird to see you being coy. And in a good mood. Both of those. Weird. Weird energy." He dipped a chunk of bagel and took a bite.

"If you double-dip that, Rondeau, so help me, you'll never eat again, except maybe through a straw."

He grunted, chewed, and swallowed. "Still, it doesn't seem right. Dipping the pen in the company well."

"The what in the what, now?"

"Shagging the help! Did you buy juice? I need a

drink. I'm not used to eating great big wads of bread first thing in the morning."

"No juice. Make coffee. Weren't you the one begging me to hire a nineteen-year-old with flexible morals as my p.a., so *you* could shag the help?"

"That's different. I wouldn't have been her *boss*. It would've been a tender understanding between coworkers, not a weird power-dynamic thing. So—did you sleep with him?"

Rondeau was her closest friend, and he was in no moral position to judge, so . . . "Yeah. I did. Last night."

"I knew it. You've been stuck to him like a bug on flypaper since you hired him, so I figured it was inevitable. Was it great? I know he's a lovetalker and all, but *damn,* I'd sleep with him, and I only like boys on special occasions."

"Yeah, it was pretty great. Until someone tried to assassinate me."

Rondeau whistled. "In flagrante delicto? Shitty timing. Anybody we know?"

"That renegade slow assassin, Zealand. As for who *hired* him, I dunno, but I'll find out. I need to call a meeting. Where's Ted?"

"In your office. He's been working since, like, six this morning." He rolled his eyes. "Just like every morning. The guy's dedicated. Hey, Ted!" he called.

Ted emerged from her office. "Oh, Marla, sorry, I didn't know you were here."

"Eat a bagel," Marla said. "Then I've got a bunch of work for you to do." Almost being killed last night had been a wake-up call. Sure, she wanted to explore this thing with Joshua, but she did have business to attend to, and she was willing to admit—at least to herself—that she'd been shirking her work a little bit in the glow of new romance.

Ted sat down with them and Marla talked while he ate. "I need a conference, ASAP. Lunchtime is fine, I guess. I need Hamil here, and you, Rondeau, and Langford, and Dr. Husch, too, but she can be on speakerphone, and this guy named Kardec, I'd like him here in person, you can find his number—"

"I have it," Ted said. He had a little personal electronic organizer—she vaguely recalled him asking for the money to buy one—and he was jabbing away at it. "I entered all the business cards on your desk here, I remember seeing his because the name was so unusual. Should I tell them it's about any particular business?"

"Tell 'em it's a matter of life and death. And I guess make sure there's some food here for us to eat. We'll have the meeting in the special conference room downstairs. I'll show it to you later."

Ted nodded. "May I use your office to make the calls?"

"Knock yourself out," she said, and Ted departed, carrying a bagel with him.

Marla cocked an eyebrow at Rondeau. "So what do you think of Ted, now that you've had some time to get to know him?"

"He's been coming down and having a couple of drinks at night, helping me close up the club, so we've hung out. I guess he's all right. I mean, given that you picked him *totally* at *random* off the street, you could've done a lot worse."

"Eh, I had a good feeling about him. And anyway, random is safest. If we'd actually put out an ad and interviewed people, there would've been spies, moles, maybe even *assassins,* the way things are going."

"So it's like a double-blind hiring process," Rondeau said. "You don't know who you're going to hire, and *they* don't know they might be hired, so everybody's surprised." He shook his head. "I guess that actually makes sense under the circumstances. Anyway, Ted's been sleeping on the futon in my living room . . . weren't you going to set him up with an apartment in your building? I mean, not to be inhospitable, but my hot water heater sucks, and since he's up early and gets first shower, my ass has been frozen the past few days."

Marla chewed a mouthful of bagel, giving herself a moment to come up with an answer. She'd totally forgotten about Ted's living situation. She hadn't even *thought* about it. Maybe she was spending a little too much time with Joshua. It was just hard to think about doing anything else when he was in the vicinity. She swallowed. "Yeah, I'll see about moving him in tomorrow, deal?"

"Fair enough. You need me this morning?"

Marla shrugged. "Be here at noon for the meeting, otherwise, I don't think so. Why?"

He waved the racing form at her.

Marla sighed. "You're still gambling?"

Rondeau shrugged. "Yeah, you know. Here and there."

"Horse racing isn't your usual thing."

"I had a run of bad luck at the other places. I'm trying to change up my games."

"What, you've been gambling at those joints what's-her-name runs? Gregor's dogsbody?"

"Nicolette," Rondeau said. "Chaos magician. It's all craps and roulette and stuff in the places she runs, no poker or blackjack or anything where skill can help. She *really* digs games of chance, and she doesn't even cheat, just draws energy from all the cascading randomness, you know? And she makes money, of course, some of which ironically ends up in *your* pockets as tribute, and maybe even gets paid right back to me in salary, who knows. But my luck was pretty lousy last time I tried one of her joints, so I'm switching things up, like I said."

"Horse racing is basically random when you don't know anything about it," Marla pointed out. "And you *don't* know, unless you've been studying and I haven't noticed. Maybe you should consider poker?"

He rolled his eyes. "Marla. It's not like I have skill. At least when I lose at craps I can blame a cruel or indifferent universe. If I lose at poker, I gotta blame *myself,* and that plays hell with my self-esteem."

Marla laughed. "Well, go to the off-track betting place down on 9th, don't go all the way to the track, I might need you."

"You mean I don't get to enjoy the unparalleled beauty of watching large herbivorous mammals run in circles?" Rondeau said. "I'm crushed, because that's where the real thrill is for me." He stuffed a bagel in his jacket pocket, waved, and ambled off.

Marla perused the tattered remnants of the newspaper Rondeau had left scattered on the table—it was just the usual sorts of bad news, nothing she needed to get upset about, and her people had thus far succeeded in suppressing reports of the weird shit Genevieve had caused. Marla had let that stuff go on too long. Being distracted by Joshua was understandable, but not excusable. She went into her office and dropped onto the couch. Ted was sitting behind her desk, just hanging up the phone. "It's all arranged," he said. "Hamil, Langford, and Kardec will be here at 12:30, and Dr. Husch is scheduled for a conference call."

Marla raised an eyebrow. "That quickly? What, didn't any of them give you shit or argue with you?"

"No. Were you expecting them to?"

"I guess not," she said thoughtfully. If she'd made those calls personally, every one of them would have pestered her with various questions and demands, but since she had her assistant, someone with no *authority*, do it, they'd just said okay. This was working out better than she'd expected. Still, she needed to get to know the guy. She should have sat Ted down for a serious talk two days ago. "Good work. So, Ted . . . now that you're hired, maybe it's time I actually did an interview. How'd you wind up living on the streets?"

He visibly tensed for a moment. Then he removed his glasses and began rubbing the lenses with a handkerchief. Marla wondered if he'd taken his glasses off so he couldn't see her as well. "I made some mistakes, and had a run of bad luck."

"Was it booze? Rondeau said you've been coming down for a drink or three every night, and I was just worried. If it was booze, well, there are things we can do to help you cope with the cravings, you know? No need to let it get out of hand."

"I'm not an alcoholic. I've never had an addictive personality, except for chess. Well . . ." He shook his head. "Listen, I've been meaning to ask *you* a few questions, about what exactly your business is, and—"

"You start paying me, and I'll feel moved to answer your questions," Marla cut in. "And if you're not comfortable working for me without those details, well, hell, I'll miss you, but there's the door. If you want to continue working for me, though, Ted, I do need some answers. It didn't matter at first, because I figured there was a good chance you'd just try to steal all the money out of the cash box downstairs and disappear into the streets. But you stuck it out, and you seem to be serious about doing the job and doing it well, so I need a little info. Not your life story, just the *pertinent* parts. What did you do before you wound up sitting on Dutch Mulligan's grate?"

He put his glasses back on. The expression on his face was somehow simultaneously shamed and defiant. "I was a high-school math teacher."

Marla twirled her finger. "And?"

He shrugged. "I was fired. My wife divorced me. I had to move into a tiny apartment. My savings ran out before I could find a new job, and when I couldn't pay rent, I was evicted. I'd been on the streets for a few weeks when you found me and I fully expected to either die of hypothermia or be murdered in an overcrowded shelter. You saved my life, and I'm grateful, but—"

"Why'd you get fired?"

"Marla, I really need—"

"Answer me, Ted. Or do I have to make a couple of calls and find out from someone else?"

"I slept with one of my students," he said miserably.

"How old?" It was an important question.

"She was seventeen. I'm not a *pedophile*. It was inappropriate, wrong, I know that, but I'm not a child molester, despite the things they said about me."

"Well, judging by the stuff I see on the Internet, you're not in the minority for lusting after hot teens, but how stupid are you? I'm not exactly reassured about your good judgment. Was it some cheerleader who wanted an A in Algebra, or what? Did your brain get too overheated from the presence of all that teenage girlflesh?"

"It wasn't like that. She wasn't a cheerleader. I was an advisor for the chess club, and she was a member. Brittney. She's very good at the game, already nationally rated, quite brilliant, really, and we fell in love, I *thought* it was love. . . ." He sighed. "But, yes, it was stupid. We talked about running away together when she turned eighteen. But . . . we didn't wait until that happened to explore the physical side of our relationship. She told one of her friends, who then told Brittney's parents, and when they confronted her, she admitted it. And that was that. Neither my bosses at school nor Brittney's parents wanted publicity, so no charges were filed. I just 'resigned.' My wife divorced me, of course. That's all."

"You still talk to the girl?" Marla asked.

He shook his head. "She went off to college this fall. She sent me one letter, to say she was sorry for everything, she'd always remember me as her first love. . . . Well, she's young. I should have known better."

"Okay," Marla said after a moment. "No fucking underage girls on my watch, okay? They slip into the club from time to time, so before you get cozy with anybody you meet down there, you make damn sure they're legal. And if I find out there's anything more to your story than what you told me, we'll have words. Otherwise, though, we don't have a problem. You did a stupid thing, and you paid for it. Just don't do *another* stupid thing, and we're cool."

"Thank you, Marla," he said, looking down at the desk. She felt a little bad for dredging up his shame, but she'd needed to know.

He'd given his true confession. Maybe it was time for hers. "You wanted to know what I do for a living. What do you think?"

Ted looked her in the eye—that impressed her—and said, "Well, you have an office above a nightclub. You go to visit associates who work in warehouses. You sent me to fetch your car from a bad part of town. You keep peculiar hours. It's hard not to draw . . . certain conclusions."

"Such as?" She was trying hard not to smile.

"I assume you're involved in some sort of organized crime."

"You're half right," she said. "People have described my job as half crime boss, half superhero."

"Superhero?"

"Come on. Easier if I show you." She rose and Ted followed her out of the office.

"Where are we going?" he asked.

"Roof."

He stopped walking, and she turned. "I'm not going to throw you off or something, Ted, gods. Come on. This'll knock your socks off."

"Just let me get a coat—"

"No. Come on." She beckoned, and he came, reluctantly. She led him down a short hallway to the stairway that accessed the roof and sent him up ahead of her. He opened the door and stepped out onto the snow-covered roof. He hugged himself against the cold and turned to face her, breath steaming in puffs from his mouth.

Marla shut the door behind them and looked up at the gray sky. Flurries of snow were coming down, not too heavy yet, but there was a storm expected in a day or two.

"What are we doing up here?" Ted said.

"Time to show you something cool," Marla said, and snapped her fingers.

The roof fell away. They rose into the air surrounded by a bubble of warmth—or *seemed* to. This was actually an immersive illusion rather than actual flight, but there was no reason to explain the distinction to Ted just yet. Ted screamed and reached out for her, and she put her arm around his waist and made a soothing noise. "It's okay, Ted. I'm fully flight-rated. This is the superhero bit, you see?" She glanced at him, and his eyes were squeezed tight. "Come on, Ted, look around. It's not a view you'll get to see every day."

He opened one eye—that was a suitable compromise, she thought—and looked down. They stopped rising a moment later, hovering high enough that they could see the entirety of Felport below them, from the towering spire of the Whitcroft-Ivory building to the giant cranes by the port, the green-and-white swath of Fludd Park and the tiny houses where the students lived near Adler College, the bigger-than-it-seemed junkyard where the sorcerer Ernesto lived, the vast iron bridges spanning the Balsamo River. Felport was a dirty, asymmetrical jewel of a place, a city with a gridlike planned core surrounded by a messy improvisational sprawl, and she adored every back road and sewer grate and abandoned building of the place. "I'm a sorcerer, Ted. And my job is protecting Felport from the sort of problems you can't even imagine. If I do my job right, you and all the other ordinaries who live here never *need* to imagine them. I figured if I just told you that, you wouldn't believe me, but if I *showed* you . . ."

He loosened his grip on her, though she didn't take her arm away. He stared down at the gray morning city, where only a few cars were slowly navigating the icy streets. It was an illusion, but it was an accurate-to-the-millisecond illusion, so even if they weren't *actually* flying, the distinction was meaningless. Except this way they couldn't fall and kill themselves. They were really just still standing on the roof. "What *kind* of problems do you protect us from?"

"Well, there was an evil sorcerer with an army of birds once. Another nutcase wanted to raise a monstrous old god from the waters of the bay. An incursion of creatures we might as well call demons came up through the sewers last spring. A serial murderer—the Belly Killer, remember that, it was in all the papers?—who the police couldn't catch, because he had magical powers. That sort of thing."

"I'm a man of science, Marla. I know that sounds like something from a movie, but this . . . I don't know how I can accept this. Sorcery?" He shook his head, but still stared down, captivated. "I can see my old house from here," he said after a moment.

"If it helps, don't think of it as magic. Think of it as bleeding-edge science. There was a time when electric lights would've been evidence of supernatural power. Nowadays you can talk to people on the other side of the globe, instantly—make a claim like that a few hundred years ago and you would've been killed as a witch. Scientists are capable of splitting apart atoms and releasing incredible destructive energies. Sounds a whole lot like magic to me. Don't even get me started on biotech, or the weirdness of modern physics. Yeah, what I do looks impressive—hell, some of it *is* impressive, and hard as hell to pull off—but if it helps you, just tell yourself I have access to a world of science beyond your understanding."

"But . . . it's not science. It's not replicable. It's not something anyone can do."

She waved her free hand. It was an argument she'd heard before. "So? It just takes a combination of skill and a whole lot of practice. I mean, you can't give a random guy on the street a scalpel and expect him to perform brain surgery successfully, but we don't say brain surgeons are magical, even though there are some people who could *never* do that job successfully, no matter how much they practiced. Some people are born with perfect pitch, and that's not something you can *learn,* but we don't say it's 'magical.' The stuff I do, that people like me do . . . it's a way of changing the world. A way of messing with the root commands of the universe. We call it sorcery because that's a useful catchall term. There's a lot of it we don't understand ourselves. Some of us consort with gods and demons, but if you'd rather call them extra-dimensional aliens, you're welcome to. It's not any more or less accurate. And so what if some of the acts we perform seem dependent on the will of the magician or some inborn capability?"

Ted actually took a step away from her. He was

remarkably adaptable—he didn't even seem freaked out by the lack of a floor under his feet. "Is it really that simple? This sorcery is just aspects of the natural world that most people don't experience?"

"If it happens, it's part of the natural world, Ted. There's nothing in the universe that *isn't* natural. We say 'supernatural,' sure, but that's not exactly what we *mean.* Think of it like light. There's a visible spectrum that people can see. But there's light at both ends of the spectrum that we can't see naturally. That doesn't mean the infrared and ultraviolet parts of the spectrum are *unnatural.* Humans are pretty stupid, Ted. We have a nasty tendency to assume our own limitations are somehow the limits of the universe. That's one of the first prejudices sorcerers have to overcome."

"Could I be a sorcerer?" Ted said.

Marla shrugged. "There are a couple things I could give you that pretty much anybody could use. The same way you can use a TV without understanding how it *works.* As for giving you real power, who knows? We just met a few days ago. Some people are never going to be world-class athletes, no matter how hard they train, and some people who have the potential to be world-class just don't have the *will.* I don't know if you do. Maybe." She snapped her fingers again, and they were, abruptly, back on the roof, back in the cold. Ted stumbled, even though they hadn't actually *moved,* and she caught his arm to keep him from falling into the snow. "C'mon, Ted. You still need to make sure there's some food for our guests, right?"

Ted stared at her for a moment, then laughed. "Yes. I . . . yes. It's going to take me a while to get used to all this."

"As long as getting used to it doesn't stop you from getting your work done, take your time." Marla thought he was handling it pretty well so far. The magic-as-science angle comforted some people. Marla figured it was about half bullshit, herself—there were some things about magic that just seemed too flat-out *weird* for that kind of rationalization—but there was no reason to hit Ted with that kind of confusing distinction. She'd ease him into things.

As they went back downstairs, he said, "So, what . . . voodoo? Does that work? Kabalistic magic? Fortune-telling? Telekinesis? Clairvoyance? Necromancy?"

"All of it," Marla said. "Everything works . . . if you do it right. But it's really, really hard to do *any* of it right. Most people specialize. My associate Hamil is a master of sympathetic magic. There's a guy named Gregor who's good at seeing the future—and before you get started on free will and shit like that, it's more a way of collapsing probability waves and seeing what's most *likely,* or what the only possible outcome of a given course of action is, you know? It's about seeing *possible* futures, but if you narrow the parameters enough, some of those possibilities become the next best thing to certainties. He's richer than god. He's got a gift for real estate speculation and the futures market."

"What's your specialty?" he said.

"I specialize in beating the crap out of people, actually. I do a little of this, a little of that. I've never been interested in choosing a niche. I get bored too easily. A lot of people think I'm an ineffectual dilettante. Some of them even go on thinking that until I show them how effective I can be. I believe in adaptability, Ted.

Sure, if I go head to head with some sorcerer in their chosen specialty, they can beat me, but I have a lot more tricks up my sleeves than *any* of them do. If I ever need really high-level specialization, I just *hire* somebody to do it for me. Easy."

"I see. And what's Rondeau's specialty?"

Marla hesitated. It was, perhaps, a bit early in Ted's magical education to explain that Rondeau was actually a free-floating parasitic psychic entity of unknown origin, which had wrested control of his current body from the previous occupant when said occupant was only eight years old. "Rondeau doesn't have a specialty. He's not a sorcerer. He knows a few tricks, but he doesn't have the skill or the will to do much more. Still, he's one of the most valuable guys in my organization, loyal and flexible and trustworthy. You should see the shit he can do with a butterfly knife, too. Anyway, come on, I'll show you the special conference room."

She led him downstairs. "What do you know about the history of Felport, Ted?"

"Not much, I'm afraid."

"You know how it got its name?"

"Wasn't there an early settlement that was lost, and rumors that it was a haunted place?"

"Yep," Marla said. "It was 'the fell port,' meaning 'fell' as in 'dire, sinister, evil,' you know? A little settlement was lost, you're right, just a trading post, but whatever nasty thing killed all those people disappeared or went underground or something when more people settled here." They made it all the way downstairs, to the dance floor, and Marla took Ted down a short corridor, past the bathrooms, to what looked like a locked utility closet. She began sorting through her keys. It was a magically variable lock, and the correct key changed every day. "But Felport kept its reputation as a place where weird forces converged, and there were stories of witches' sabbats, weird rituals, places in the woods where no grass would grow. Things like that." She found the right key and opened the door, revealing a space that looked like a broom closet until she pressed the doorjamb in the right places to make the illusion of disinfectant and mops disappear. Ted gasped, and Marla grinned. "This club was built on top of one of those places where no grass would grow, a dead zone. Specifically, the room right in front of us is over that spot." The room itself was nondescript, just a conference table, a few chairs, and a bright lightbulb hanging from the ceiling. "It's funny, because people think places like that are dangerous, but this is actually the place where you're safest from magic. You can't cast spells here—it's like trying to light a wet match, it just doesn't work. It's also impossible to magically eavesdrop in here, or use clairvoyance to see inside, or find someone hidden here using magical divination. It's pretty sweet. We do dangerous business here, have sit-downs, things like that. Though it doesn't seem to hurt inherently magical things. Telepaths can still read minds, as long as they're all standing inside the room. But a telepath standing right outside the room can't read the minds of those *inside,* and a telepath on the inside can't read the mind of anyone outside. It's like the place is insulated somehow." Joshua's powers would work in there, too, or so Hamil assured her—lovetalkers had been used for negotiations there in previous regimes. "We don't understand how the place works, or why it has the limitations it does, but we're happy to take advantage of it. There are a few places like this scattered around the country, and we're lucky to have one under our control. We'll have the meeting here, okay?" Marla closed the door, gave Ted the keyring, and explained how the lock worked. They returned upstairs.

Back at her office, she checked the time and said, "I'm going for a little walk. I'll be back in time for the meeting. Hold down the fort." Ted nodded, still clearly preoccupied by what she'd shown him. She wondered if he'd still be there when she got back. She thought he probably would. He said he didn't have an addictive personality, but she suspected Ted *was* addicted to learning new things, and he must realize there was a whole world of wonders opening up before him now. Marla remembered how that sense of wide-open possibility felt, herself. It felt pretty fucking great.

Marla found Joshua at the Wolf Bay Café, sipping something from a small black ceramic cup and tapping away at a tiny silver laptop. He closed it when he saw her approach, beaming up at her, and Marla sensed everyone else in the café, male and female, looking at her with jealousy for a moment. Then they all went back to staring at Joshua, more-or-less obtrusively. *He must be hell on workplace productivity anyplace he goes.* Looking at him certainly didn't incline *her* to do any work. "Good morning," he said.

"It is now," she agreed, sitting next to him.

"A café au lait for my friend?" he called, and a barista with a pierced nose hurried to fill the order, ignoring the people waiting in line. This café didn't actually have table service, but that wouldn't stop them from bringing anything Joshua asked for, of course.

"Do you even pay for your drinks?" Marla asked, amused.

"Sometimes I try. It's seldom accepted. I can't help it. I'm likeable."

"Good. I'll need your likeability soon. I'm having a meeting at 12:30, and I'd like you to be there."

"I hope it won't run on too long. I have plans this afternoon."

She felt a stab of entirely inappropriate jealousy, which immediately dissolved under the pleasure of his gaze. "Oh? For what?"

"I'm visiting a friend. What's the meeting about?"

"Crazy sorcerers and failed assassins, mostly."

"No delicate negotiations? Then why do I need to be there?"

Marla paused. Why *did* he need to be there? "Well, you were there when the assassin attacked, so you might have something to contribute. And I'd like to introduce you to some of my other associates. . . ." She trailed off. Neither of those were very good reasons. She just *wanted* him there. But she couldn't say that without giving up the power in their relationship. So she just grinned and said, "And because I'm your boss. Maybe I just want to make sure you remember that, in case last night gave you some other ideas."

"Oh? You didn't seem much like a boss last night."

"I never said I was *only* your boss. Just that I'm *also* your boss."

He nodded, conceding the point.

"But I've got a couple of hours before the meeting. . . ." She realized everyone in the café was listening to her, and the barista was hovering just a step away from the table with her drink. Marla glanced up at her, and the girl put down the cup and scurried away. "You could come join me for a little mid-morning exercise."

"Are you asking me as my boss, or as something else?"

"Does it matter?"

"I suppose not." He rose. "We'll need to-go cups, please," he said sweetly, and three customers leapt from their seats to bring them cups and lids.

"I'll go in alone first, if you like," Joshua said, pausing in the doorway of Rondeau's club. "I understand if you'd like to maintain the illusion of propriety."

Marla checked the buttons on her shirt again, half-convinced she'd walk into the meeting partially undressed. "Yeah, might be better. I don't care if people know we're involved, but I don't want that to be the focus of *this* meeting."

Joshua kissed her cheek and went through the door, giving Marla a moment alone on the street to collect herself. How had her love life gone from vibrator-and-alone-time to midmorning-delight-with-a-lovetalker so quickly? She knew it was partly Joshua's magic that made her willing to open herself up to him, physically and (at least a little) emotionally. Was she just drawn to his magic, or to the man himself? Marla felt lucky to have Joshua in her life, though. He was fulfilling parts of her she hadn't realized were wanting. And yet, she considered love spells coercive, and wasn't Joshua really a walking, talking love spell? How could Marla possibly judge this situation objectively when she was *inside* it? She couldn't.

This whole thing was something to ponder later. She had more pressing business now. Supposedly the powers of lovetalkers were impossible to resist, but maybe Langford could come up with a countercharm. If so, Marla could examine her feelings for Joshua unclouded by his pheromones or aura manipulation or whatever. She'd ask.

Marla went inside, and found Ted at the foot of the stairs. "Sorry I'm late. I got busy. Is everyone here?"

"Everyone but Rondeau."

Marla scowled. "Damn it, I told him this was important. Call his cell."

"I have, several times. It goes straight to voicemail. I'm sorry, Marla."

She sighed. "It's all right."

"There have been phone calls. From, ah, your various other associates. They're all concerned about what's happening with the city. The . . . Genevieve problem, they call it?"

Marla groaned. "That's part of what I'm here to deal with. Are the others in the conference room?"

"Devouring sandwiches as we speak."

"Good man." Marla went to the secret conference room. Ted had installed a new multiline phone in the center of the table and had a little sideboard set up with trays of bread and meat. Langford was standing, shoving rolls of meat and cheese into his mouth, while Hamil focused on the carbohydrates, sitting at the table and chewing his way methodically through a heap of croissants. Joshua had a little plate of grapes before him on the table, and Kardec stood, arms folded, against the far wall, where he could see the door. They were all trying not to stare at Joshua, but only Kardeç was doing a halfway decent job. "Thank you all for coming. You there, Husch?"

"Yes," the voice crackled from the phone.

"Great. I have some separate-but-overlapping stuff to talk about, and it was just easier having all of you here at once. Kardec: I found your boy. He tried to assassinate me last night."

Kardec whistled. "Did you kill him?" He sounded both worried and hopeful.

"No such luck. I incapacitated him, but he teleported, or something. Disappeared right out of my hands."

Kardec's brow furrowed. "That's a new trick."

"I kept some of his things, though." She gestured, and Ted brought over a box with Zealand's stun gun, pistol, and garrote. "Think you can track him with these, Langford?"

Langford came over, his mouth still full, poked through the objects in the box, then nodded. "Shouldn't be a problem."

"Good. When he finds Zealand, Kardec, I'll let *you* know, if you promise to get him the hell out of my city, *and* if you swear to find out who hired him and let me know. It's no surprise I've got enemies, but it would help if I knew which shoulder I should be looking over, you know?"

Kardec looked annoyed, but said, "Fine."

Marla sat down at the head of the table. "Yeah? I don't need to take you out back and throw a circle of binding around us, do I? To make sure you're telling the truth?"

"I give my word as a slow assassin."

"Ah," Langford said. "You're a slow assassin? I've always wanted to ask about some of your more exotic poisons—"

"Later," Marla interrupted. "Okay, Kardec, I'll take your word. Langford: any luck finding Dr. Husch's fugitive?"

"She appears intermittently, then disappears." He unfolded a map of the city with a scattering of red dots drawn all over it. "There is no pattern apparent yet. But . . . her effects are being noticed." He nodded toward Hamil. "He can tell you more."

"Yes," Hamil said, his voice heavy with gravitas. He always sounded like he was intoning the voice-over for an Academy Award–winning movie. "My spies at street level have been present for several of her appearances. Genevieve Kelley typically lurches out of an alley, or from around a corner, and looks around in fear and bewilderment. Every once in a great while she brushes up against someone, and when she does . . . they fall down. Unconscious, but only for a little while, a few seconds sometimes, never more than a couple of minutes. The victims wake up and go on about their business, seemingly unaffected . . . at first."

"Have you followed any of them after that first contact?"

"Yes." Hamil sighed. "They disappear. Sometimes within a few minutes, sometimes later. There's no discernible pattern, which is annoying, but then, her power is linked to dreams, and dreams are notoriously unpredictable. But the victims all vanish, and later they reappear, elsewhere in the city. At least, some of them.

Maybe all of them, but we haven't *seen* all of them reappear."

"I assume they're disappearing into Genevieve's dream world," Dr. Husch said. "That when she comes into contact with people, she . . . drags them into her gravity. Or loosens their bonds with consensual reality. I'm not sure."

"Yeah," Marla said. "Sounds like what happened to *me,* all right, and it fits in with those people Joshua and I ran into the other night, the ones from the hospital waiting room. Huh. I wonder if Zealand ran into Genevieve, if that's why he disappeared. He might be dream-poisoned, too, I guess. . . ." She shook off the thought. There was no way to prove or disprove the hypothesis, but she'd keep it in mind. "So, Langford, any conclusions yet? Is it bird flu, or black plague?"

"So far it seems more like bird flu," he said. "Only the people Genevieve touches are infected, if 'infection' is the right word. There's an initial reaction—passing out—and then a variable incubation period before the full onset, signified by the disappearance from this world. I've seen no sign that the infected pass the condition on to others. But from what you told us, people can be swept up by the parts of her dream world that intrude into *our* reality, even without encountering Genevieve directly. Which means it's impossible to extrapolate the extent of the damage Gevenieve's presence could do if left unchecked."

Marla nodded. "We have *got* to get this woman in custody. Assemble a strike team, Hamil. As soon as Langford can zero in on her—or detect a pattern so we can predict where she'll be—we'll get her. Somehow. Nets, tranquilizer darts, psychic dominators, anything and anyone we can think of. Get in touch with the other sorcerers, they must know there's something going on by now, tell them we're conscripting people to deal with 'the Genevieve problem.'" She turned back to Langford. "This is priority one, okay? Getting Genevieve. Zealand can wait."

Langford shrugged. "I can run the searches in parallel. There's a lot of time spent waiting for data to process anyway."

"Be gentle with Genevieve," Dr. Husch said. "Remember, she's *sick,* she's not your enemy. Try not to frighten her. Sedate her, and I'll pick her up and bring her back home. I think the familiar environment will soothe her."

"Like the doc says," Marla said. "Okay. I think that's it for the *pressing* problems." She glanced at Joshua. "But I still have a city to run. How goes scheduling for the big meeting, Hamil?"

"Two nights from now, at darkest midnight, on neutral ground, in this case the gazebo in Fludd Park. Everyone will have their requests for Susan's possessions turned in by 6 P.M. tonight, and I will help prioritize them for you. Of course, there will be a certain amount of arguing at the actual meeting. Susan's holdings were impressive, outshone only by yours and Gregor's, and everyone wants a piece. There are great opportunities to make alliances here, Marla, and with Joshua there to smooth over any bumps in the negotiations . . . I wouldn't worry too much." He hesitated. "Except. Well. We haven't heard from Gregor."

"Okay," Marla said. "He's been incommunicado lately. I need to look into that. Maybe he just doesn't want anything of Susan's."

"Perhaps," Hamil said, but she could tell he was thinking the same thing *she* was: maybe Gregor was the one who'd sicced the assassin on her, and that was why he was laying low. Though, if that was the case, shouldn't he be trying to act *more* normal, so she wouldn't suspect him? Maybe he was just deep into some spell that required his full attention. She'd find out. "You up for the big game, Joshua?"

"I serve at your pleasure," he said, a little cryptically, a lot sexily.

Marla cleared her throat. "Anything else?"

Silence, and then everyone began to leave, Joshua leading the pack. That's right. He had "an appointment," whatever that meant. Marla told them all to let her know when they discovered, well, *anything*, and soon she was left alone with Ted.

"Dr. Husch needs to speak to you privately," he said, gesturing to the phone, and then left.

Marla frowned and picked up the phone. "What is it, Leda?"

"I've been investigating Jarrow's escape attempt. It wasn't an accidental breach. She had outside help."

"Say *what*?"

"Jarrow's cell is wrapped in binding spirals, the walls chiseled with the sorts of orderly symbolic progressions that negate her powers, inlaid in gold. Someone released a bunch of microscopic rock-eating bacteria, programmed to deform the spirals by actually changing the surface of the sigils that surround her cell. By *eating* the metal. They've been at it for a long time. I discovered the creatures this morning, when doing a close inspection of Jarrow's cell. I managed to neutralize the bugs, but . . ."

"You're sure they were deliberately introduced?" Marla said.

Husch sighed. "I'm no expert on extreme organisms, but I spoke to Langford—who is—and he said creatures like this live in caves and gold mines, not in *houses*, and they don't usually behave the way these did. Someone else was controlling them. I have no idea whom, but they wanted Jarrow to escape."

"What kind of nutcase would let Elsie Jarrow out? She's like a pissed-off genie—she'd be more likely to kill whoever helped her escape than she would be to reward them." Jarrow was a living malignancy, a woman who'd transformed herself into the embodiment of chaos and increasing disorder. She was like cancer with a mind.

"I don't know," Husch said. "I'm redoubling security on her cell, of course. But I thought you should know, *someone* wants her to go free."

"Thanks, Leda." Marla stabbed at buttons until she managed to hang up the phone. This was *great*. She wanted nothing more than to curl up in her apartment with Joshua and a variety of entertaining implements, but it was not to be. At least, not until she cleaned up this whole mess of messes.

And where the *hell* was Rondeau?

"Ted!" she called, and he appeared. "Come on. We're going out to walk the right of way."

"Uh . . . like, walking along railroad tracks?"

"Not exactly. I'm walking *my* right of way. I go out every day, if I can, and walk part of the city. It's important, keeps me connected. I draw power from the city—in some ways, it's an extension of me—and in return, I have to give the city my attention. You looked down on Felport with me from on high earlier. Now you're going to see it from street level. We're going out to do some good. And you wanted some magic, right?" She went into her office and opened the bottom drawer. Ted had straightened things up, but he hadn't moved anything, and she found the tiny glass vial with the dried brown spider inside. She handed it to Ted. "Hold on to that. If we run into Genevieve Kelley, or the guy who tried to kill me, I want you to squeeze that thing in your fist and break the glass and crush the spider, okay?"

He stared at the vial like it might be poison. "Won't the glass cut me?"

"It's freezing outside, Ted. I figured you'd be wearing gloves. Besides, if it does make you bleed a bit, that's fine. A little blood won't hurt the spell. Might even boost the signal."

"What, exactly, will it *do*?"

She grinned. "It's better if you see it. Seriously. Way more impressive that way. Come on, let's see if I can find some gloves for you in Rondeau's room."

11

Want to earn your keep, Zealand?" Nicolette leaned in the doorway, the bib of her white overalls smeared with either blood or food. Zealand turned down the corner of the page he was reading.

"Not particularly." He reclined in the armchair beside the bed. The room they'd provided him was nicer than the one at the hotel where he'd been staying.

"Come help, or you don't eat," she said. "I hate seeing a killer with time on his hands."

Zealand sighed and rose. "I don't kill without recompense."

"Apparently you don't kill even when we pay you half up front, judging by your performance with Marla. Besides, I just want you to throw a scare into this guy. He thinks he's got me outsmarted, but I'm gonna show him otherwise." She led him down the hallway.

"Is this a boyfriend who cheated on you, Nicolette?"

"Nah. Just a well-connected little fuck who owes me money and thinks he doesn't have to pay. I picked him up on the street this morning."

"I find this all so very interesting," Zealand said. "Please just point me to the person I'm supposed to menace, so I can get back to my book."

Nicolette pulled open the door to a windowless conference room, and Zealand looked inside to see a Hispanic man, perhaps in his late twenties, tied to a chair. He was wearing a summer-weight seersucker suit and he looked more bored and annoyed than frightened, which perhaps explained why Nicolette wanted Zealand's help—the unknown was often more frightening than the known, and Zealand was very good at being scary.

Nicolette winked at him and swaggered in. "Hi, Rondeau. I brought a friend to meet you."

Rondeau. Zealand had never seen him up close, and so hadn't recognized him, but this was Marla's closest confidant and right-hand man. Zealand cleared his throat—unless they planned to kill this man, it probably wasn't a good idea to let him discover Zealand's identity. Word would surely get back to Marla, and any consequences couldn't be good.

"He's a little old to be a goon," Rondeau said, eyeing Zealand without apparent recognition; good. "Unless he's a *very* smart goon. What, is he your sugar-daddy, Nicolette?"

Nicolette put her hands on the arms of the chair and leaned in, putting her face close to Rondeau's. "Maybe you haven't noticed—I know you don't keep up with current events—but I have you tied up, in a fortress, and you owe me a figure that's fast approaching one hundred thousand dollars. So maybe you'd better try to be more polite."

Rondeau belched in her face, and Nicolette stood

up quickly. "If anything happens to me," he said, "Marla will come down on you harder than a zombie apocalypse. She'll be picking pieces of you out of her teeth two hours after I'm dead. Now, untie me before—"

"I wouldn't *kill* you," Nicolette said, not quite purring. "I know all about the *real* you." She turned to Zealand. "That's not his body, not really. He's a *what*, not a *who*, a psychic parasite, a floating intelligence—if you can call that intelligence—who stole this body you're looking at from a little kid years ago. Just like he's stealing from me *now*. I guess it's just his nature. He's stuck in this body, but if it dies he'll just pop out and steal another one. Maybe mine. Maybe yours. So murder's off the table. But maiming . . ." She reached under the table and came up with a big metal toolbox, ominously red. A cliché of a gesture, Zealand thought, but he appreciated the old standbys as much as anyone. He cracked a few of his knuckles by way of contributing to the general atmosphere, then surreptitiously scratched at the back of his hand. There was still a little patch of green there, and no matter how he scrubbed, it wouldn't come off. He assumed—he *hoped*—it was just some persistent plant pigment that would flake away in time.

"Let's see you throw dice with no fingers," Nicolette said. She flipped up the latches holding the box closed.

"Marla—" Rondeau began.

Nicolette snapped her fingers in his face, startling him into silence. "You're done hiding behind Marla's skirts. I'm gonna take a finger or a toe for every thousand you owe me. And unless you're a polydactyl . . ." She shrugged. "I'm gonna run out of digits. We'll figure out market value for your eyes and ears and cock and balls and kidneys when the time comes. You can live for a *long* time on dialysis in my basement."

"You *can't,*" Rondeau said, as if trying to explain a simple physical limitation, like the laws of gravity or the concept of inertia, to a small child. "I'm protected."

"Oh, it'll be bad for me if word ever gets back to Marla that I touched you. But, see, she won't ever know. I haven't left a psychic signature on this box of toys—they're new, just bought yesterday, and I won't be the one using them on you. My friend here will do that. Hell, I'm even going to leave the room before he starts, so none of your little forensic bitch Langford's investigative techniques will find *any* connection to me." She patted his cheek. He did look a little more afraid now, and Zealand scowled and looked appropriately menacing.

"I'll tell her you did it," Rondeau said. "You think I won't?"

Nicolette snorted. "My friend here knows a lot about *brains,* Ronnie. Once he's done hurting you, he'll put a needle right here"—she tapped the inside corner of his eye—"and *shove.* Ice-pick lobotomy. Old school. Then he'll poke a few more holes for good measure, maybe break your spine when he's done hurting you, too. You won't be telling anybody *anything.* I know you don't really think with your brain—your mind is a cloud of weird particles, or a persistent resonating field, or something like that—but try using that body you inhabit when its brain is all fucked up. You won't be able to keep from shitting yourself, let alone talk to Marla. And Gregor tells me he's pretty sure you can't do the body-switching thing at will, that you're stuck in this body until it dies, and like I said, we're going for a fate worse than death here. So toodles. You guys enjoy getting to know each other."

Zealand considered his options, annoyed that Nicolette hadn't given him more time to prepare. He could spend a fair bit of time rattling the toolbox, selecting implements, and presenting them for Rondeau's terror, drawing out the suspense in hopes that Rondeau would break before it became apparent he was in no real danger. At least, not from Zealand. He wasn't about to actually *hurt* Rondeau. He was an assassin, not a torturer. That was part of why he'd left the slow assassins in the first place—their focus on psychological torment struck him as fundamentally distasteful.

Nicolette started toward the door, and Rondeau drew a breath—though whether it was to shout defiance or beg for mercy Zealand didn't know, because Gregor flung open the door just then. "There you are—" he began, and then saw Rondeau. He went very still. "Rondeau," he said, and then turned stiffly to Nicolette. "Please tell me this is some consensual sex game, and *not* that you have the chief sorcerer of Felport's closest associate held hostage."

Nicolette looked down, scowling, and Rondeau began to grin.

"It's personal business," Nicolette said. "He ran up a bill at some of my gambling parlors, and he won't pay."

"Nicolette, you *know* better," Gregor said. "Untie him." Nicolette flipped open the toolbox and took out a knife—*that* made Rondeau flinch—but she only used it to cut the ropes that bound him to the chair.

"There are proper avenues for conflict resolution

when it comes to collecting debts from those in the employ of prominent citizens," Gregor said. "I swear, your love for chaos can be most *vexing.*" He bowed to Rondeau, who was ostentatiously straightening his suit. "Do convey my apologies to Marla for any inconvenience your detainment may have caused her." He narrowed his eyes. "Since you work for her, I'm sure she understands the problems that headstrong assistants can cause. I'll escort you out. *You* stay here," he said, jabbing his finger at Nicolette. He put a solicitous arm around Rondeau and led him away.

"Ouch," Zealand said after a moment.

"Nothing like getting dressed down by your boss in front of a victim to put some piss in your cornflakes," she said, sounding surprisingly cheerful. "But it's okay. Next time I snatch up Rondeau, and take him someplace my boss doesn't visit, he'll *know* I'm serious, and he'll sign the deed of his nightclub over to me quick-snap."

"Mmm," Zealand said. Was Nicolette really getting so worked up over money? Property? That was disappointing. He'd always hoped sorcerers would have more rarefied interests.

Gregor stormed back in. "Hey, boss," Nicolette began, but he backhanded her sharply across the face, knocking her back against the conference table. Gregor was not a large man, and Zealand wondered if he'd put some magical wallop behind the strike, or if he was really just *that* pissed.

"Stupid wretch," he snarled. "You know what a delicate time this is for me, that the auguries point to

Marla as my downfall, and you bring her *best friend* here?"

Nicolette pushed herself back up. Zealand attempted to look unobtrusive. So Marla was prophesied to be Gregor's doom. That explained why Zealand had been hired to assassinate her. He'd assumed the reasons were merely political.

"Sorry, boss," Nicolette said. "I thought I was allowed to pursue my own business however it suited me."

"Don't be deliberately dense," Gregor said, smoothing his hair, which had come disarrayed in the violence of his entrance. "You *do* have that freedom, when it doesn't interfere with *my* interests. We—" He appeared to notice Zealand for the first time, and frowned. "We'll discuss this later. Come. We need to visit our friend in the basement."

"Okay," Nicolette said, all unfazed again. "Just let me get some oatmeal cookies." She patted Zealand on the arm. "Thanks, Z. You make a good hatchet man."

They left, and Zealand started to go to his room. He paused by the door, thinking. Gregor and Nicolette were going to the basement. This was a very tall building, and he was very high in it now. They might well be gone a long time. He had no prevailing *need* to snoop, but it was in his nature to gather intelligence. And he *was* curious about one thing—Reave. The strange mushroom-white man he was, supposedly, meant to battle. He crept up the hallway toward Gregor's office. The leaded glass door was locked, but even Zealand's feeble lock-picking skills were up to the task—Gregor trusted in other means of defense, and considered his whole building an impregnable fortress. Once you were inside, getting around was easy.

Gregor's office was illuminated only by the sunlight beyond the tall windows, looking out on the cold clear city below. There was no sign of Reave. Zealand closed the door behind him and went toward Gregor's desk. Maybe there were papers, documents, e-mails, something to indicate the nature of his relationship with Reave, and, more important, information about the strange woman who'd spoken to Zealand in that *other* place.

He'd rifled through one filing cabinet without success and had moved on to the second when the stain on the back of his hand began to itch abominably. He scraped at it with his nails, but they were clipped too short to provide much relief, and the itch was maddening, so intense it made his eyes water and his bowels tremble in sympathy. He lifted his hand to his mouth and *gnawed* it, scraping his teeth across the green stain, and that provided some measure of relief, at last.

A sudden shadow fell across the room, and Zealand looked up. Had a cloud gone over the sun, or—

He turned to the windows. A black tower rose beside this building, where no structure had been a moment before, its bulk blacking out the light. Zealand went to the window, slowly, and put his hand against the cold glass. The tower was made of cracked black stone, tall, vast, and—he was no student of architecture, but still—almost ludicrously phallic. It seemed to swarm with shadows, and the occasional windows were only arches revealing slightly lesser darkness inside. The balconies looked small and likely to crumble away, railings topped with twisted figures that might have been gargoyles carved crudely in coal. He remembered a snatch of Genevieve's hurried words—"*He lives in the black tower. He marshals nightmares.*"

This was sorcerers' business. But the tower was so *ridiculous,* like the comic-book idea of a dark lord's keep. It was the architectural equivalent of those idiots who put on long black trench-coats and dark glasses and think the wardrobe makes them into badasses, when actually becoming a badass required working very, very hard. Gregor's fortress was a modern skyscraper with reasonable functions, doubtless magically enhanced, but still. Zealand couldn't help but think Reave's castle was the fortress of someone with an overdeveloped sense of the dramatic. What the hell were the ordinary people down there on the street *thinking* in the face of this apparition?

His hand had stopped itching. But now it pulsed, strangely warm, and when Zealand held his hand before his face he saw the green had spread across the back of his hand, tendriling up to his fingers and around his palm. "What the hell," he muttered, and then the light burst in on him again, the tower abruptly vanished. He shaded his eyes against the onslaught of sunlight, blinking reflexively.

"It's almost there," came a grating voice at his back.

The door hadn't opened. Zealand would have heard it. More sorcery. He turned to see Reave, with his long shiny coat, his soft-boiled-egg features.

"Before long, it will achieve immanence. We just need to stabilize certain conditions." Reave smiled. His teeth were yellowed, and bits of something leafy and green were stuck between them.

"Do let me know if I can be of service," Zealand

said. Without thinking about why, he kept his green hand in his pocket. The itching was gone, but the warm pulse was intensifying. Something to worry about later. Had he caught some strange disease in that other place? "I'm between jobs at the moment, and my rates are competitive."

Reave sniffed. "I suppose we might let you guard a door, later. Once we've got something to lock up behind it. Now run along. You aren't supposed to be here."

"I love your coat," Zealand said, utterly deadpan. "Wherever did you find it?"

"In her dreams," Reave said, and flicked his hand toward the door. "Go away. Wait to be useful."

Zealand bowed his way out of the room. *In her dreams*. Well. That certainly failed to clear anything up.

A great wind rushed down the street toward Marla and Ted, a channeled blast that whipped stinging snow toward them. "Shit!" Marla shouted—even with her eyes slit against the wind she could see the huge black tower, suddenly just *there,* in the middle of the street. It was Reave's tower, the tower from her interlude with Genevieve, but she hadn't entered the woman's dream world—this was a real street in a real city, *her* city. This made a few spontaneously appearing orange trees look like *nothing*.

"That—that—that . . ." Ted sputtered. Marla grabbed his arm and tugged him along after her. "What is that?" he finally asked.

"A big pile of dog shit right in the middle of my

day," she said grimly. This was bad. It was the middle of the day, downtown, and even snowbound, the city was alive. Hundreds of ordinaries were going to look out their office windows and see that impossible thing rising up in the middle of the street. There were no pedestrians in sight, and traffic was light on this particular side street, but a couple of streets over it would be a different story. She could already hear the sound of honking horns, and that oddly soothed her—even confronted with an impossible fortress of black stone materializing in the street, the people of Felport were mostly annoyed by the way it held up traffic. Gods, she hoped it hadn't crushed anyone.

As she got closer to the tower, Marla saw that things were both better and worse than she'd expected. From the size of the tower, she'd assumed it must be pressed tight up against the surrounding high-rises, but it actually had plenty of room around its base.

Unfortunately, it had plenty of room because it had hacked away at Euclidean space. It had somehow . . . made room for itself. The street was split on either side of the tower, just as wide as ever, but divided in two. The tower hadn't just popped into existence in her city. It had brought a little of its own reality with it, a bit of ground from Genevieve's dream world.

Materializing a tower in the middle of a city was big magic, but Marla could have done it, with some prep. Altering physical reality to make space in the middle of a city to set the tower down without disturbing the surrounding area . . . that was way beyond her. It was way beyond anybody, except a reweaver, somebody who could make reality roll over and play dead. Somebody like Genevieve.

"Marla, what should we do?" Ted was staring up at the tower. People were getting out of their cars and staring up. This was exactly the sort of thing Marla was supposed to keep from happening. They were being invaded by a madwoman's nightmares. A few orange trees, and even skittering things that kept to the shadows, could be ignored. But a tower appearing downtown was a pretty hard-core intrusion into consensual reality. There wasn't enough forget-me-lots potion in the city to dissolve this problem.

Marla had no idea how to fix this. She needed to find Genevieve, but the immediate problem, the big dose of unreality in the middle of Felport—where to begin? Fuck it. There was a tower in front of her. She'd just *storm* it, and deal with whatever she found inside.

Then the tower disappeared with a huge rumble of thunder, air rushing in to occupy the space where the building had been. "Oh, thank the gods."

"What are all these people going to think?" Ted said.

Marla shook her head. "It was there for less than a minute. They'll think mass hysteria. They'll think it was an illusion, a weird weather effect, viral marketing for some new video game, who knows? They'll come up with some explanation. People always do."

"And if it had stayed there for an hour?" Ted said.

"Then we'd be in trouble. I'm going to get a call from the mayor and the other sorcerers anyway. I wish I had something useful to tell them. But it's not too dire, as long as there aren't any more—"

Another tower appeared, and where the first had been a blunt instrument bludgeoning reality on the skull, this one seemed almost to sidle in, precipitating out of the air and gracefully easing the surrounding buildings out of the way, the only change in the air a gentle breeze. People gasped and pointed, and a few even—bizarrely—applauded, as if the tower were an impressive special effect. It was made of opalescent stone, rising high, with arched windows and silver flag-poles protruding irregularly, flying yellow banners. A fairy-princess sort of castle.

Marla had let one castle disappear in front of her. Not again. "I'm going in," she said.

"I'm coming, too," Ted said.

"I don't know what I'll find in there. You could get eaten by giant spiders or something."

"I'm your assistant," Ted said, and since Marla didn't dare waste the time it would take to restrain him, she just sighed and ran, hoping she'd outrun him. But Ted was pretty spry—the cancer cure must have worked—and he kept up with her. She rushed through the wide-open archway, into a hall of gleaming pris-matic marble dotted with pillars, the floor so highly polished it mirrored the vaulted ceiling. Ted puffed af-ter her, sliding to a stop, and they both looked back toward the archway in time to see the street and the baffled citizens and their cars disappear, replaced by a rolling field of clouds under a clear blue sky. It wasn't winter here, too warm for the heavy coats and gloves, and Marla shed hers immediately. Ted followed suit. They could always get new coats when—*if*—they made it back to Felport.

"We're in it now," Marla said, turning away from the pile of discarded clothes. "Come on."

Ted just stared at her. "What—we—how do we get *back*?"

"We worry about getting back after we finish up here. One thing at a time."

He looked around. "Where do we go?"

"It's a tower, Ted. We climb." Not that she saw any obvious place to begin. She walked through the chamber, her boots clicking on the floor, and did a mental inventory of her assets. She had her dagger of office, and her boots—which were reinforced with steel toes and enough inertial magic to allow her to kick a hole in a concrete wall if necessary—and her wits, and that was about it. "See if you can get a signal on the cell phone," she said.

"Ah, one bar. And it's flickering."

"Crap. That phone's got magical augmentation. Langford told me it could get a strong signal on the *moon.*"

"So what does that mean?" Ted said, pocketing the phone.

Marla shrugged. "It means we're a lot farther away than the moon, I guess. I think this is Genevieve's place in the country. The *dream* country. I'm hoping she's here, and that I can talk to her, get her to chill out, come back to the Blackwing Institute, and put a lid on all this craziness."

"You think that will work?"

"Dunno. She wasn't too lucid last time we talked. Maybe she's more sane here, in her own castle. We'll see. I wish Joshua was here—he's good at talking to people."

Ted grunted. "So where are the stairs?"

Marla spied another archway, beyond a rank of smooth columns. In the absence of other options, she would take whatever presented itself. "Come on." She walked through the arch into an open courtyard filled with orange trees, the smell of fruit strong and somehow heartbreaking. The courtyard went all the way to the top of the tower, with walls rising to the vanishing point on all sides, dotted with occasional windows and balconies. She sighed. "Remember when we floated up above the city, Ted? That was pretty cool, right?"

"Sure." He looked worried.

"Well, that was fake. Just illusion. Now we've got to fly for real. I don't do it much, because it makes me puke, usually, and I don't think having a passenger will help. It's not as cool as it looks in the movies. Throwing off the constraints of gravity pisses off reality, and it's not much fun for me, either. Maybe the rules are . . . looser here. I hope. Come, grab on."

"Do I just . . . hold your hand, or . . ."

"This isn't *Peter Pan.* You have to do more than touch me. I'm going to rise up in the air, and if you don't hold on as tight as you can, you'll fall off and go splat on the ground. I'm not going to try to go all the way, just to that balcony." She pointed to a protrusion about three floors up. "Let's hope there's a staircase in there, or at least a freaking intercom."

Ted awkwardly approached her from behind and wrapped his arms around her waist. Marla wished she'd brought some rope or a grappling hook, or something, but she hadn't expected to be storming a castle. "Hold tight." She bent her knees, closed her eyes, and whispered a bit of incantation that she was told translated into an incredibly graphic and cruel insult to gravity itself, in the flutelike language the fundamental forces of nature spoke. As always, she didn't so much rise from the earth as get *thrown*, and Ted gasped and clung to her way too tightly, his locked hands digging in above her pelvic bone. She gritted her teeth and tried to exert some control over her flight, lurching hard to the right, almost crashing into the balcony she'd been aiming for. She grabbed the edge of the railing with both hands and felt her legs rising up, like a balloon lifting away on a tethered string. Ted scrambled off her and grabbed the rail, heaving himself over the edge, and Marla shouted the ritual apology to make gravity embrace her again. She slammed down hard against the edge of the balcony, the rail hitting her rib cage just below her breasts, hard enough to bruise. She groaned, and Ted helped pull her over the side. "See?" she said, leaning on the rail. "Superman is full of shit." The balcony led to another archway, to a library of high dark shelves and dusty old tomes, with a deep armchair beside a brass lamp, and a decanter of brandy on a small side table.

"I could use a drink," Ted said.

"Neither eat nor drink here," Marla said. "First rule of traveling in dreamlands, fairy realms, the underworld, all those places. Food and drink can have weird and terrible consequences. Besides, for the moment, we're housebreakers, not guests, so we don't get hospitality. In the normal world, we have manners and etiquette to grease the wheels of social interaction. In places like this, there's etiquette to keep you from being killed or enslaved." She went to the big table in the center of the room and flipped open one of the books there. She whistled when she read the neat penmanship on the inside cover. "Property of St. John Austen. He was Genevieve's teacher. She made his whole house disappear and replaced it with an orange grove. But maybe she just took his house *away,* and put it here, inside the palace."

"That's right, more or less," said a cultured voice. Marla turned, her dagger in her hand, expecting the bald man with the knives, but finding instead a thin man with gray hair in a ponytail, sitting in the armchair.

"Who the fuck are you?"

"St. John Austen." He paused. "More or less." He poured himself a glass of brandy and sipped, never taking his eyes off Marla. "Thank you for coming. Genevieve is waiting upstairs. She'd come downstairs and see you herself, but down on these levels, there are . . . bad memories. She's more comfortable at the top of the tower."

"You didn't die?" Marla said. "You've been, what, living here, in her dream world?"

"Oh, no. I died. Starved to death here, actually. There's nothing to eat in this library, just an eternally replenishing decanter of brandy. My bones are secreted around the room, behind books, on top of shelves. Genevieve feels guilty about killing me, but she couldn't help it. She was asleep when I passed away." He shrugged. "But no one Genevieve gets to know well *really* dies. We get into her mind, and she can't get us out again. We lodge there, like bits of shrapnel, and because of her powers, we are occasionally . . . expressed. Some of us have limitations. I have some of my memories, and most of my mind—as far as I can tell—but I exist only occasionally, and cannot leave the palace. Unless Genevieve pays particular attention to me, I can't even leave the library. Ultimately, I'm just a dream Genevieve has sometimes. Reave, though . . ."

Marla sat on the edge of the big mahogany table. "Take notes, Ted," she said, and he pulled out his PDA.

"Reave. He was the man who assaulted her, who drove Genevieve crazy?"

"Not exactly. The man who attacked her was named Terrence Reeves. It was . . . a terrible experience." He shuddered delicately. "Genevieve is a very sensitive psychic, but her power opens a two-way conduit. She gets into your head, yes, but you also get into *hers.* When Terrence raped her, she learned his name, and felt his emotions, even his physical sensations, losing her sense of self, blurring the distinction between victim and attacker, and the horrible intensity of that experience made a stronger-than-usual impression on her. A version of Terrence got stuck in her mind, but he was also *amplified* there, the cause of her most terrible trauma, the source of her worst pain, the bringer of nightmares. The reality of the rapist—just a squalid, terrible man—was merged with her image of him as a monstrous destroyer of worlds, implacable, merciless, villainous, misogynistic. He became an *epic* villain, and after some years of living in her mind . . . he declared his independence. He renamed himself Reave, king of nightmares, and turned some measure of Genevieve's power to his own purposes. He created a tower. He created nightmares to serve him. Now he assaults this beautiful castle, the home of Genevieve's heart, on a regular basis, and it's all she can do to hold him at bay. Of course, she's not here all the time—sometimes she wakes up and finds herself in the real world, where she's vulnerable in other ways."

"How can he have any power of his own, if he's just a figment from her dreams?" Marla said.

"He only has the power Genevieve gives him," St. John said. "But haven't you ever been hurt so badly by someone that they gained power over you, took up space in your mind, stole your sense of well-being away? Hasn't anyone ever rooted themselves so deeply into your soul that nothing could tear them out?"

"Yes," Ted said softly, and Marla nodded, too. "But what's his *goal*? Why is he trying to get to her?"

"He wants to lock her up, I imagine. Her real, physical form. Keep her alive and torment her to increase his own power in her mind, and, thus, in reality. He wants to crawl out of her mind and into the real world. Genevieve is usually good at fighting him off, but something happened to her, something woke her up all the way and disoriented her, sent her wandering. There was snow, and snow is terrible for her, as it reminds her of the night she was attacked. Now the barriers between her dreams and reality are flickering. Reave is taking advantage of that, and moving at large in the world, looking for Genevieve, for her real physical form. If the walls between dream and reality crumble totally, I have some small hope that I might be able to walk out of here, into the real world, and regain my life. But I don't think I have enough independent agency." He sighed. "Even now I wonder if I'm really myself, or just a mouthpiece Genevieve is using to tell you things more clearly and lucidly than she could manage on her own."

"I'll do what I can to help you," Marla said, though she doubted that was much. "But tell me—how do I stop Reave? I mean, *really* stop him? How do I help Genevieve?"

St. John shook his head. "I have no idea. If I did—if *we* did, if *she* did—don't you think we'd try to do it ourselves? How do you kill a nightmare, Marla, without killing the dreamer as well?"

Marla didn't twitch a muscle when he said that, but perhaps her stillness was a giveaway of its own, because St. John widened his eyes. "No," he said. "No, no, no, you *can't* kill her, she's an innocent, she doesn't deserve execution—"

"She's infecting my city," Marla said, deciding honesty was the only course—Genevieve, who was doubtless listening, could read minds anyway. "She's taken a wrecking ball to reality. If I can't get her quarantined . . . we'll have to do something else. Otherwise, she could unravel everything. She's a Typhoid Mary, spreading some kind of dreaming sickness, making people fall into her world, letting bits of her nightmares out. I want to help her. I'll do everything I can. But . . . I'll do whatever's necessary to stop the infection."

"That's it, then," St. John said sadly. "She thought you might be able to help her, that you might be a champion. But she's afraid of you now. I can feel her fear radiating down from the rooms above. Now she'll have to rely on the green knight to protect her."

"The green what?" Marla said. "What the hell are you talking about?"

"Good-bye, Marla Mason. And good luck." He disappeared, the glass of brandy in his hand falling to the floor.

"That didn't go well," she said. "I really wish Joshua had been here to smooth things over. I guess we keep trying to go upstairs—"

"You'd really kill her?" Ted said. "After everything she's been through?"

"Damn it, it's not my first choice, but if there's no other alternative. What, you'd rather I let this Reave guy set up shop in the middle of my city? He calls himself the *king of nightmares*—you think his leadership is what Felport needs?"

Ted just shook his head. "It's not right."

"My job isn't about 'right' and 'wrong' so much as it's about 'necessary' and 'unavoidable,' Ted. Now, come on—"

The tower tilted, and not gently. The floor became a ramp, and Marla and Ted both lost their footing and slid toward the open archway and the balcony. Now the inner courtyard was gone, and only clouds hung below. The tower kept turning, and Ted and Marla slammed into the low wall of the balcony. The tower kept going, and they started to slide. Marla grabbed Ted by the wrist with one hand and grabbed the railing with the other, and soon they were both dangling from the rail, only clouds beneath their feet.

The tower *shook,* like someone shaking a bag of potato chips to get out the last crumbs, and Marla lost her grip. She fell, and Ted screamed, and she lost her grip on him, too, and they plunged through the bank of clouds. She Cursed gravity again, but it had no effect—Genevieve had managed to wrest control of that spell in her domain, it seemed.

Marla's next-to-last thought in that world was of Joshua, and his beautiful face, which she'd never see again. But her last thought was of her city, and how it would fare or fail without her when she splattered to death below.

12

Zealand looked up from his book and saw that his rooms had disappeared. He was in a library now, with a decanter of brandy on a table beside him. "Sorcerers," he said, and looked back down at his book. Nicolette was behind this, or Gregor, or Genevieve, or *someone*—he wouldn't give any of them the satisfaction of watching him twitch.

"Mr., ah, Zealand? My name is St. John Austen. I work for Genevieve Kelley."

Zealand closed his book. "I'll need to get that back," he said, setting it on the table. "Don't go shelving it with all these other things, all right?" He stood up, scratching at the moldy patch on the back of his hand. "I assume Genevieve wants to see me?"

"Yes," St. John said, seemingly relieved. "Come." He led Zealand out of the library, into a hallway with photographs in dusty frames. Zealand paused to peer at them, and saw they were all of a girl at various ages, probably all Genevieve. He leaned close to one photograph—a teenaged Genevieve proudly holding a tray of cookies—and stepped back when the scent of chocolate chip cookies filled his nostrils.

"They're happy moments in her past," St. John said. "Frozen on the wall, so she can visit them when things are especially bad, when the sky turns black and monsters ride the currents in the air and siege engines assault her castle."

"Nice trick," Zealand said. "Shall we go on?"

St. John beckoned, and they walked down the long hall—Zealand caught whiffs of chlorine from summer swimming pools, the scent of pot and incense from all-night college parties, and the smell of oranges, of course. "You have a daughter, don't you, Zealand?"

Zealand didn't flinch. The existence of his offspring was a well-guarded secret. If the slow assassins knew he had a daughter, they would kill her just on the off chance it might bother him. "I'm not interested in women, I'm afraid, Mr. Austen, so natural children were never in the cards for me, and adoption is impractical for a man in my business."

"You don't need to lie. We're not threatening you or your family. And Genevieve knows what's in your mind."

"Then why are you talking to me? Why waste my time, when you know it all?"

"You have a daughter, grown now. You may not be interested in women, but in your youth you tried, because it was expected, and you did have a child, though you hardly knew the mother. You've made sure she's well taken care of financially. She must think she's a very lucky young woman, winning contests she never entered, finding lottery tickets in her mailbox, receiving windfall inheritances from dead relatives she's never even heard of—and who don't, in fact, exist."

"My life is mostly about killing people, Mr. Austen. It amuses me to do some good with my time as well."

"You sometimes kill women, but you never torture them," Mr. Austen went on.

"I detest torture in general. It's a bad way to get information, and it's also uncivilized. Some people need to die, and I provide that service. Occasionally people pay for . . . extra services, it's true. For a particular mode of death, usually an unpleasant or even gruesome one. If I never perpetrate such acts against women, it's only coincidence." Zealand followed his gut when it came to taking assignments, and sometimes he turned down jobs without fully understanding why.

"Well. At any rate, Genevieve believes you are a good man who does evil things, and she hopes you will consent to do some evil things for her, in the service of good."

"'Good' being defined as 'good for Genevieve,' I suppose?" Zealand said. He wondered how long this hallway was.

"We all have our biases," St. John agreed.

"Why are you telling me all this, and not her?"

"Her mind wanders. I understand what she wants, deeply and all the way through. She's been in my mind for a very long time, and I in hers."

"She wants me to kill Reave?"

"She wants you to *protect* her from Reave. Killing him is probably impossible. Keeping him away from her is important, though, and stopping his imperial aspirations in the mortal world is also a good idea. Driving him back if he approaches these walls is imperative."

"Mmm. So I'm to be a palace retainer, then?"

"Well. There is one other thing she'd like you to do, if you can."

"Which is?"

"Kill Marla Mason. She's made it clear that she'll murder Genevieve if she gets the opportunity."

Zealand stopped. "Really. You know, killing Marla Mason is the reason I came to Felport."

"We know."

"Marla wants to kill Genevieve? Whatever for?"

"She feels she has good reason. We disagree."

"Ah," Zealand said. "You know, I've faced Ms. Mason before, and it didn't work out well. And now she's on the lookout for me. I'm not sure . . . well. I hate to deride my own talents, but she may be too much for me."

"I've given you a present, though," Genevieve said, appearing from nowhere, as if she'd walked in from a side passage, but there were no side passages. She wore yellow, and her hair was a crazy cascade. Her violet eyes were lovely, and, yes, they were the same improbable color as his own daughter's; how had he not noticed that before?

He bowed to her, slightly. "A magical sword? A cloak of invisibility? One of the classics like that?"

"No," she said, and touched his hand.

The green spot bloomed, and his hand was soon covered in a thick, crawling glove of mold. He shook his hand, and a strand of mold flew from his fingers and struck the wall, spreading over it, covering it in a green pool. He twitched his hand, and the mold pulled away, bringing chunks of stone with it, opening a hole in the wall, onto darkness. He stared at his hand, and the mold subsided, drawing in on itself, until it was only an itchy spot again. "A magic sword might have been less disturbing," he said finally.

Genevieve frowned, turned, and walked down the hallway, disappearing around a corner that wasn't there.

"She gets distracted," St. John said apologetically. "As for the mold . . . well, she doesn't have very fine control. It's all associative, symbolic, a jumble of images. Genevieve was attacked by a man, and that man had spinach or something in his teeth, and so she associates a bit of green with something profound, powerful, terrifying . . . it's an odd weapon, I know, but it could be useful."

"The man who attacked her, that was Reave?"

St. John hesitated. "Yes."

"You're sure?"

"It's complicated. But, yes, Reave assaulted her. He's responsible for the way she is now, her mind wandering—"

"Her bad dreams spilling out into the world. Hmm. Which is why Marla wants to kill her, I suppose? Because they're *Genevieve's* bad dreams, and Marla only cares about saving her city, even if Genevieve can't help what she does, even though she's a victim herself." He grinned at St. John's stunned expression. "You see? I don't even need to read minds to figure some things out." He made a fist, and the mold crawled around his hand, twining in his fingers; it was a strange power, but power of any sort wasn't to be scoffed at. "All right, I'll kill Marla. But I plan to kill Reave, too. Being on indefinite guard duty doesn't sound very appealing. Though I wouldn't mind a permanent guest room in this lovely palace. I'm sure I'll retire someday, and this is a pretty spot."

"Killing Reave could be—"

"Impossible, yes. Well, I won't have anyone saying I didn't *try*. Rapists offend me, Mr. Austen. But Marla first, you think? Fine, fine. Just let me out somewhere near downtown Felport. I'll find my way."

"We can't thank you enough," Austen said. "Truly."

"Genevieve can make dreams come true, can't she? I'm sure you'll come up with some way of showing your appreciation."

Marla fell into a snowbank, and Ted fell on top of her. The impact wasn't bad—as if she'd fallen a couple of feet, not the thousands of feet she *knew* she'd fallen. They'd dropped for long enough that Ted had even stopped screaming, the uprushing ground beneath them changing again and again. First it was black ocean, then a vast plain of yellowish-white specked here and there with green, and later giant cobblestones. Ted had squeezed his eyes shut when the ground far below turned into red-and-yellow flames consuming the bones of a city-sized animal. Marla kept her eyes open, though, because a glimpse into any of the subcontinents of Genevieve's mind could prove useful, if they were lucky enough to survive this fall. So she'd seen the vast forest of trees—doubtless orange trees—and the rolling hills dotted with black tombstones, and the crystal palace of broken domes, and the mushroom jungle, and a place with dinosaur-sized monsters made of segmented bones, stepping with the delicacy of water-birds through a swamp of steaming shit.

But when they landed, they landed in a deep bank of snow, in Felport, right beside Rondeau's club. It couldn't have been coincidence, but Marla wasn't sure whether or not it was actually mercy.

She sat up, groaning, and elbowed Ted off of her. He sat up, teeth already chattering, and looked around. "I thought we were going to die," he said, his voice a croak from all the screaming.

"The night's young. We still might." She rose, a little shakily, and offered Ted her hand. His cell phone was ringing, but they both ignored it as they brushed snow from their bodies and made for the sidewalk. The sky was darkening to dusk, which meant time had passed differently in Genevieve's realm, or else they'd been falling for so long that Marla's usually reliable internal clock had failed.

They reached the door to the club, and Rondeau swung it open. "Holy shit! Where have you guys been all afternoon, making snow angels?"

Marla grunted and shoved her way past him. "If you'd showed up for the meeting this afternoon, you would've been *with* us, and you could've seen for yourself. I need a drink, and so does Ted. Rustle up something. We've been working for a living." She plopped down on a bar stool, and Ted settled in beside her while Rondeau poured them each a brandy.

"Look, about this afternoon," Rondeau began, and Marla waved her hand.

"Explain later. I need to know what's happened while I'm gone. And if you tell me 'nothing' I'll kiss you on the cheek."

"Ah," Rondeau said. "Well, no, it's not nothing. It's a lot of things. Phone's been ringing off the hook. It's getting wild out there, Marla. A couple of *castles* appeared in the middle of traffic downtown. People are passing out right on the street, and when they wake up, they're talking about crazy shit, places full of fire, places full of monsters, places full of nicer things, too, but mostly what I've been hearing about is the bad things. There are creatures running around down by the docks, things with too many legs and not enough eyes, and the Bay Witch says there are things *under* the water, too, and that there's some kind of ruined palace down there, deserted as far as she can tell, but with a big black stone door that doesn't open, and she hears a kind of thumping behind it. Ernesto called to say there's a black tower in his junkyard—"

"Interesting," Marla murmured, and waved her hand for Rondeau to continue.

"Viscarro called from the Bank of the Catacombs to say two extra vaults have appeared, and the doors won't even open for *him,* and he's pissed. The little border gods say something's straining against the edges of the city from the *inside,* and they wonder if they should try to expel it, or what—I told them to just hang tough until I heard from you. That moron Granger says sinkholes are appearing in the park, and do we have a magic shovel he can borrow to fill them in faster? The Chamberlain even called down from the Heights to say the ghosts of the founding fathers are sensing a disturbance in the ether, and she's worried about property values. The—"

"Wait," Marla said. "Tell me who *hasn't* called."

"Gregor," he said promptly, then winced.

"Huh. And one of those towers appeared *right next to* his building. You'd think he would've been the first guy on the phone. Kinda . . . suspicious."

"Ah. I might have an explanation for that," Rondeau said.

Marla raised an eyebrow. "Do tell."

"The reason I missed the meeting is Nicolette kidnapped me."

Marla sat up straighter. "What? Why, to get to me?"

"Oh, no. When Gregor found out she'd taken me, he threw a hissy fit and sent me on my way, and probably gave her hell. He seemed pretty terrified that you'd be pissed."

"He may have good reason. So why *did* she take you?"

Rondeau looked down. "I mentioned that bad run of luck I had gambling. . . ."

"Shit, Rondeau, how much do you owe her?"

"See, the bitch of it is the compound interest. . . . She wants my club. This club. That'd just about cover it. I think she must want the special conference room."

Marla put her head in her hands. "I don't know why I ever stop slapping you, even for a minute."

Rondeau cleared his throat. "Yeah, so she was pressuring me, and I invoked your name, you know, to encourage her to give me a little more time, but I guess she got impatient, so . . . but Gregor told her to ease off, not to bother me, because bothering me bothers *you*."

Marla frowned. "It's not like him to be that considerate, but fuck it. We've all got bigger things on our minds. *If* we get through the next few days in one piece, we'll figure out a way for you to square things without losing the club. Maybe you can do some work for Nicolette. Ted, you fill Rondeau in on what happened to us today, okay? You took notes, right? I've got to make some calls."

"Want me to make them?" Ted said. He sounded exhausted, and it was a wonder he hadn't pissed himself during their long fall—or maybe he had, and the wind had dried it. Marla shook her head. "No. These calls, I have to make on my own."

She headed upstairs as Ted began to tell Rondeau about their adventures in dreamland. He'd probably get St. John Austen's speech word-for-word. Ted wasn't magical, but he was pulling his weight anyway. She called Hamil from her office. "We need a gathering," she said. "*Everybody.*" Hamil said he'd see to it—he didn't need to ask why.

She sat at her desk, wondering if she should call Joshua. She wanted him for the comfort he gave, and she wanted to make sure he was okay, but she was afraid that calling him would be a show of weakness she couldn't afford. She would need him for the meeting, but Hamil knew that, and would make the arrangements. She'd just wait.

Hamil called back twenty minutes later. "Gregor says he can't come, something about a delicate spell that needs his physical presence in the building."

"Fuck that," Marla said. "Tell him we'll meet at his place, then."

Hamil didn't speak for a moment. "And if he refuses?"

Marla picked up a silver letter opener from her desk. It gleamed in the lamplight. Anything could be dangerous in the right hands. "Tell him I'm not asking. It's a matter of Felport's security, so he doesn't *get* to say no." She hung up, sighed, and called Langford.

"Your city is undergoing some unpleasant transformations," he said.

"I noticed. Any luck finding Genevieve?"

"She's in the city. Intermittently, though, and not for long. I'm narrowing the parameters. I have my search protocol slaved to a minor oracle, and so far it's been hit-or-miss at predicting her next location, only accurate five percent more often than chance. Wait, six percent now. It's getting more accurate on an exponential curve, though, so by . . . hmm . . . tomorrow in the early afternoon I should be able to predict her next appearance with better than ninety percent accuracy."

Marla whistled. That was better than she'd hoped for. "Langford, you're a genius."

"Sometimes, when the wind is right," he said. "Get a strike team ready to mobilize. I may not be able to give you a lot of advance notice about her materialization." He paused. "And, of course, all bets are off if an army of monsters from a nightmare destroys my lab."

"Get all your defenses online," she said.

He cleared his throat. "That's *expensive*."

"I'll pay the bill."

"Yes, ma'am. Do you still want me to come to your meeting?"

"No, I guess not. I figured I'd need you as a science advisor to assure them that everything we *could* do was being done, but you gave me an actual timetable, so I'll be able to shut them up."

"Knock 'em dead," he said.

"How about our buddy Zealand? Have you tracked him down?"

"Not yet. He is very effectively hidden. He hasn't left the city, but beyond that, who knows. There are a few places in the city that are impervious to scrying, and he must have found one of them."

She sighed. "Which means he was hired by a sorcerer, who's now hiding him. Well, I'm not surprised, but it sucks. You'll keep trying? He has to go out *sometime.*"

"Yes, of course. I'll let you know if he turns up."

"Good enough," she said, and hung up.

Hamil rang in soon after, to tell her the meeting was set for nine o'clock at Gregor's, and he would meet her there. She thanked him, stood up, paced around the office, looked out the window at the snow, tried not to think about the crazy shit that might be happening out there, and even tried meditating, but she just couldn't get her head straight.

Screw it. She'd call Joshua, too, even though Hamil had already confirmed he would be at the meeting. After the day she'd had, she deserved a little lovetalk.

But his phone just rang and rang, and he never picked up, and she couldn't think of anything to say to his voicemail that wouldn't sound desperate and weak.

Zealand spent an hour at a construction site, seeing what his mold could do. It wasn't all that disgusting, really. He felt a bit like Spider-Man, but when he gave in to the temptation to sling a rope of vinelike mold at a steel girder and swing, he nearly crashed into a pile of rebar. He had more luck using the mold to tangle things up and pull them down. He startled a nest of rats, and the mold went after them without his conscious thought, spraying out from his hand and immobilizing them, and a few moments later, when the mold turned brown and blew away, there was nothing left beneath them but tiny white bones. Creepy, but creepy was Zealand's stock and trade. At some point, the mold had migrated to his other hand as well, which was faintly disturbing, but meant he could send waves of crawling fungus in more than one direction at once. He slammed his cocooned fists into a heap of cinderblocks and punched them into powder, without feeling the impact on his hands, the force of the blow absorbed by his furry green gloves. The mold kept him warm, too. It was a surreal sort of superpower, but he welcomed any advantage when it came to fighting Marla.

"Not sure how it helps against knives, guns, and Tasers," he said, musing, and the mold surprised him by crawling up his arms, under his clothes, across his chest, around his back, down his legs—covering him in a rippling green second skin that made his clothes flutter. "Huh," he said. "Can you . . . hear me?" The mold didn't respond, but how could it have? He thumped his own chest a couple of times without feeling any pain, but couldn't think of a way to test the mold suit's protective powers without endangering his life. "Guess I'll just have to trust you," he said. He checked his watch—the mold obligingly scurried aside—and saw it was going on eight o'clock. Marla surely had sorcerers magically searching for him, but that kind of work took time, so if he moved quickly, he should be able to proceed before being detected. He wondered if

Nicolette and Gregor had missed him yet. He hoped not. He wanted to slip back into the building unnoticed and have a go at Reave, after he was done with Marla. It would be a long night, but something—adrenaline, or perhaps some quality of the mold—made him feel energized.

The mold shot out of his sleeves and snatched something out of the air. Zealand drew in the tentacle of green and frowned. The mold had caught a shuriken, a throwing star, blacked so it wouldn't reflect light. He sighed. "Hello, brothers."

"Zealand," said Kardec, from somewhere near a heap of cinderblocks. "How nice of you to come out and play."

"I'm impressed. How did you find me?"

"We have eyes everywhere. The sorcerers can peer into their scrying mirrors or crystal balls or bowls of mercury all they like, but we simply keep our eyes on the streets."

"Mmm," Zealand said. "Antiquated. Inefficient. Sounds like the slow assassins. Push off, gentlemen, and let me do my business, and you will be allowed to live."

Kardec chuckled. "It was a nice trick, snatching the shuriken from the air by magic. I would have simply used my hands. You've been consorting with sorcerers too long. You've forgotten the fundamentals."

Zealand lifted his hands and threw out a rope of fungus, smashing through the cinderblocks, powdering a few of them to dust. Kardec grunted, and Zealand raced in his direction, leaping over the blocks, but the slow assassin was gone. "You're a bureaucrat," Zealand said, looking around the dark construction site. "You haven't been in top fighting form for years. I trust you brought a few others to help you?"

Someone gurgled behind him, and Zealand turned to find a black-clad man scrabbling at his own throat, trying to pry off the mold that choked him. Zealand smiled. The mold had sprung from the back of his neck. He did have eyes in the back of his head. The assassin fell, either dead or unconscious, and the mold drew back to Zealand's body.

A great whizzing filled the air, and tentacles of fungus shot out from his hands, his throat, the cuffs of his trousers, through the buttons of his shirt, in all directions, snatching crossbow bolts, arrows, poison darts, and even a couple of bullets from the air. "The same back at you," Zealand said, though he wasn't sure it would work. He should have had more faith in the fungus, he realized, because the tentacles reared back and whipped their lethal projectiles through the air, back toward their original owners, and he heard a few gasps and cries that suggested at least some of the weapons hit their targets. "Really, brothers, you're wasting my time," Zealand said. "I'll tell you what. I know the death of your operative was distressing. I certainly didn't wish for that to happen. I'll make a generous donation to your organization, what do you say?"

"Money is not our object," Kardec said, perhaps from the direction of a backhoe, perhaps from behind those steel barrels. "You betrayed us. You must be punished. We must make an example of you."

"I'm sure it's hard, after all those centuries of being the most feared and dangerous killers in the world, to have me come along and outclass you," Zealand mused. "Why don't you *stalk*—me for twenty years, hmm? Let everyone know you're pursuing me, and that my come-uppance will come—oh, yes, in a time of your choosing. You can save face that way. Truly, Kardec, you *annoy* me. How many of your men must I kill tonight to make you leave? I know each is a tremendous investment of time and effort. Why waste them just to waste *me*?"

"I will slit your throat, Zealand," Kardec said levelly.

"Poor Kardec," Zealand said, almost sad for him. "You want to be my nemesis, don't you? My arch-enemy. But you're so unimportant to me, I can scarcely believe I'm bothering to talk to you now. You think your pursuit of me is the story of my life, but you're barely a subplot." While the words were true, Zealand also hoped they would be upsetting enough to make Kardec attack him directly, so Zealand could kill him. The slow assassins were a conservative organization, and if Zealand killed one of their top operatives, they might hesitate to send another force against him. But Kardec didn't answer, and Zealand sensed that he was now alone. They would wait for another opportunity. Well, good for them. Zealand hadn't worried *too* much about his former brothers before, and now that he had the mold protecting him, they were barely an irritant. Still, Kardec and his killers had wasted Zealand's valuable time, and he needed to get a move on, before Marla's seers and diviners discovered him.

He walked the few blocks to Rondeau's club, the mold shifting eagerly across his body. The building was nondescript, marked only with a sign that read "Juliana's" over the door. It wouldn't open until nine at the earliest, so—assuming Marla was here, as she usually was in the evenings—he had time to slip in and dispose of her without drawing a crowd. And if she wasn't here, he'd beat her location out of Rondeau or one of her other associates. Charging in through the front door didn't appeal, so he crept around the alleyway, looking for a side door with a lock he could pick. Unfortunately, the only door he found had no handle or lock on the outside, just a buzzer, which didn't help him. He started to turn away when his hands began to tingle, and fine threads of mold spun down from his fingertips and began waving toward the door. He pressed his hand against the door, and the mold slithered through the cracks around the jamb; a moment later it clicked and opened far enough for him to hook his fingers on the edge and swing it wide. There was only darkness beyond the door, and the murmur of voices, and he slipped in quickly, letting the door shut behind him. A wire dangled loose above the emergency door, and he realized that it was alarmed. The mold had thought—could it *think*?—to pull loose the wires and prevent the alarm from sounding. Extraordinary. It was like having an accomplice he could carry with him.

He was in a dark corner of the club, near the stage; this door was probably used to load in the DJ's gear. The only lights came from the vicinity of the bar, which was invisible from here—the club was in the shape of an L, and the bar was situated along one wall of the short arm, with the main dance floor here before him. Voices came from around that corner, along with the light, and Zealand slipped quiet as a cockroach across the floor, the mold swarming out over his shoes to soften each step. He paused in the shadow of the wall, right around the corner from the bar, and listened.

Marla said, "It'll all be over tomorrow afternoon, one way or another, unless we fuck things up seriously."

"You're going to try to help her, aren't you?" Rondeau said. "I mean, killing her . . . that's a last resort, right?"

Marla sighed. "Ted, when I asked you to tell him what happened, I didn't ask you to editorialize."

"Sorry," said a stranger's voice—presumably Ted. "It seemed important."

"I'll do whatever I have to do to save Felport," she said. "If that means killing Genevieve, well, that sucks, but better her than everybody and everything else."

Zealand scowled. He didn't pretend to understand much about Genevieve, but he had no doubt she was a *victim*, not a villain. He took a dentist's mirror from his pocket and used it to look around the corner. Marla was at the bar, her back turned, and Rondeau was standing behind the bar, messing around with bottles. Ted was hunched on a bar stool several seats down from Marla, effectively out of the picture. If Zealand timed it right, he could get to Marla before Rondeau knew what was happening. He reached into his pocket for a garrote, but the mold flowed across his hands, forming a tough strand of choking vine. He grinned. This was truly versatile stuff. He crouched, and felt the mold tighten, acting as a second set of muscles. Marla didn't stand a chance.

A phone rang, then stopped. Marla said, "Yeah, Langford?" Her voice changed, becoming more intense. "You got a fix on him? Well, then narrow it down. Tick-tock, Langford. What do you mean he's right on top—"

Zealand launched himself around the corner.

Langford, on Marla's phone, said, "I mean Zealand is right *there*," and then Rondeau was shouting and pointing, and Ted was turning around on his stool in her peripheral vision, and she started to turn, just fast enough to see Zealand flying through the fucking *air* toward her, his fingers dripping some kind of green shit, more green creeping up his cheeks and neck. He was going to hit her, and there wasn't time to dive out of the way, there was barely time to flick a dagger out of her sleeve and into her hand, and to raise her hands to meet him, before the impact—

Which never came. Zealand hung still in the air, arms outstretched, ropes of slimy green spiraling out toward her, the nearest one inches from her face. A dozen tendrils, budded from the end, waved impotently, and she knew without a doubt that they were going for her eyes, her nostrils, her mouth, ready to fill her and suffocate her. Marla slid from the bar stool and off to the side, Zealand's eyes the only mobile thing in his body, tracking her, wide and furious. "What the *hell*," she said.

Ted held up his hand, which was bleeding, and winced as he picked bits of glass out of his palm. "The glass vial you gave me, with the spider in it," he said, almost apologetically. "You told me if we saw Genevieve or Zealand, I should crush it—"

Marla grabbed Ted by the shoulders and kissed him on the lips; he was so startled he emitted a little peep. "You get a raise," she said. "Rondeau! See this man gets a raise! Did you see that?" she said, turning to Rondeau. "He crushed that thing and cast that bug-in-amber spell like *that*." She snapped her fingers. "Ted caught that motherfucker in *midair*."

"Good shooting," Rondeau said. "Do you think

we should, I don't know, *restrain* him before the spell wears off?"

"Oh, sure," Marla said. "We've got a few minutes, though, and he'll fall straight down like a rock when it gives. All his momentum's gone." She walked around Zealand, prodding his body, frowning. She lifted up his coat and tugged his shirt out of his waistband; his skin was swarming with fungus. "You hooked up with some kind of crazy herbomancer?" she said finally. "That's . . . weird. I heard you weren't a big fan of magic." She circled back around to his front, took out her dagger of office, and cut the vines of vegetation away from his fingers. The severed mold began to turn brown right away, and within seconds it was just flakes of gray dust, impossible even to hold in her hands. She brushed it away, frowning, then met his eyes. "Look, why are you so determined to kill me? How much can they possibly be paying you? I believe in taking pride in your work, but if you keep this up, I'm going to have to execute you, but only after I have my friend Langford put his nasty mind-reading helmet on you. It doesn't kill you when it sucks out your thoughts, but it makes you *wish* you were dead—it's like a hangover turned up to eleven."

"You can't kill her," he said, speaking through his involuntarily clenched teeth. "I won't *let* you kill her."

"Kill *who*?" Marla said. "What are you—" She stopped. "Shit."

"The green knight," Ted said.

"You're the green knight," Marla said, cocking her head. "You work for Genevieve? Why would she hire you to kill me? I only decided I might have to kill her a few hours ago!"

"She didn't hire him," Rondeau said, and Marla turned, because this was information from a quarter she had *not* expected. "Not at first. I didn't recognize him right away with that green crap crawling up his face, but this guy was at Gregor's today, when Nicolette had me tied up. She brought him in to torture me, or at least to scare me into *thinking* he would."

"Now, *that's* interesting. You work for *Gregor*?"

"Once," he said. His lips moved a little more now, which meant the spell was fading. "No more. He's working with Reave, and I won't let them hurt Genevieve, either."

"I'll be godsdamned," she said. She'd been suspicious of Gregor, but he was an expert in divination, a jumped-up fortune-teller who'd gotten rich by abusing the stock market. She'd never taken him for a throne-toppler. "What's gotten into him? He's allying himself with my enemies, trying to kill me? No wonder he hasn't been returning my calls—though if he had any sense, he'd be pretending everything was normal. Hell. This is a whole new wrinkle. Look, Mr. Z, me and you shouldn't be enemies, all right? We have some common ground here—we both want to stop this Reave guy."

Uncertainty flickered in his eyes, but only for a moment. The green on his hands was beginning to move by itself again, just a little. "You lie. You want to kill Genevieve."

She sighed. "I've been *willing* to kill Genevieve, because she's the root of all the crazy shit happening out there. Look at you, Zealand—you're covered in magical *mold*, and I'm guessing that's her doing. There are towers appearing and disappearing on the streets. There are monsters running loose, people dropping unconscious on the street and disappearing and reappearing, bringing bits of Genevieve's nightmares back with them. From an urban management standpoint, it's a bad situation! But I don't *want* to kill Genevieve. I want to *help* her." She sighed, rubbed her forehead, and said, "Look. Will you help me if I promise not to kill Genevieve?"

"How can I believe you?" The spell slipped another notch, and he dropped an inch, but still hovered some height above the floor.

"I'll swear it on the name of my city," she said. "I'm a *sorcerer,* Zealand—we don't go around breaking oaths. We do our best to never make them, but our word is all we have. You must know that."

"Oaths are nice, but hardly unbreakable. You may even be sincere now, but circumstances could change your dedication."

She sighed. "Okay. We'll draw a binding circle—I'll swear not to kill Genevieve, or cause her to be killed by my actions or orders, or allow her to be killed by my willful negligence, and you'll swear not to kill *me* or cause my death, etc. And if either of us breaks our word, poof, it means *we* die. Big magic. Okay?"

He considered. "That is acceptable. Why the change of heart?"

She shook her head. "Well, for one thing, I can't get much done with you constantly trying to kill me! You're pretty badass, and an alliance with you could do both of us a lot of good. For another, these two have been giving me shit for the whole killing Genevieve thing, too, and I'm starting to think maybe all of you have a point. My first loyalty is to Felport, but if I start committing atrocities to keep the city safe . . . that's a pretty slippery slope. You think I don't feel for her?

Hell, I wish I had the time to track down Terry Reeves and punch his face into a crater, just for the principle of the thing."

"Terry who?" Zealand said.

"Reeves. He's the, what would you call it, *inspiration* for Reave, Mr. King of Nightmares. He raped Genevieve, and she's such a powerful psychic that his traumatic memory became a living thing with its own nasty hopes and dreams. Reave is like a monster-movie exaggeration of this genuine asshole Terry Reeves." She shook her head. "Reave is the dangerous one. Help me find a way to stop him. And maybe let Genevieve know that I'm *not* planning to kill her?"

The spell died out, and Zealand fell to the floor, but he didn't sprawl inelegantly as Marla had expected; the mold must have helped him somehow, because he landed in a graceful crouch, then rose and nodded. "Very well. But Reave is with Gregor. How will you reach him? Gregor's building is a fortress. I know—they were hiding me there, to keep you from finding me, and I only escaped through Genevieve's intervention."

"Oh, we can get in," Marla said, grinning. "We're having a meeting there in about forty-five minutes. But first, Ted, bring me the red chalk and the jar of black sand from my office. I need to draw a binding charm here, so Zealand and I can cross our hearts and hope to die."

13

When Joshua slid into the back of the Bentley, it took all Marla's willpower not to jump him. He settled in beside her and gave her one of his dazzling smiles. "I missed you," he said.

"Good. It's good to be missed."

"You lovebirds behave back there," Rondeau shouted from the driver's seat. "This isn't some kind of taxicab-confessions mobile hedonism unit!" Ted, riding up front beside him, paid no attention, but just murmured into his phone, probably taking care of problems Marla hadn't even noticed yet.

"So what's the plan, my liege?" Joshua asked. "Hamil told me this is a big meeting of all the sorcerers. I thought that wasn't scheduled for a couple more days."

"This is something different. An emergency-session sort of thing to deal with the whole people-getting-sucked-into-dreamland thing."

"I assumed such were the natural hazards of working in a city full of sorcerers."

Marla snorted. "*Most* cities of any size are full of

sorcerers. But we usually do a good job at keeping the magical disruptions to a minimum, and try to hide our actions from ordinary people. One of my main jobs is keeping a lid on things like mysterious disappearances and spontaneously appearing orange trees. Things are getting out of hand. There's an end in sight—I hope—but it's going to get worse before it gets better, and I need some damage control. In times of crisis, the chief sorcerer can compel the assistance of other sorcerers in the city. Think of us as a bunch of crime families, with alliances and allegiances to make it easier to do business. I'm going to call on the other big noises in town so we can lock things down before they get worse. What I need *you* to do is smooth the passage. Nod when I say something, frown and shake your head whenever anyone disagrees with me—nothing too overt, just enough to show that your support is unconditionally with me—and it should have a dampening effect on the usual explosive bullshit that happens anytime more than two sorcerers get together in a room."

"Understood. Anything else I should know?"

She considered telling him about Zealand, who was even now approaching Gregor's building from a different direction, and about Gregor's alliance with Reave, but they were pulling up to the building, and there wasn't time to get into everything—especially when it came to explaining that she was now allied with the assassin who'd tried to murder them the night before. "Just trust me, and if something unexpected happens, roll with it. And if something *violent* happens, get yourself out of the way. You're not a fighter, and you're no good to me dead. Okay?"

"Yes, ma'am," he said, and she couldn't help herself—she leaned over and kissed his delicious lips. *For luck,* she told herself. Then she opened the door and stepped out into the cold.

Zealand broke into Gregor's building without much difficulty, thanks to a combination of his natural skills and the ever-increasing genius of the mold, which managed to slip through a crack in the service entrance and crawl several meters down a hallway to disable the security system through the simple expedient of choking the wiring with vegetation; the mold wasn't smart enough to crack keypad codes yet, it seemed. Getting back up to the higher floors was more difficult, since the elevators were monitored, and the stairwells, too. Zealand called his mold back until all that remained was a spot on each hand and a fuzzy cummerbund against his skin, hidden by his clothes. He made his way to the building's kitchen and began rummaging through the big industrial refrigerators, finding a platter of roast turkey covered in Saran wrap, a commercial tub of mayonnaise, and a loaf of bread. He made himself a little feast at one of the big prep tables and waited.

He was halfway through his second sandwich when Nicolette appeared with a clatter of braids. She'd added several objects to those previously tangled in her hair—glass beads in the shape of tiny white skulls, knots of thorns wired together, coins with holes punched in their centers, a cat's-eye marble bigger than a grape in a wire cage.

"Want a sandwich?" he asked.

"How the fuck did you get down here without security noticing?"

"Have we met? I'm Zealand. I was trained by the slow assassins."

She shook her head. "If you were hungry, why didn't you just ask for something to eat?"

He hazarded a guess. "There seemed to be a certain, ah, buzz of activity about the place, and I didn't want to disturb."

Nicolette picked up a piece of turkey and munched it. Her shoulders slumped, and Zealand realized with something like horror that she was about to *confide* in him—she must consider him a friend! Or else she was convincingly pretending she did, for her own reasons. She was a chaos magician, which made analysis of her behavior difficult. She drew her power from disorder, so she couldn't be counted on to do *anything*, not even to act in her own self-interest. Zealand found her far more terrifying than Gregor, who was as predictable as a bullet trajectory.

"Things here are fucked," she said. "Gregor told me to find you and make sure you stay out of sight. Marla Mason is coming here, in about fifteen minutes, along with every other big bad sorcerer in Felport. Some of those fuckers scare *me*."

"Why the gathering? Monthly quilting circle?"

Nicolette laughed. "These are good times for chaos, Z. Reave has brought a whole lot of craziness with him, and things are getting wild out there. You wouldn't know, being all tucked up safe and sound in here, but there are buildings appearing out of nowhere, people disappearing, monsters roaming the outskirts . . . it's a big beautiful wonderful mess. I'm positively *crackling* with power. But Marla's worried about the state of the city. So she's called us all together to make a game plan, probably, or at least quarantine the mess."

"Marla is coming *here* to figure out how to stop Reave, who is allied with your master? I suppose you'll be keeping *him* under lock and key, too, hmm?"

"Reave is a free agent, but he knows it's better to stay away for a few hours, yeah. The boss and me will pretend to go along with Marla—we already had to roll over and let the meeting happen here—and keep, ah, pursuing our own agenda on the side. Gregor figures it's a calculated risk—the relevant prophecies say he's safe as long as he doesn't leave the building, so he thinks it's unlikely that Marla will attack him here." She shrugged. "Typical backstabbing sorcerer shit, but on a bigger scale than usual, I gotta say."

"Your own agenda? And what, exactly, is Gregor helping Reave *do*?"

Nicolette waved her hand. "Conquer the world. Crush all opposition with iron boots. You know, guy stuff. Very linear, very top-down."

"I see," Zealand said. He didn't think he could get her to be any more specific than that—Nicolette was no fool—but he knew enough. Genevieve was somehow the key to Reave's ambitions, and Zealand would make sure Reave didn't get to her. Simple, really. And he was happier being on Marla's side, for the moment, than he'd been fighting against her. He made another sandwich. "Shall I retire to my room, then?"

"Double-quick, and don't come out until I tell you." She escorted him upstairs.

Once he was alone in his room, Zealand settled down to wait. Marla had a plan, and he knew his place in it. He reached for his book—and realized he'd left it in the library in Genevieve's palace. He sighed, but there was nothing to be done about it. It wasn't as if he'd never read *The Art of War* before. He just found the familiar pages comforting.

Marla rode up the elevator with Rondeau, Joshua, and Ted. She tapped her foot and stared at the ceiling and thought murderous thoughts. She hated getting together with the other leading sorcerers. It always turned into a pissing contest.

"You look nervous," Rondeau said.

"I'm not so good at diplomacy. But that's why Joshua's here."

The elevator opened, and Marla strode out into the hall. She wore more finery than usual, with her white cloak across her shoulders—the lethal purple side turned inward, for now—fastened at the throat with a silver pin in the shape of a stag beetle. Her white cotton shirt and pants were loose and allowed great freedom of movement. Her reinforced boots were shined, and she had six rings on her fingers (only half of them magically imbued). Her dagger of office hung in a sheath at her belt, the hilt wrapped in alternating bands of white-and-purple electrical tape. The other sorcerers would be pretty much equally armed, everyone more comfortable with mutual assured destruction in the event of a fight than they would have been with some bullshit restriction on bringing weapons, which everyone would have ignored anyway. Marla wasn't wearing makeup—she still had her limits—but she'd washed her hair before coming over. Right now, she was the leader of the sorcerers of Felport, first among equals, protector of the city, and it paid to look her best.

The meeting room was appointed with couches, club chairs, and stools, and Nicolette was unfolding extra chairs as they arrived. The place was jammed with Felport's most prominent handful of sorcerers and their retainers, and they all turned to stare at Marla when she walked in.

Viscarro sat in a far corner, peering at her through his gold-rimmed monocle, his skin paler than the snow outside. He wore a velvet smoking jacket from another era, though it might have been fashionable the last time he emerged from his vaults into the wider world.

Ernesto, a big man wearing a tuxedo with grease-stained lapels—for magical purposes, not just because he was a slob—sat on a stool popping olives into his mouth, and he grinned at Marla and waved. He was still happy with her because she'd given him a contract to clean up pollution in the bay, and allowed him to use the resulting filthy residue to make a pollution golem to patrol his junkyard.

The Chamberlain stood by the window in a long black evening gown that revealed the smooth length of her back, her skin dark and lustrous, and she turned to regard Marla with a glance of infinite pity and scorn; Marla never felt more like a dirty child pretending to be a grown-up than she did in the Chamberlain's presence, but the Chamberlain wasn't exactly an enemy. She hadn't brought bodyguards, but she had the ghosts of Felport's founding families at her beck and call, so she hardly needed backup.

The Bay Witch wore her usual dark blue wetsuit, her blond hair was disarrayed, and she dripped water in a spreading puddle on the carpet. She kept casting anxious glances toward the eastern wall—she didn't often leave the bay, and was clearly uncomfortable this high up.

Granger—that idiot Granger—sat picking his nose, oblivious to the gravity of the situation. He was a hereditary sorcerer with no particular intelligence or wit, but his family had been the caretakers of Fludd Park back when it was just the village commons; he was tied to the land, and had power to go with it. Nature magic made Marla uncomfortable—she was a city woman by choice—but he was unquestionably important enough to have a seat at the table, even if he didn't do anything with that seat but wipe boogers beneath it.

Gregor stood as far across the room from Marla as he could get, and he looked unhappy. If Marla hadn't known about his plans to kill her, she would have assumed he was just pissed about the Bay Witch dripping all over his carpet—Gregor was a notorious neat-freak.

Hamil was here already, and he gave her a nod from the vast overstuffed armchair where he'd installed himself. He gestured toward another chair, apparently left unoccupied as a courtesy for her. The chair faced all the other seats, which meant she could address everyone easily, but it also looked a little like a hot seat.

"Hello, everyone. Thanks for coming." Marla sat, and Joshua stood a bit behind her, where everyone could see him. Rondeau and Ted stood back against the wall with the other assistants, apprentices, and assorted hangers-on. "You all know why you're here. There's a woman named Genevieve Kelley wandering the city, and her bad dreams are intruding into our reality at an exponential rate, probably because of all the stress she's under. Worse, one of her bad dreams has a mind of his own. Reave is dangerous, but if we can reach Genevieve and get her back to Dr. Husch at the Blackwing Institute, I think we can get Reave under control, too." Marla wasn't sure of that at all, but getting Genevieve out of the city couldn't hurt the cause.

"Why don't we just kill her?" Viscarro said, his voice harsh and grating from long disuse.

"You want to make it our policy to kill insane sorcerers, instead of confining them to the Blackwing Institute?" Marla said, and Viscarro flinched. He'd been confined in Blackwing himself for a few months after having a nervous breakdown many years before, but he'd recovered.

"Of course not," the Chamberlain said, and everyone turned to give her their attention. She could have been chief sorcerer, if she'd wanted, but she wasn't interested in the job—she only cared about the Heights, the historic and hoity-toity area of the city where her ghostly extended family lived among the oblivious yuppies and nouveau riche. "Killing the mentally ill is bad policy. But if there are no other options . . ."

"There *are* other options," Marla said. "I have a good lead on Genevieve, and expect to have her in hand tomorrow afternoon."

"What lead?" Ernesto asked.

"You all know Langford, the technomancer. He's found a way to track Genevieve, and—"

"Nonsense," Gregor said. "I've been trying to track her myself, and she only pops out of her dream world for a few minutes at a time. She can't be found."

"Are you calling me a liar?" Marla asked, and she

noticed Joshua from the corner of her eye, frowning and shaking his head at Gregor. Good boy. "Langford uses different methods from yours, Gregor, and he's got some of Genevieve's personal possessions to work with, too. You're the best when it comes to traditional methods of divination, no doubt, but Langford's got a gift for improvisation on the fly. He says he'll have Genevieve's location by tomorrow—actionable intelligence, info we can *use*—and he's not the type to boast."

"All right," Gregor said. "My apologies. Go on."

"The more immediate problem," Marla said, "is the whole city going to hell. We need to deal with containment and quarantine. Right now, Genevieve's little reality-alterations are confined to a few areas, but they're spreading, and we don't want them to get beyond the borders of Felport. We need to cut off communication with the outside world, and keep people from getting in *or* out. Any ideas?"

"The border guardians can whip up a blizzard," Hamil said. "Bad enough to close the roads. And if things get really bad, beyond the ability of our own forces to contain, we can always activate the secret oaths—the police force will help us without even realizing why they're doing it."

"Cutting communication is easy," Ernesto said. "Consider it done." Marla nodded; Ernesto was good at infrastructure.

"I'll secure the sea route, not that there's a lot of oceangoing traffic in this weather," the Bay Witch said.

"It would be good to get more of our people out on the street," Marla said, "to deal with shit before it gets too bad. Things have been glimpsed in alleys and backstreets, and while they haven't attacked any people yet, it would be good to have defenses ready." Marla outlined the neighborhoods she wanted defended, and delegated people to cover each, and the grumbling was surprisingly minimal, thanks to Joshua's nodding and beaming at her every word. He was worth his weight in platinum.

"I'll get the mayor to declare a state of emergency, ostensibly because of the blizzard, and advise everyone to stay home," Marla said. "We'll close the airport, train station, bus depots, everything. It wouldn't kill us to get some sort of soothing stay-home vibe going through the city, too." None of the current ruling cabal was particularly adept at such mental magic, but many of them had projecting empaths and the like in their employ. "Not that people are necessarily safer inside their homes, but so far most of the big interruptions in reality are happening outside." She went over a few more specifics, assigning tasks and offering compliments or incentives or threats where necessary, but by the time she finished, she felt things were well in hand. Damage control was never fun, but it could have gone a lot worse—without Joshua's silent yet charismatic support, there would have been a lot more bitching and moaning.

"If we're done here—" Marla said.

"When are you going to divide up Susan Wellstone's assets?" Viscarro said. "Her property, her interests in local business, it's all just sitting, going to waste. Making money for *you*."

"The income from Susan's businesses is held in trust, and you know it. We'll meet on that subject in a couple of days, assuming the city isn't a smoking hole in the ground by then. Perspective, people. I don't *want* Susan's shit, so stop suggesting otherwise." She didn't bother to hide her irritation. Viscarro wanted *everything*. He was a classic hoarder. Rumors said he was part dragon, but Marla didn't believe in dragons. He was just a greedy fuck.

Viscarro scowled, rose from his chair, and stalked off. The others left, too, most pausing to shake her hand and exchange a few words, taking their entourages with them. When only Marla, Hamil, and their people were left, Gregor approached them, frowning, with Nicolette at his side. "If you're done imposing on my hospitality, I have to clean up the water puddles and grease stains left behind by our esteemed guests."

"We need to chat, Gregor," Marla said. "You've been a naughty boy."

He had enough self-control to keep his expression calm. "I've been nothing but cooperative, while you've let the city fall apart. I have half a mind to—"

Marla kicked him in the knee, and Gregor fell, gasping and clutching at his leg. Nicolette reached for one of the charms in her hair, but Hamil was already winding a piece of string woven with a stolen strand of Nicolette's hair around his finger, and the sympathetic magic bound up the chaos magician, too, freezing her in mid-motion.

"What's going on?" Joshua said, alarmed.

"Don't worry, baby," Marla said. "Just taking care of some traitors in our midst. Gregor here hired that assassin to attack us."

"Lies," Gregor grunted.

"I got it from the man's own mouth," Marla said.

"I made him repeat it in a circle of binding, and he told the same story even under the truth-compulsion."

"Impossible," Nicolette said. "You couldn't have talked to him, he's been here the whole—" Her eyes went wide, and Marla couldn't help but grin. Nicolette probably had a lot of fine qualities, but apparently she wasn't the sharpest arrow in the quiver—at least, not under stress.

Gregor snarled. "You idiot!"

Marla crouched down beside him. The rings on her fingers would vibrate if he tried to cast any spells, but he wasn't much of an offensive magician anyway—he was much better at plotting from the shadows. "I don't mind you trying to kill me, really. It's part of the business. I mean, I'll squash you flat for it, but that's part of the business, *too*. What I can't condone is your alliance with Reave. He wants to destroy the city, Gregor, and remake it in his own rather fucked-up image. What were you *thinking*? What, did he promise you land and titles and all that usual dark-lord-of-the-night bullshit?"

"Of course he did," Gregor said, sounding rather subdued. "But that's not why I did it. I did it because I had no choice. The auguries were clear. If I didn't ally myself with Reave, my death would result. I won't apologize for trying to preserve myself."

"Well, I gotta tell you, things aren't exactly looking good for you now," Marla said. "Nicolette doesn't have to die—she's in your employ, and I understand loyalty—but shit, Gregor, what choice have you given me? I'd banish you, but this is basically wartime, and you're an enemy collaborator. The rules about that kind of thing are pretty clear."

"You will release them now," Reave said, stepping from a dark corner of the office. He had those long knives in his hands, and the expression on his mushroom-white face was one of profound annoyance. "They are in my service."

"Baldy!" Marla said. "I was hoping you'd show up. Now, Zealand!" she shouted.

That should have been the cue for Zealand to come leaping from concealment, fungus flying, with enough force to at least distract the king of nightmares while Marla and her cohort piled on.

But Zealand didn't appear.

The floor-to-ceiling windows behind Reave shimmered like water and vanished, revealing a ramp that led to darkness—a darkness that contained scuttling, onrushing things. The king of nightmares grinned. His teeth were horrible, and flecked with green.

While the meeting droned on beyond the door, Zealand waited in the closet. He'd hidden himself there just before the guests arrived, and he was waiting for his moment. If Reave arrived—or if Gregor and Nicolette put up more of a fight than Marla was prepared for—he would step in. Simple enough, really.

Then a light appeared behind him, and with a sinking feeling, Zealand turned. The back of the closet was gone, and a new path extended before him, a long narrow footbridge over dark water, leading to a small wooded isle. There were two moons in the sky, and the smaller of the two was threaded with red, like a bloodshot eye. Something flew over the water off in the distance, a seabird the size of a small plane. A tall dark tower rose on the horizon, disagreeably phallic.

Zealand considered leaping out of the closet, but that didn't seem prudent. Better to sit tight, and see what happened. In the past he'd been swept up and taken to Genevieve's dreamland whole, but this was different, a bridge built between the real world and the dream. Perhaps that was Reave's approach, making connections, loosening the boundaries, making reality and nightmare blend ever more easily together.

Then the king of nightmares himself stepped onto the far end of the wooden bridge, and Zealand didn't hesitate, just raced forward, the mold flowing over his body and giving his muscles extra power. He snarled, his teeth bared—

—and Reave waved his hand, making a wide section of the bridge ahead vanish. The water began foaming, alive with things Zealand couldn't see, but which he suspected were full of teeth. He stopped short, two steps from plunging off the end of the broken bridge, the mold helping arrest his motion just as it had helped propel him. Reave regarded him across the gulf, and sighed. "We could have been friends," he said. "You seem more a thing of nightmares than sweet dreams, Zealand. It's not too late. Join me."

"Never. I *detest* your kind."

Reave didn't have eyebrows to arch, but he looked surprised. "My kind? What kind is that?"

"Rapists."

Reave waved a hand dismissively. "The seed of my creation may have been a rapist, but I have transcended that. I have no interest in the flesh of women; I *despise* women. My greatest regret is that I owe my existence to a woman, a weak vessel like Genevieve. You find no appeal in the flesh of women, either, isn't that true, Zealand? We are not so dissimilar."

"Being gay isn't the same thing as being a misogynist, you ass," Zealand said.

Reave shrugged. "I suppose you've told Marla about my relationship with Gregor?"

Zealand grinned. "Does that worry you, mushroom man? Are you scared of a woman like Marla?"

"Not at all. I'm not afraid of buzzing flies, either, but they can be an annoyance. I'll brush her away. But I *am* disappointed in you, Zealand." He turned his eyes skyward, contemplatively. "You could have—"

Zealand saw his chance and threw out his hands, flinging ropes of fungus across the gulf, striking Reave and binding him, dragging him down off the pier and into the foaming water.

But Reave didn't sink, and the things thrashing beneath the surface didn't harm him. He stood on the water as if it were concrete, and tore the vines away from himself contemptuously. "This isn't *your* world," he said. "This isn't Genevieve's palace, either. This is *my* territory, and you are at my mercy." Knives dropped into his hands from his sleeves—or from *nowhere,* since reality was his to alter—and he climbed up onto the pier. Zealand backed away, recognizing that he was outgunned, and turned to run down the bridge, back toward the closet. But the closet, of course, was gone, with only an endless expanse of bridge before him, stretching over the water as far as he could see. Reave was behind him, his feet slapping wetly against the boards, and even with the mold giving him a burst of speed, Zealand couldn't run *forever,* and how long before Reave made the boards in front of him vanish, too?

It didn't come to that. Reave's knives went into Zealand's back, right through his kidneys. Zealand had been stabbed before, but this pain was indescribable, a pair of hot lances transfixing him. He went down face-first on the boards, and Reave crouched on top of him, pressing his knees against the wounds. The world faded, went black, returned in a burst of white agony. "My dear Zealand," Reave said, right in his ear, intimate as a lover. Or an assassin. "You will be missed, by someone, I'm sure."

Then the world tilted, a vertiginous twist that was becoming as unpleasant and familiar as a red-wine hangover, and Zealand could see just enough to know he was back in the library of Genevieve's palace. St. John Austen was there, reaching out, looking pained and anxious, and Zealand wanted to say something, make some apology or explanation, but the darkness returned before he could.

"Back, guys, get back," Marla said, drawing her dagger of office. It wasn't really a weapon for streetfighting, but it could cut through *anything*. She held the knife in a reverse grip, like an ice pick, the blade up against her forearm, where she could flick it out without Reave seeing where the strike was coming from. Reave held his own weapons in a straight-up grip, and didn't carry them like a knowledgeable knife-fighter, but that didn't mean he wouldn't be dangerous. Rondeau tossed her a dish towel—who knew where he'd gotten it?—and she wrapped it around her other forearm, so she could absorb some of Reave's knife-strikes. "Rondeau, Hamil, stand with me. Ted, you and Joshua get out of here." Nicolette was still bound, and Gregor was in no position to walk, not with the kick she'd given his knee. They would keep.

Reave seemed in no hurry to rush them. He was waiting for his backup, which came slithering, scuttling, and wetly dragging themselves along a ramp from another universe. They were childish nightmare things, jumbles of spider and crab and squid and serpent, all pincers and eyes. Marla was confident she'd be able to squish them. Rondeau stood at her shoulder, his butterfly knife open in his hand, and Hamil murmured to his bodyguards, enormous stitched-together corpses that only passed for real humans at a glance. They were actually more of Hamil's sympathetic magic, puppet-bodies guided by his real employees, who were safely ensconced several blocks away. Each meat golem had a little vial of hair and blood from its operator sewn deep inside its armored chest, and they'd all go on fighting until those vials were destroyed. They were blunt instruments, but that was fine with Marla. She didn't want to join combat until Ted and Joshua were safely away, but Joshua was arguing with Ted, and she didn't want to wait too much longer, so she launched herself at Reave, leaping over Gregor.

Who reached up and grabbed her ankle, sending her crashing into Nicolette, and knocking her down. Marla kicked backward viciously at Gregor, hoping to cave in his skull with her magically reinforced boots, but her foot didn't connect. Nicolette was still paralyzed at least, still in her same posture, but now supine on the floor. Without looking back, Marla regained her feet and went for Reave, who wove his knives around in a lazy pattern. With a thought Marla could reverse her cloak and become an implacable killing machine, but the cloak's magic was intensely dangerous, and it had to be a last resort—while in that haze of violence, she would just as likely turn on her friends as her enemies, and she couldn't risk hurting Joshua. *Or the others,* she thought, only a little belatedly. Besides, she figured Reave was all flash and no substance, though the blood on his knives worried her—who had he been stabbing before this? And where the hell was Zealand? The thoughts fit together uncomfortably well.

Reave came at her with the knives, and it was just too easy. She stepped in, blocked his knife-strike with her towel-wrapped arm, grabbed his other wrist, turned, and used Reave's own momentum to plunge the knife into his belly. She pressed down on his arm, expecting to feel the hot spurt of blood against her own stomach, but Reave just grunted and shoved her back. She went, putting her weight on her back foot, bringing her dagger up.

Reave wrenched the long knife out of his stomach and poked at the dry, open hole. "Bitch," he said, almost meditatively, and Marla's heart sank; he wasn't human, he didn't bleed, and sticking a knife in him had been like stabbing a loaf of bread. Maybe he was soft enough to tear into pieces, to decapitate and dismember—would that stop him? She'd need a bigger knife, or an axe, or sword, or machete. . . .

Then the monsters arrived, most the size of large dogs, squishing and lashing and squealing as Hamil's bodyguards and Rondeau stomped and stabbed and wrestled them. Reave faded back, as if content to let his monsters do their work, but Marla wasn't going to let him off that easy. It would be hard to get his head off his shoulders using only her dagger of office, but she was up to the challenge.

"Marla, watch out for Gregor!" Ted shouted, and Marla turned, annoyed that he was still here. Gregor was moving in her direction—he dragged himself over to Nicolette, and reached out to snatch a charm from her hair. Marla swore, and went to stop him, but then Reave was coming at her again, taking advantage of her inattention to stab at her, and it was all she could do to deflect his blows. There was a tinkling crash behind her, and she kicked out at Reave, forcing him back a step, long enough to steal a glance. Gregor had unleashed some little charm of Nicolette's, and now Hamil was on the ground and groaning, the magic strand that bound Nicolette dropped from his fingers. Nicolette rose and snatched another charm from her hair, dashed it to the ground, and swept up Gregor bodily—she must have given herself a burst of strength. Nicolette ran from the room, carrying her boss, and Marla didn't have time to be pissed, because Reave was on her again. She dropped and swept his legs out from under him, sending him toppling, but before she could leap on him for the coup de grâce, one of his tentacled nightmare things tangled up her legs and tried to pull her toward its slavering maw. She doubled over and hacked at the tentacles—wait, were they *tongues*?—with her dagger, severing them and making the monster squeal and draw back on itself.

Struggling to her feet, she turned back to Reave, and saw Joshua walking up to him as if they were old friends. Reave looked startled as Joshua laid a hand on his shoulder, leaned in, and whispered in his ear. Reave's eyes glazed over, and he began to nod. Marla felt a brief stab of jealousy and mentally kicked herself—being mixed up with a lovetalker led to all kinds of inappropriate feelings. Once she pushed the jealousy down she felt relieved—Joshua was lovetalking Reave, distracting him. She beckoned to Ted, and they helped get Hamil to his feet. Rondeau joined them, his outfit spattered with black-and-green streaks of nightmare blood. The two bodyguard meat-golems held off the remaining nightmares. Marla hesitated in the doorway, but Hamil said, "Joshua can take care of himself. Come on, we should go, before this gets any worse." Reluctantly—she hated leaving Joshua even more than she hated leaving a fight unfinished—she followed. Reave didn't even glance after them.

"I'm sorry, Joshua just wouldn't leave," Ted said as they hurried to the elevators. "He said he could help, and I told him it was too dangerous, but he insisted."

"I guess it's good he stayed," Marla said, "or some of us might not have made it out of there alive."

"That was pretty much a disaster, wasn't it?" Hamil said, puffing to keep up.

"We've had finer hours," Rondeau said. "But once we get hold of Genevieve tomorrow, we'll be able to shut this guy Reave down, yeah? Dr. Husch can pump Genevieve full of heavy-duty sedatives, put her down so deep she won't dream, and Reave will just fade like . . . well, like a bad dream in the morning, right?"

"I hope so," Marla said. "If we find Genevieve before Reave does, yeah. I'm just glad Langford is better at divination than Gregor is."

They rode down to the lobby, Hamil lamenting the

likely loss of his meat-golems, hoping they might survive in enough of a state to stumble home. Their death would be traumatic to their operators, too. As they left the building, Marla's phone rang; it was Joshua.

"Are you okay?" she said.

"I had to promise Reave I'd sit at his right hand when he takes over the world, but yes, I'm okay. Are you out?"

"We just left the building."

"I'm halfway downstairs now. I convinced Reave that he can destroy you at his leisure, and told him I'd meet him later." He paused. "Men really will believe *anything*, won't they?"

"You're a treasure. Come back to the club as soon as you can." She snapped her phone shut. "That wasn't exactly a win," she said, climbing into the Bentley. "But we haven't lost yet."

"Yeah, yeah, Joshua is the greatest guy ever, even though he totally ignored your order to leave, and never mind that I got spider crab squid goop all over my pants," Rondeau said. He sighed. "Of course, the worst thing is, whenever I see Joshua, I think he really *is* the greatest guy ever."

"Jealousy is such an ugly thing," Marla said. "Envy, too."

Nicolette hid with her boss in their deepest subbasement, the equivalent of a well-appointed bomb shelter. "That was close," she said, working on Gregor's knee. Her chaos magic wasn't *just* about increasing disorder, it was about *shifting* disorder, and tilting the balance. She drained off the chaos of his shattered knee into a series of highly ordered crystals piled in the corner. As the crystals shattered and snapped into dust, his knee jumped back into place, his wounds knitting, stealing the order from the crystals. It worked fast—Nicolette was positively thrumming with power. There was a *lot* of uncertainty for her to feed on in the current situation in Felport.

Gregor grunted as his knee realigned. "There's no turning back now," he said, flexing the leg. "Marla knows I'm her enemy, and I'm sure she'll get word to the other sorcerers soon. If Reave doesn't win . . ." He shook his head. "He *has* to win. We have to find Genevieve before Marla does."

"We can't outpredict Langford," Nicolette said. "He does some seriously weird mojo, you know? I don't know how we'll locate Genevieve before he does."

"I know I can't predict where Genevieve will be as accurately as Langford can," Gregor said, "but I can predict *what Langford will predict.*"

Nicolette frowned. "You taught me yourself that you can't predict predictions—even trying to do so introduces too much uncertainty into the system, and the results are lousy, worse than plain guessing would be. Right?"

"Oh, yes," Gregor said. "Trying to predict someone else's divination does lead to great uncertainty. But I have *you,* my dear, to draw that uncertainty away, dump it somewhere unimportant, and replace it with certainty. Yes?"

"That's . . ." She was going to say that was too difficult for her, the equivalent of making the falling rocks in an avalanche land to form an exact scale replica of Buckingham Palace, but was it really beyond her?

"You're stronger than me now," Gregor said, matter-of-factly. "You're rising up on the madness in this city like you're riding a geyser. You have the power."

"Yeah," she said. "Yeah, I can do that."

"Do what?" Reave said, appearing, as he did, from nowhere.

"Is Marla dead?" Gregor asked. He was getting cabin fever, Nicolette supposed, and was tired of staying in his building, where he was safe. She glanced at his bare knee. Well, relatively safe.

"Not yet," Reave said, flicking his hand as if the issue was of no consequence. "What is it you said you can do?"

"We can find Genevieve before Marla does. Tomorrow afternoon." Gregor's voice was weary, and Nicolette felt an unexpected pang of pity for him. She shoved it away. There was no room in her life for pity right now.

"Good," Reave said. "I'm going to try storming her castle now."

"Why?" Nicolette said. "We told you, we can get her tomorrow, and you know you'll never break into her palace."

"I will not answer a *woman,*" Reave said. "Dare to question me again and I'll skewer you, however useful Gregor thinks you are."

Nicolette regarded him coldly. If this was the new world order, it did not agree with her.

"I'm curious, too," Gregor said. "Why waste your energies on a fruitless attack?"

"I attack her every night," Reave said. "Why let her know anything has changed? Besides, I don't waste my energies. Every time I assault her palace, she becomes more afraid of me, and I grow more powerful. When I have her locked up in a room, to torment at my leisure . . ." He shivered, clearly delighted by anticipation, and Nicolette shuddered in disgust. "My power will only grow, and the world will be made over in my image."

"All cheesy dark towers and nightmare armies like a little kid would be afraid of?" Nicolette said, incredulous. "*You're* going to rule the world? What kind of economic system are you going to implement? How are you going to deal with sewage? Road maintenance? Health care for your slaves? What are you going to do for food? I know you're bringing your dream stuff into this world, but this world isn't going to turn into the dream world completely. There's practical matters to—"

"Silence!" Reave roared, but Nicolette only fell silent when Gregor put his hand on her shoulder.

"I will have her head on a pike," Reave said.

"No you won't," Gregor said. "Behave yourself. You need us." To Nicolette he said, "You have a point, of course, but it's something we've considered. He needs *me* to help him run things, Nicolette, and I need you. All right? You'll always have a place with me."

Reave spat and turned away.

"The feeling's mutual, asshole," Nicolette said, and Reave vanished into the shadows.

14

Zealand woke on a white daybed in a room filled with yellow light. He smelled oranges. Genevieve sat beside him, her hands clasped in her lap, her head cocked to the side, watching him.

"I'm not dead," Zealand said, reaching tentatively to touch the place on his back where Reave's knives had gone in. The wounds felt . . . strange.

"The mold saved you," St. John Austen said, coming in through a doorway Zealand hadn't noticed before (perhaps it hadn't existed before). "It filled in your wounds. For all I know it took over the function of your kidneys. The stuff is part of you now, not just armor, but flesh."

Zealand considered that. Perhaps it should have repulsed him, but it didn't. He was merely glad to be alive. "Then I owe Genevieve a great debt for giving me such a gift."

"You fought him," she said, eyes wide. "You really fought him."

Zealand sat up and swung his legs over the side of the bed. He felt fine, really, a bit tired, a bit sore, but not at all as if he'd been skewered through both kidneys. "For all the good it did. I'm afraid I couldn't do much to him on his own ground, he controlled the rules of reality there, and—"

"You *fought* him," Genevieve said again, and reached out, as if to touch his face, though she let her hand fall before making contact.

"Genevieve is still a bit astonished at the notion that Reave *can* be fought, that you were brave enough to face him," Austen explained.

Zealand shrugged. "He's only a man. Not *even* a man, I realize now, just an idea of a man with delusions of independent reality." He remembered. "Good Lord, did he hurt Marla? We were supposed to work together to stop him, but I was attacked before the plan could go into effect." He grimaced. "She'll think I deserted her for sure."

"You were trying to help Marla Mason?" Mr. Austen was alarmed, and Genevieve stood up and backed away.

"You misunderstand her," Zealand said. "She has had a change of heart. She no longer wishes Genevieve's death. I don't believe she ever *wished* it—she just thought it might be unavoidable. She wants to help you now, Genevieve, and stop Reave, and all the terrible things happening in her city. That's what she told me, and I believe her. She swore an unbreakable oath."

St. John Austen frowned. "She wants to lock Genevieve up again, you mean, sedate her, keep her in this dream world forever."

Zealand spread his hands helplessly. "Isn't that what Genevieve wants? I thought she was only vulnerable when she woke up in the real world? Here, she can hold him off indefinitely, yes?"

"That's no way to live, Zealand, cowering here in her palace," Austen said. "She wants Reave *gone*. She wants her life back, but she never believed that was possible until she saw you attack him."

Genevieve wandered away, leaving them alone. Zealand sighed. "No offense—I'm rather fond of her—but she's *mad*, Austen. Isn't it best if she's confined someplace where she can't hurt herself, or others? Because Reave attacking her . . . in a way, that's just her hurting herself. He only has the power she gives him."

Austen shook his head. "She can't bear it anymore. Something shocked her, woke her up in that hospital, but she could have stayed, could have let the doctor come and give her a shot to calm her down. But she chose to act, to try to effect a change. She doesn't even know how long she was in that hospital. *I* don't know. Seeing you actually fight Reave . . . it had a great impact on her. You don't spend time with her like I do, but I see the change, she's more lucid, more interested, more *hopeful*. She thinks of him as an unstoppable nightmare, but if we can chip away at that image, let her know Reave *can* be beaten, it may help her finally purge his presence from her mind."

"Marla could help with fighting Reave, assuming he hasn't killed her already," Zealand said. "She's very formidable."

Austen shook his head. "Genevieve doesn't trust her. She tried to trust Marla Mason, tried to enlist her as a champion, but Marla had murder on her mind . . . you must understand, Genevieve doesn't trust easily.

She saw something in you, I don't know what, something in the shape of your dreams, something that made her believe you might put her needs first. But Marla would *never* put Genevieve's needs first. If Genevieve had wandered to Cleveland or Pittsburgh or Milwaukee instead of Felport, Marla wouldn't care in the slightest."

"I can't argue with that. But circumstance makes strange allies, Austen. I think we should meet with Marla."

"Try convincing Genevieve," he said with a shrug. "In the meantime, she'd like you to stay here, to protect her against Reave. He'll be attacking soon."

"How do you know?"

Austen looked at him strangely. "He attacks every night, Zealand. He's the king of her nightmares."

At the club, Marla checked in with Langford one more time—Zealand had vanished again, he said, but things were on track with finding Genevieve—and made Rondeau and Ted eat something. She sat on the couch in her office and listened to the radio, filled with late-night advisories for the oncoming blizzard, which the border wardens were even now whipping up magically. The things at the borders were not human, but were imbued with minds, and drew power from Marla's own energies to protect the city—they weren't some great magic of hers personally, but rather a protection set up long ago that came with her job. Even so, the weight of their work made her tired, and as the snow fell thicker and heavier and snowplows on the edge of town suffered mysterious breakdowns and phone lines fell under the weight of sudden icicles, she slumped deeper and deeper into the cushions. She had to sleep. Sleeping here was not ideal. She should, at the very least, fold the sofa out into a bed. But getting up was too much trouble.

Tonight had gone badly. She knew "plan" was just a four-letter word for something that doesn't work, but she'd been hopeful. Maybe Zealand's presence would have tipped the scales in their favor, and they could have taken Reave apart. Now Zealand had run away, or betrayed her, or been killed by Nicolette and Gregor—who knew?

Someone entered the room, and Marla opened her eyes. It was Joshua, cheeks red from the cold, smile warm as a hearth. She reached out to him and pulled him down to the couch with her, and they nestled together, snugly, for a few moments.

"Did I do good tonight?" he asked, and Marla knew she'd been playing this right all along—because who else in the *world* would Joshua ever feel the need to ask *approval* from? She was opposed to playing games in relationships, both on principle and because it seemed like a waste of time, but if aloofness was the only way to make Joshua see her as more than another toy to use and send on her way, she'd keep it up.

She kissed his forehead. "You did really good." Deep down, though, part of her rankled at her own retreat. Maybe she *could* have reached Reave and cut him down. It might have been pointless—maybe he had a whole mushroom-grove of new bodies waiting for him to put on like fresh clothes—but it might have bought them some time. The meat-golems and Rondeau had been holding his monsters back. She could have killed

Reave, she thought. But Joshua had seen her fall, and come to save her, and she could hardly fault him for that. "So you, what, professed your love for him?"

"Oh, I just told him I saw which way the wind was blowing, that I thought it was clear his side was going to win, and that he shouldn't even worry about you, that you weren't important, he could deal with you later. I get the feeling he doesn't have a very high opinion of women. I told him I'd join him after he won."

"Wow," Marla said. "And he believed you. I wasn't sure something like *him* would be susceptible to your charms."

"Oh, all men and women love me, Marla," he said, snuggling in closer. "Being mostly imaginary is no defense."

"I can't imagine what it must be like to have your power. Some of the most important formative relationships in my *life* are based on hatred. Hamil says that pride is my engine, that I'm just too proud to *fail*, but before I had anything to be proud of, it was hate that drove me. Hate that let me leave my fucked-up family, hate that made me take a job waitressing in a topless bar—I hated men back then, so it pleased me to pretend to like them and take their money." She shook her head. "I don't know how I would have lived a life of love, love, love."

"Well, just because everyone loves me doesn't mean I love everyone, Marla. I can hate as well as the next man, I imagine, though admittedly I have less cause." His hand slid down to her hip, fingers tucked into the waistband of her pants, a casual intimacy that almost made tears come to her eyes. She hadn't been this unguarded with anyone for years, except for the incubus, and that hardly counted.

"A lot of what I do is because people hate me," Marla said. "I went to San Francisco last month because someone was trying to kill me, and the only thing that could save me was hidden on the other side of the country. At least this mess with Genevieve doesn't feel *personal* that way, though it's getting there. It's kind of funny that Genevieve hates me *and* her sworn enemy hates me. The enemy of my enemy is my enemy, too, apparently."

"You could use a love potion and make everyone adore you."

"That only works for a little while, and there are diminishing returns—it's less effective with each application. Besides, that kind of stuff, that mind-and-emotion control, it's immoral."

He chuckled. "You think I'm immoral."

"You didn't choose to become what you are, Joshua. You didn't decide you wanted to control people and then work magic to make that happen. A hammer can be a tool to build something, or a weapon to kill something. Your power is the same way. Motive is what matters, and so far as I can tell, you're mostly on the side of the angels."

"I'm not entirely unselfish. I am used to getting what I want."

"Sure. But you don't do so at the expense of others."

"I've never considered my power an excuse to be cruel. I can see what you mean, though. Better if you go on as you have."

"Feared by many, hated by some, loved by few."

"It will all work out," he said, and leaned in to kiss her cheek, her chin, the tip of her nose, finally her lips. He looked into her eyes, his own just inches away. "You have me. Let's take you home, and get some rest. Tomorrow is a big day, yes?"

"Yeah," Marla said. "I'd like you to come with us tomorrow. I've got tranquilizer guns and stuff like that, but the best way to get Genevieve might be to have you stand up and say 'Come here, sweetheart,' you know?"

"Of course. Should I go get the car?"

"I think I'm too wiped out to leave, and it's probably better if I'm here first thing, in case Langford calls earlier than expected. The couch folds out into a bed. It's not too comfortable—it's a little like sleeping in an iron maiden—but for one night it might not be so bad."

"As long as you're sleeping with me," Joshua said, and rose to help her make their bed.

Zealand dragged himself to the library, sore, exhausted, knowing he'd be bleeding from a dozen places if not for the mold acting as a natural bandage. St. John Austen opened the door for him, ushered him in, and offered him water.

"That was the most bizarre fight I've ever had in my life," Zealand said, sinking into the armchair, grateful for the rest. He wasn't sure what he'd expected, but he hadn't been prepared for the reality—or surreality—of the battle. Reave's black tower had appeared on the horizon and approached over the sea of clouds like a pirate ship, black banners flapping. Genevieve had stood beside Zealand on the highest balcony, and he'd watched as she closed her eyes and mustered her defenses, people and creatures appearing on the balconies all down the length of the palace, weapons at ready. The defenders of her castle were a bizarre mishmash of pop-cultural references and the plainly surreal. There were familiar superheroes in capes and tights; an archer who might have been Robin Hood; a Cheshire Cat as big as a tiger, with a grin like a scythe; a black stallion with flaming hooves; a titanic, ten-foot-tall version of St. John Austen clothed in shining plate armor; angels riding astride enormous locusts; and more, all conjured from her subconscious, things she'd imagined as protectors or heroes. And the attackers from Reave's tower, throwing grappling lines from their balconies to Genevieve's or buzzing the parapets, were equally strange: hordes of literally faceless men with flashing silver knives, riding astride monstrous blackbirds; things like the marriage of squids and spiders and crabs; babies with gigantic heads and needle-sharp teeth; women in bloody wedding dresses armed with razor-edged cake knives.

The defenders on the balconies drove back the attackers again and again, and Zealand was happy to stay out of the bloody battle and beside Genevieve as her personal bodyguard. The towers rocked a little, like ships at sea, and Robin Hood fell from a window and spiraled down through the clouds. A giant blackbird snapped a giant locust in half with its beak. The faceless men hurled the needle-toothed babies across the gulf like projectiles, and they landed biting. St. John Austen's giant counterpart swung a warhammer and knocked down a dozen enemies at a stroke. The battle was an even match, with neither side gaining, and Zealand began to see how this could happen every night with no decisive result. Of course,

Genevieve's side wasn't trying to gain ground, just hold it, which he thought was a tactical mistake. If he was going to be here for a while, he might try to talk a little strategy with Genevieve, get her to put her men on the offensive. It was possible she'd just sing a snatch of song at him, or ignore him entirely, but if he repeated himself enough it might penetrate. At any rate, the battle was almost boring once you got past the bizarreness of the fighters—

Until Reave appeared on the balcony directly opposite theirs. The two towers were separated by a gulf of only a few yards, just a bit too far for a normal man to leap, and so they could see each other clearly. Zealand stepped forward with his best grin. Reave looked stunned. "I *killed* you—"

Zealand didn't chitchat, though the urge for banter had never gripped him more strongly. Instead he flung out a dozen ropes of twisting vegetation, tangled Reave up, and jerked him off his balcony. Genevieve gasped, then clapped her hands like a little girl who's just seen a magic trick. Zealand twisted his hands around the vegetation to get a surer grip, then leaned out a little, looking over the edge of their balcony, where Reave dangled, knives in his hands.

"Go ahead and cut yourself free, then," Zealand said, swinging the vines a little, starting a pendulum motion that set Reave swaying and spinning. The man wasn't very heavy, really, and the fungus gave Zealand's muscles extra power anyway, so he was in no danger of being pulled off himself. "Go ahead, I don't mind." Genevieve came, hesitantly, to stand beside him, looking down at her enemy. "See, he's just a stupid little yo-yo at the end of a string," Zealand said. "Nothing to be frightened of."

Two of Reave's giant blackbirds fell dead from the sky, taking their riders with them. Zealand grinned. So this *was* getting through to Genevieve. "Shall I let him drop, fling him out, and send him down through the clouds, my dear?" he said, and Genevieve clapped her hands again.

Reave jerked at the vines. He was *climbing* them, even as he swung, even though the vines were wrapped around his own body. With a dismissive sniff, Zealand flicked his fingers, and let the vines fall free.

He expected Reave to plummet, but the man fell at an angle from the pendulum swing, and snatched on to the edge of a balcony on his own tower, a few floors below. He clambered over the rail, shouldered his way past his fighters, and disappeared inside.

"Gone to lick his wounds, I expect," Zealand said, but a second later Reave was back on the highest balcony, *running* out, and leaping.

The jump was too far for a normal man. Zealand could have made it, with the help of his mold. Reave apparently had augmentations of his own, because he cleared the gap easily, and landed to perch on the railing. "I will eat your champion's *eyes*," he said. Genevieve fell back with a cry. Zealand shoved at Reave, trying to knock him off the rail, but Reave wouldn't budge. He'd been a lightweight before, but now he was dense as marble.

"Genevieve, get inside!" Zealand said. If she didn't *see* Reave getting stronger, maybe she wouldn't *let* him get stronger. Genevieve hurried inside. Zealand's only weapon was the mold, while Reave had his knives, and they came flashing as Zealand danced away. The blades nicked him lightly here and there, but the mold was ready this time, and it bound up Reave's wrists, first slowing them and then wrapping them together. The mold crawled up Reave's face, gagging him, and Reave just chewed methodically and spat the mold out, almost fast enough to keep up. Zealand kicked at Reave's knee as hard as he could and heard a satisfying snap. The king of nightmares lurched over, unable to support his own weight, and Zealand gathered him in his arms. The man must weigh five hundred pounds now, and it took every ounce of Zealand's mold-augmented strength to lift him up and dump him over the parapet. Reave fell, shouting as the mold in his mouth turned to dust, and disappeared through the clouds.

Zealand didn't believe for an instant that he was dead. Genevieve was right. It wasn't that easy. The black tower disengaged, though, pulling away and bobbing off into the distance. The defenders vanished like dew in the sun. Zealand went inside, but he wasn't on the top floor anymore, and Genevieve was nowhere to be found. He'd trudged to the library instead, where St. John Austen gave him water.

"You threw him over the side," Austen said. "Genevieve is *very* impressed."

"Mmm," Zealand said. "How many times will I have to throw him over the side before Genevieve decides he's really no threat at all, and his power dissipates?"

"Well," Austen said. "That is the question."

Joshua and Rondeau sat at the beat-up old table outside Marla's office, playing War, because that was the only game where "Joshua can't cheat me blind," Rondeau had said. "If it's not pure luck, he can work his wiles. Not that I mind—I like it when his wiles work me over—but it's more fun this way." Marla was sitting out the game, waiting impatiently for Langford to call. It wasn't yet noon, so he wasn't late, but she was tired of sitting idle. She'd made a few calls, checked on a few business ventures, cast some precautionary auguries, trying to keep up with her *other* responsibilities, but the whole magical community was focused on the Genevieve problem, so she hadn't accomplished much.

She paced around, finally ducking her head into her office, where Ted was at her desk, on the phone. "Hey, Ted, I'm going upstairs to take a look at the city. You want to come?"

He put his hand over the mouthpiece. "I do, I really do, but I'm trying to track some things down, and I'm getting close, so next time, okay?"

"Sure," she said, a little miffed, but not willing to show it. Yesterday he'd been dazzled nearly into speechlessness by the sight of the city spread out below them, but now he'd rather make phone calls. She wondered what he was working on, but she prided herself on *not* being a micromanager, and he'd already proven himself trustworthy. He was probably just liaising with the sorcerers, making sure all the plans to quarantine the city were going smoothly.

Marla went to the roof—fuck, it was cold, but that was the point, wasn't it?—and worked the spell. The roof dropped off below her, and she hovered above Felport, the illusion refreshing constantly, giving her a true view of events in the city with only a millisecond of lag between her vision and reality. It wasn't snowing much in the city proper, but the snow was a solid curtain all around the perimeter, sealing the place off. Repair crews couldn't get out to fix the phone lines, and the mayor was urging everyone to stay home and wait it out. Amazingly, power hadn't failed in the city—Marla had made sure of that. She didn't need people freezing to death or hospitals shutting down. With luck, the state of emergency would be over by this evening. Still, there were kids out sledding in Fludd Park, and a few pedestrians walking around. There were patrols of apprentices and cantrip-throwers and press-ganged alley witches out there trying to keep people safe. She saw a few scurrying things in side streets, and down by the waterfront, but whenever she zoomed in for a closer look they were gone. Reave's nightmares weren't getting stronger in the city yet. Good.

She zoomed in on Ernesto's junkyard, a vast hell's acre of crushed cars and scrap metal, which shimmered a little in her vision—he had non-Euclidean stuff going on in there, folded space and hidden pockets of choked-off reality, and it was hard to look at the place directly. As Marla watched, Reave's black tower flickered and disappeared between two stacks of crushed cars. Ernesto said the tower had been appearing there pretty often. It had popped up other places in the city, too, but most often in the junkyard, so she wanted to keep an eye on the spot. She checked out Gregor's building, and Hamil's meat-golem guards were still there, watching the entrances. Gregor was safe inside—deep in subbasements too well defended to breach easily—but he couldn't leave.

Except he probably had escape tunnels. Marla certainly did. But, hell, she couldn't cover *every* contingency. Once Genevieve was safely ensconced in the

Blackwing Institute, Marla would smoke Gregor out and banish him. Then she could divide up his holdings *and* Susan Wellstone's, and enrich all the sorcerers who'd remained loyal. It wasn't so different from being a medieval warlord. You rewarded the retainers who served you well, and stripped the assets from those who didn't. It wasn't a particularly enlightened or progressive form of government, but so much of being a sorcerer was about personal power, and benign dictatorship was the best you could hope for.

There were still weird sinkholes in Fludd Park, but Granger had them cordoned off, so the kids playing there were *probably* safe, unless shit started to come crawling out of the holes, but there were people watching for that. While she looked down, no more buildings appeared or disappeared. Reave was still out there, but he hadn't gotten his hands on Genevieve. If he did, Marla thought the face of the city would begin to change rapidly. Genevieve was the ultimate power source for Reave, and Marla had to keep her away from him.

Marla settled back to the roof of the club, and went inside. Ted was at the table now with Rondeau and Joshua, and they were playing Oh, Hell, having tired of playing War. Somebody had picked up a pizza from the little restaurant around the corner, and there was an untouched medium with everything on it, waiting just for her.

"Deal me in," Marla said, and sat with them to wait.

Langford called at 2:30, which saved them from listening to Rondeau beg them to play strip poker—he just wanted a look at Joshua in the altogether, and while Marla wasn't opposed to seeing that, Joshua wouldn't have been the one getting naked; he could bluff every hand and never lose.

Langford said, "Genevieve will be at Fludd Park, near the bandstand, in twenty-three minutes. She'll be conscious for between five and seven minutes, so you won't have much of a window before she disappears back to dreamland." Fludd Park wasn't far, and with the likely lack of traffic they should get there in ten minutes.

"I owe you a fruit basket for this," Marla said, and hung up. "Ted, call Hamil and have him send his guys, then call the other sorcerers, let them know what's happening. Rondeau, get the tranq gun, Joshua, put on your game face. Let's get going." She put on her cloak, just in case Reave showed up. She hated wearing it, but it was the most powerful weapon she had. The price it extracted was one she was willing to pay if it would help save her city.

Ten minutes before Langford called Marla, Gregor looked up from the metal bowl of mercury, images shimmering on the surface of the poisonous liquid. An elaborate toothpick model of the Taj Mahal lay in broken shards near the bowl, all the disorder Nicolette had bled off the divination poured into its destruction. "Genevieve will be in Fludd Park, near the bandstand, in about thirty minutes."

"I can get there in five," Nicolette said. One of the escape tunnels came out in the park, near the duck pond.

"You have maybe twenty minutes before Marla and her crew arrive," Gregor said.

Nicolette grinned and heaved a heavy knapsack, bulging with nasty goodies, over her shoulder. "Plenty of time."

"We should not trust Nicolette," Reave said from his corner of the shelter. He'd been pissy all morning, though he wouldn't say why. Nicolette didn't really care. The king of nightmares might take over the city—she didn't really believe he could take the *world*—but Nicolette was already thinking about possible palace coups. "I should go collect Genevieve myself."

"If Genevieve even senses your presence, she'll run," Gregor said. He sat with his back against a pile of boxes, emergency rations stockpiled against some possible calamity in the world above. "This prediction isn't proscriptive, it's *de*scriptive, it's a most-likely scenario. It's so likely that I trust it's basically a certainty, but your presence could change that. Nicolette is better. Genevieve doesn't know her, so her presence is unlikely to cause immediate alarm."

"If she fails, I *will* destroy her," Reave said.

"You can try, baldie," Nicolette said.

"We're wasting time," Gregor said. "Go. I want this *over*, so I can finally get the fuck out of this building and go *outside*."

Marla didn't like it, but she hung back in the tree line with Rondeau, and the rifle. He was a better shot than she was, so she didn't *need* to be there, but Genevieve didn't trust her, so it was better if Marla didn't show her face, or bring her mind too close. Marla looked through a pair of binoculars and saw Joshua making his way toward the bandstand, where Genevieve was supposed to appear. He would call to her, calm her, and then Rondeau would hit her with a tranquilizer dart for good measure. Hamil had half a dozen meat-golems hanging around—dressed in huge winter coats to hide their inhumanity and fooling around in a snow-ball fight—to deal with any contingencies. "I think this is going to—" Marla began, but then Joshua threw his arms up in the air and fell backwards, vanishing into the snow without so much as a cry. Marla was up and off like a shot toward him, but something clotheslined her, and she went down, hard, staring up at pine needles and gray sky. She sat up, carefully, slowly, and saw a cage of glowing blue lines being woven around her in the air. *Magic.* She looked down at her feet at a scattering of fortune cookies lightly covered with snow. She'd stepped on them, cracking them open. She picked one up, and looked at the fortune, which was in an unfamiliar language—some spell of binding and holding she'd never seen before.

"Rondeau!" she called, pushing against the blue webbing, which was still growing and thickening—the strands yielded under pressure, but they wouldn't break. "Hold your position!" Rondeau didn't answer. Was he doing as she said, or had something happened to him?

The meat-golems were still throwing snowballs, and one of them hurled a snowball at one of his fellows—and blew his head off in a shower of red and gray. The snowball had become a lethal projectile at some point in midair. The meat-golems just stared, then started walking, but they must have triggered some hidden trap, too, for they all went down in different ways—one's legs disappeared from the knees down, and another bent all the way backward, like a yoga practitioner in bridge pose, then went farther until his spine cracked. Three of them began mindlessly tearing at one another, driven into a frenzy by some hidden magic. What had happened to Joshua? Was it as lethal as those traps?

Marla finally thought to draw her dagger of office, which could cut through anything, material or magical, and cursed herself for being taken by surprise—she'd wasted seconds by not thinking to use the dagger right away, but she'd been so stunned by seeing Joshua go down that she wasn't thinking straight. The dagger sliced through the blue webs easily—and just in time, since they were drawing tighter, to mummify or crush her. She forced herself to make her way carefully toward Joshua, avoiding the little traps she now knew to look for, a few marbles in the snow here, a trip wire there, a row of thumbtacks glowing faintly yellow here. She finally reached Joshua, who was knocked out cold, his legs tangled in a chain of rubber bands that were climbing his body, pinning him, trying to choke him.

Marla cut his bonds away with her dagger and patted his cheek, but he wouldn't wake up. She threw him over her shoulder in a fireman's carry and retraced her footprints back the way she'd come, toward the relative safety—she hoped—of the trees. In her mind, a mental clock tick, tick, ticked. Genevieve would be appearing in less than a minute. If Rondeau was still there, still looking through the rifle's scope, they could still get her.

But Rondeau was facedown in the snow and

groaning, his rifle gone. Marla put Joshua down, and touched Rondeau's shoulder. He rolled over halfway. "Nicolette," he said. "She hit me in the head with something. I saw her take the gun. Couldn't stop her. She . . ." He trailed off.

Marla slapped his face, and he gasped. "Stay awake, you might have a concussion, damn it." She took a handful of snow and shoved it down the front of his pants, and Rondeau gasped, eyes wide; that would keep him awake for a minute, at least. She stood up and looked toward the bandstand, and there was Genevieve, her caramel-colored hair, her pale yellow blouse, her black scarf. The snow was melting all around her feet as she stared blankly around. Marla hesitated—should she run down there, shouting, and risk scaring Genevieve away? If she could get close enough she could manage a bug-in-amber spell, not as powerful as the one Ted had used when he trapped Zealand in mid-leap back at the bar, but good enough to hold Genevieve for a few moments. She started down the hill, trying to simultaneously hurry and keep her eye open for Nicolette's booby traps. Fuck, she'd been outplayed here. This was beyond bad. But it was still salvageable.

Until Nicolette stepped from the trees behind Genevieve, lifted the tranquilizer gun to her shoulder, and fired. Genevieve started to spin around and then fell to the snow. Marla hoped against hope that Genevieve would disappear, even though Dr. Husch said that, while sedated, Genevieve seemed to stay in this world—under the influence of such drugs, Genevieve simply didn't dream.

Nicolette waved to Marla, then dropped the rifle

and picked up Genevieve. Marla snarled and put on an extra burst of speed. She considered reversing her cloak, letting the cloak's violent magics seize her and make her into a living weapon, impervious to pain or mercy. She'd rip Nicolette to shreds, and she only hesitated because she might kill Genevieve, too, and she was bound not to do that. Then Marla stepped on something that cracked like dry twigs, and she was immediately engulfed in fire.

"I lit that bitch *up*," Nicolette crowed, back in the basement. "You should have seen it, Marla went up like a roman candle soaked in rocket fuel."

"Is she dead?" Gregor said. "Please, tell me she's dead."

"She had on that cloak," Nicolette said, shaking her head. "For a minute I thought I was screwed, that she would reverse it and let the purple side show, and tear me apart." Marla's cloak was legendary. Some whispered that the only reason she'd managed to become chief sorcerer was because she'd lucked into an artifact of such power. Nicolette thought that was uncharitable. Marla hardly ever used the cloak, and anyway, it took a skilled wielder to use a weapon like that. Nicolette had nothing against Marla; she even admired her a little. They just currently had incompatible agendas. "But even with the white side showing, the cloak's powerful, and it will heal her burns." Being set on fire while wearing the cloak would slow Marla down and cause her a lot of pain, but it wouldn't kill her. "Still, we got Genevieve, so I call this a win." Nicolette said. Gregor nodded, but didn't seem happy about it. "I'll check with the Giggler and see if this changes things," she said. "Maybe now Marla's no danger to you, and you'll be able to leave the building without worrying about dying."

"Perhaps," Gregor said. "But I thought the same thing when Reave showed up in my office, and the Giggler still affirmed the prophecy—if I leave this building, Marla will kill me."

"Marla will be dead by morning," Reave said. Genevieve was sprawled beside him, faintly moaning. "Tonight, everything changes."

"When Genevieve wakes up—or goes to sleep, or whatever," Nicolette said, "why won't she just, like, flit away to her palace again? It's a dream, right? She can do anything."

"She will regain her senses and find herself in my power. She will *believe* she is in my power, that she is helpless, that she cannot be saved. And so it will be true." Reave sounded utterly confident. Which was part of the point, Nicolette supposed.

"So what's the next step?" Gregor said.

"I take Genevieve to my tower. She wakes and sees where she is. She submits to my power. Then? Conquest. Subjugation." He grinned, showing his hideous teeth. "I've been looking forward to this all my life."

15

"She's gone," Austen said, materializing from wherever he was when he wasn't in the library. "I think something's happened."

"Maybe Marla found her," Zealand said. "She was going to sedate her. Genevieve may wake in the hospital, safe."

"I suppose," Austen said, though he paced around and wouldn't relax. As the minutes stretched into hours, Zealand worried, too. He tried to read, but the books in the library were incomplete, making sense for only a few pages at most before trailing into gibberish or blank pages. Austen said the books were made up of whatever Genevieve could remember from things she'd read, so nothing was wholly there, and even the fragments were inaccurate and misremembered as often as not. He couldn't find his lost *The Art of War* anywhere, and Genevieve's version turned into limericks three pages in.

A great rumble shook the palace, and Zealand went to the balcony. There was nothing around them but clouds—until a chunk of masonry fell from the top of the palace and whistled past him, plummeting through the cloudbank. More chunks followed, and soon Zealand retreated inside to keep from being smashed. "Austen, it's all coming apart!"

"She's been captured, then," Austen said, shaking his head. "By Reave. He always said the first thing he would do was tear down her palace, to show her there were no more safe places in all the world. We're doomed."

"The hell we are," Zealand said. "How do we get out of here, back to the real world?"

Austen shrugged. "I don't know. I've never left. I'm not sure, even now, that I could leave, that I'm . . . cohesive enough . . . to survive out there."

"It's leave, or have this place come down around us." Zealand grabbed Austen by the shoulders and shook him. "Come *on.*"

Austen nodded. "We can jump down, through the cloudbank. Marla fell through the clouds that way, and she landed all right."

Now Zealand hesitated. "Just . . . jump?" As if responding to the word, the books began leaping from the shelves and falling on the floor. The whole palace was vibrating now.

"Unless you can think of a better option," Austen said.

"Nothing ventured," Zealand said, and took Austen's hand. "It's been a pleasure serving with you, sir."

"Same to you. Once upon a time, I was a probability-shifter, and even though this body is just borrowed from Genevieve's mind . . . well, I'll exert myself as much as possible to give us good luck. It's possible to survive falling out of an airplane, if you land just right."

"Assuming we don't just fall forever through dreamspace," Zealand said.

"Assuming that."

They made their way to the balcony—the tower was listing hard to that side anyway, so gravity helped. Zealand looked down, and couldn't see anything but white clouds. He took a breath, then let it out. "Over the side," he said, and jumped, followed a moment later by Austen.

They fell through the clouds, and the Earth—only it wasn't the Earth—was far below, a vast expanse of ivory-yellow dotted with bits of green. Tears flew from Zealand's eyes as he slitted them against the wind, and he turned to look at St. John Austen, who was falling alongside. But something was happening to Austen, bits of him tearing away, turning to dust and gossamer. He dissolved like sugar, feet vanishing, legs vanishing, hands and forearms and elbows and biceps unspooling and trailing away like smoke. He turned his head to Zealand, and opened his mouth as if to make some final apology or promise, but his head disappeared, and his body, and then Zealand was falling alone. He shouted, "No!" but the wind stole his words away. Austen was right. He hadn't possessed enough personal substance to survive beyond the boundaries of Genevieve's palace.

As he fell—he fell for so long—Zealand wondered what would happen to him. Could Reave force Genevieve to dispel the mold that had sealed Zealand's wounds and saved his life? Would he die from the knife wounds in his back? Did it matter at all? Would he smash to pieces on the hard plain below?

He landed in the water. From that height, hitting water should have been like hitting concrete, but it was no worse than a belly-flop into a pool, except for the cold. The mold swarmed over his body, insulating him from the worst of the icy waters, and he kicked and flailed to the surface, looking around, blinking water from his eyes, trying to get his bearings. The city on the shore there—was it Felport? It was hard to tell through the snow, and the approaching gloom of dusk.

A blond surfer-girl in a blue wetsuit surfaced beside him. "You're all green," she said.

Zealand stared at her, then laughed. "Yes, I am. Isn't it a bit cold for surfing?"

She shrugged. There was no surfboard in evidence. "I get by."

Zealand cleared his throat while he tread water—the mold was doing all the physical work for him, moving his arms and legs in perfect form. "Are you some kind of . . . sorcerer?"

"I'm the Bay Witch. This is my bay. I noticed you fall in. I didn't see where you came from."

"Ah, yes." It was surreal, having a polite conversation five hundred yards from shore, in the freezing bay of Felport in the middle of winter. "Marla Mason mentioned you." He improvised a little. "She spoke quite highly of you."

"You know Marla?"

"I've been assisting her with the recent unpleasantness."

"The lady who has bad dreams. What are you doing in my bay?"

"I fell. From another world. I landed here."

"Lucky. You could have landed on top of a wrought-iron fence or something."

"I am counting my blessings even now. I should get to shore."

"It's not very pleasant up there," she said. "There are monsters in the streets. I saw them, when I swam in close. There's an army of men with shadows for faces. The word is, Marla failed, and now we're all fucked." She shook her head. "There are terrible things under the waves. I'm fighting them, but they're coming up out of caves that weren't here this morning, and there's no end to them. I should get back. Tell Marla I'm doing my best to keep the waters safe."

"I will," Zealand said, and she dove beneath the waves. He began kicking his way toward the shore. If he encountered any of Reave's men, he would fight them, and if Genevieve had been captured, he would just have to rescue her. What else could he do? He'd chosen his side, and he wouldn't do anything differently if he could. But if he could get Marla's help, so much the better.

"Rondeau, I don't know what to do," Marla said. She sat at the bar, drinking a weak vodka tonic. She couldn't afford to get drunk, but she couldn't cope sober. The cloak had healed her burns, but it hadn't helped the memory of pain. She'd never been fully engulfed in fire before, and it was probably in the top five most horrible things that had ever happened to her. Nicolette had really gotten the drop on her, but at the same time, Marla had to admire her skills—the booby traps were effective, and she must have set them up in a hurry. "At this point I'm just glad I'm not on *fire* anymore, and that's setting the bar pretty low."

Rondeau sat beside her. He was her oldest friend, the only person she felt comfortable being even halfway open with, apart from Joshua. When Rondeau saw the flash of flame, he'd gotten up, busted head and all, to dump snow on her. By the time Joshua woke up and joined them, Marla's burns were healed, and she was basically naked under the cloak except for her boots, all her non-magical clothing burned away. Her hair was singed, but it had been short anyway, so the harm wasn't serious. Without the cloak, she would have been killed. Joshua had doted over her like a mother hen until she finally sent him to get some rest on the couch in her office.

"We've never been fucked at quite this angle before, that's for sure," Rondeau said.

Marla drained the glass, considered having another, and thought better of it. "Reave is digging in. His tower is in Ernesto's junkyard, and his army is coming out of it. I mean, we can fight him. Viscarro has all kinds of nasty shit down in those vaults, stuff that hasn't seen the light of day in decades. The Chamberlain can stir up her ghosts. We can push back the army. But . . . I'm not sure it would *help*. I mean, he's not going to run out of fighters. He creates these things from *nothing*, from Genevieve's nightmares."

"As long as he's got Genevieve, we can't beat him," Rondeau said. "Not for good. So, I mean, there's no question of what to do—we go in and rescue Genevieve."

Marla considered. He had a point. "I can mobilize

the other sorcerers, get them to fight Reave's forces directly, let him think that's the approach we're taking. And I can take a small force, handpicked guys, make my way into Reave's tower, and get Genevieve out. He must have her locked in a room somewhere, tormenting her. Even if she falls asleep from sheer exhaustion, he's destroyed her palace, convinced her there's no safe place she can hide, not even in her dreams."

"What's locked up can be unlocked," Rondeau said.

Hamil came down from upstairs. "I just talked to the mayor. He says there's looting and rioting, and he's blaming it on the bad weather and the state of emergency, the usual. People are staying inside, mostly. But Marla, if Reave's people start kicking down doors . . ." He shook his head. "We can't hide this from the populace indefinitely. Eventually, the governor is going to wonder why he hasn't heard anything from one of the largest cities in the state for a while, and who knows what will happen then?"

"We have to act fast," Marla said. "I get that. Call Ted down here. I need to talk to everybody."

"Even me?" Zealand said, coming in from the side door. He was wet, and though the water was mostly frozen, he began dripping as soon as he entered the heat of the club.

"You're alive!" Marla said. "Where the fuck were you last night? Why are you wet?"

"I ran into Reave. He attacked me in the *closet,* and got the better of me. Genevieve scooped me up and took me to safety. But she disappeared, and her palace began to crumble, and when I jumped, I fell in the bay. Eventually." He spread his hands.

"What about St. John Austen?" Marla said. "Did he . . . ?"

Zealand only shook his head.

"Well, I'm glad you're here," she said. "We're going to go bust Genevieve out of Reave's tower. Tonight."

"That's *exactly* what I wanted to hear," Zealand said.

Marla assembled her strike team: herself, Zealand, and Ernesto, who had insisted on coming, because, as he said, "That bastard has his tower on *my* real estate, and I want to kick him out." Marla had refused to let Rondeau or Joshua come; they both had useful skills, but while Rondeau was an adequate brawler, he wasn't meant for this kind of quasi-military operation. And Joshua would just be a distraction to her. She'd be so worried about his well-being that she'd have a hard time focusing on the task at hand. There had never been any chance of Ted coming, of course, though he was in charge of calling the other sorcerers to coordinate the diversionary action.

They made their way to Langford's warehouse, fighting with a squad of Reave's shadow-faced men right on his doorstep. The things didn't even leave behind corpses when they died, only puddles of viscous black slime. Langford let her group into his heavily reinforced warehouse, and now Marla was considering his available firepower.

They hadn't exactly come unarmed. Marla had her boots, her rings, her cloak, and her dagger. Zealand had the preferred tools of his trade, pistols and knives, though his best weapon was the weird crawling fungus he wore like a second skin. Ernesto had a little jar of sludge that, when opened, would release his pollution-golem, a vicious creature. He also had an array of junk-yard magic, powers of decay and destruction and disintegration. Of all the sorcerers in Felport, Ernesto was the one Marla trusted most in a fight, except perhaps the Chamberlain, but she was more valuable in the diversionary action. Even now, the other sorcerers of Felport were putting together their forces, tame ghosts and golems and shapeshifters, pyromancers and poltergeist-handlers, assassins and thugs. The Four Tree Gang and the Honeyed Knots were even lending a hand. There would be battle on the streets, Felport's finest sorcerous warriors standing against Reave's horde. But all that was just misdirection. The real operation would take place at Reave's tower.

Ernesto was admiring a trident coiled with copper wire, as Langford explained that it could shoot lightning. Zealand had looked over the blendings of tech and magic and sniffed at it all, checking his pistols instead. Marla didn't want to burden herself with lots of trickery—it could be distracting to have too many options in a tight situation, and it was better to have a few weapons she trusted utterly. She'd come here for another reason.

"Langford," she said, taking him aside. "We need to get to the top of Reave's tower, fast. I think that's where he's keeping Genevieve. He's a top-of-the-tower kind of guy. But if we try to fly, especially carrying Zealand, we're going to be puking our guts out by the time we get all the way up there. Flying is like motion sickness turned up to eleven, and Ernesto's even worse at it than I am. Do you have, like, jetpacks or something? A helicopter you can strap on your back? That kind of James Bond bullshit?"

"As flattered as I am to be your Q, I'm afraid I don't have anything like that," Langford said. "But . . ." He tapped his finger against his lips. He sighed. "I have something. It will cost you when this is over, but . . . come here." He led her to a big silver refrigerator, and opened the door, revealing a vast array of bottles, jars, and tubes. He took a small vial of red liquid from a shelf. "This," he said, "is gorgon blood."

"You mean like from *Medusa*?"

"That's exactly right."

"Well, that's pretty cool, Langford, but how does it help me *fly*?"

"Pegasus was born from Medusa's blood," Langford said. "The flying horse. Of course, a giant was born from it, too, and many snakes."

She frowned. "You're telling me that if you drop that blood on the floor, a flying horse is going to spring into existence? Magic's magic, Langford, but that's some mythic shit."

"Medusa and Poseidon mated, but their offspring were not born until Medusa was beheaded, and her blood spilled into the sea. This blood, I am reliably informed, was caught in midair, and never touched earth or water. Thus, its potency remains. Pour a drop into the sea, and a new son of god and monster will be born." He shrugged. "I've never tested it, though I did a DNA test . . . don't ask where I got an exemplar for comparison, it's a long story—but it's real. I always thought it was something I'd experiment with in my retirement."

"You're *sure* you don't have a jetpack?"

"No. But I have a device that can override conscious will and give you direct control over another creature. Of course, you have to fasten it on the creature's head first. So if you do manage to make a flying horse, or something like it, you can control it, and make it fly wherever you wish."

"Like the magic bridle Bellerophon used to tame Pegasus?"

Langford shrugged. "It's a hobby. I like the old myths, even though the gods in those aspects are mostly obsolete and long vanished. I thought, in my retirement, I might conjure a winged beast and travel the world. Perhaps find a monster or two to slay." He gave a little half smile, and Marla felt she was seeing a new side of Langford. She knew him as an obsessive perfectionist who seldom left his lab except to acquire new research materials, but apparently, inside him, there was a world-wandering warrior waiting to get out.

She could explore her new understanding of Langford's character later. The matter at hand mattered more. "What if a *giant* gets born, instead of something that flies?"

He shrugged. "A giant could perhaps lift you to the top of the tower. It's just an idea. You don't have to do it. Of course I'll charge you dearly if you do. I could use a new laboratory."

"This feels a little like letting a bunch of cobras loose in your house to take care of your mouse problem," Marla said. But she took the vial.

"One drop," Langford said. "You don't want a horde of monsters rising from the surf."

"Okay. What am I supposed to do with my magical

flying whatever after we're *done*? I can't exactly donate it to the Felport Zoo."

"You could bring it back to me for dissection. I'm sure it would be very interesting."

Marla blinked at him. So much for Langford's romantic streak. "We should get moving."

"Oh, you'll want these," he said, and rummaged in a drawer until he came up with a pair of aviator goggles. "Just say the word 'zoom' and they'll become binoculars. 'Unzoom' and they'll go back to normal." He gave that half smile again. "I guess I'm a bit like Q, after all."

She took the goggles and called Ernesto and Zealand over. "Come on, guys. We have to go down to the beach."

"This seems ill advised," Zealand said, standing in the dark on the snowy beach, watching as Marla waded out up to her ankles. There was enough light from the streetlights on the hill behind them to provide some ambient illumination, and Marla had her night-eyes working, sucking up stray light to make her vision almost as good as it was in daylight.

"I think it's great," Ernesto said. "We pussyfoot around too much trying to be safe. I didn't become a sorcerer to be *careful*. Let's see some miraculous shit!"

"Yeah," Marla said. She opened the vial, put her fingertip over the opening, and tipped it over. She righted it and lifted her finger away, a drop of blood shining on the fingertip. She awkwardly stoppered the vial one-handed and slipped it into her pocket. "You guys ready?"

There was a small chorus of anxious yesses. Zealand was prepared to fling vines and pin down whatever came up out of the waves. Marla hoped like hell it had wings, and was big enough to carry three people. Ernesto held the tangle of straps and metal that Marla thought of as a magic bridle and Langford called a mind-control device. Though it wasn't really mind control—minds were *complicated.* It was more of a manual override. Marla would be able to control the creature like one of her own limbs. She expected the experience to be very disorienting, but so many things about her job were.

"Here goes," she said, and bent down to dip her blooded fingertip into the cold bay. The water began to roil, and she stepped back to the shore, afraid that if she stumbled into the heaving water, she would become entangled in the birth of a demigod.

It took a surprisingly long time. Marla had always imagined Pegasus springing full-blown from a drop of blood, bursting into life. This was different. They all stood on the snowy sand, watching as the water bulged and bubbled for two minutes, three minutes, four. Finally something came shoving up from under the water, bursting out into the air as if it was being born. "Zealand, now!" she shouted, and he flung out his hands, vines springing forth and hitting the water, binding up the thing in the waves.

Zealand grunted and dug his feet into the sand. "It's strong!" he shouted. Marla snatched the bridle from Ernesto and waded back into the water. The creature was big, larger than a horse and white as salt, and it did have wings, though the details were hard to see in its thrashing. The head was beaked—was it a gryphon?

The beak whipped down toward her, and Marla leaned aside and grabbed for its neck, wrapping her arms around it. The thing lifted its head and Marla rose almost entirely out of the water before being slammed back down into the waves, but she didn't release her grip. Zealand got another vine around its head and held it steady, so Marla could get her feet under her. She clipped the leather strap around its neck, and managed to get the bit into its beak without losing any fingers. Once she'd cinched up the harness, she grabbed on to the reins, which were wrapped with silver wire.

An electric jolt passed through her, and then it was like she had a whole extra set of limbs. "Whoa," she said, and climbed onto the thing's back, which felt a little like climbing onto her *own* back, and settled against its feathered neck, her legs straddling its body in front of the wings. When Zealand saw she had it under control, he let his binding vines fall away. Marla walked the creature forward, out of the waves, onto the sand. She saw double, through her own eyes and through the beast's, and she felt the sand crunching under her . . . hooves? But lions didn't have hooves. What was this thing?

Perhaps noting her disorientation, Ernesto said, "It has the body of a white bull, and the head of a seagull."

Marla had to concentrate to answer, and before managing to speak, she made the chimera squawk harshly, a gull's cry amplified by enormous size. "Makes sense," she managed finally. "Bulls were associated with the god of the sea, just like horses. And seagulls fit, too, as much as anything."

"Our good luck it's a seagull," Ernesto said, in a tone that suggested he was trying to joke. "We're going to my junkyard, and seagulls love that place, so it shouldn't have any trouble finding the way."

Marla let go of the bridle and slid off the beast, which was just a beast again, and not an extension of herself. It stood docilely, the bridle making it into a sort of switched-off robot, and Marla felt a stab of guilt. Was it just an animal? Or was it sentient? Confused, or terrified, or furious? It was the child of a long-dead monster and a long-vanished god. Who knew what its capabilities were? She walked around the chimera, patting its wide flank, squatting down to see if it was, ah, anatomically correct—yes, it was a bull all right, and bigger than most. Great size aside, the body wasn't too shocking, but that head—glassy black eyes, yellow beak with a darker hook at the end, smooth white feathers—it was bigger than a horse's head, and terrifying, even if it was a scavenger bird and not a predator like a hawk.

"If we need the element of surprise, I'd say we've got it," Ernesto said. "Reave won't expect us to come flying in on a white bull. Should we . . . ah, how do we get on?"

"Can you fashion some kind of harness for us, Zealand? Something we can grab on to?"

"Gladly," he said, and his mold crawled from his outstretched hand to the beast and began weaving a net around its body, keeping well away from the wings. Strands of the mold ran back to Zealand's body—if he broke contact, the mold would dry up and blow away. Marla climbed on first, settling herself behind the beast's neck again. She wanted to whisper in its ear, tell it she was sorry and that she'd set it free soon, but she wasn't even sure where a bird's ears were located. She wasn't going to let Langford dissect it when the job was done, though. The chimera was too strange and beautiful. She'd find a home for it somehow, maybe on the grounds of Blackwing. For now, Marla settled for stroking its feathers. Zealand got on behind her, and Ernesto at the back.

"Everyone got a good grip?" she said. They did, so she put the goggles over her eyes, gripped the chimera's reins, and learned how to fly.

Nicolette didn't like Reave's tower. It was dark and cold, and the corridors were designed to be claustrophobic and disorienting, with spikes protruding at odd angles. The whole place was just *stupid*, not a functional living space at all. Dream architecture wasn't meant to exist in the real world. She made her way to Reave's throne room, a hall of polished obsidian floors, with chandeliers made of rib cages. He sat on a throne made of *skulls*—how cliché was that? It looked like the cover to a pulp paperback novel from the '70s. At least there weren't beautiful female guards in chain-mail bikinis, and he didn't have Genevieve chained up in a golden collar at his feet. Not yet anyway.

"Bow before me," he said when she reached him.

"Suck my ass," she replied, and grinned when he snarled. "Gregor sent me with a message. You know we have a spy in Marla's camp?"

"Her new employee, yes? I saw him with her at the meeting last night."

"Right. He called with some info. You know how all the sorcerers are getting their shit together and taking the battle to the streets?"

"Oh, yes," Reave said, leaning forward. "They're fighting my warriors most bravely, trying to hide the battles from the ordinary humans by attacking under cover of night. They cheer when they vanquish a group of my fighters. Fools. They might as well try to soak up the sea with a sponge."

"Well, all that crap is just a distraction. Our source says Marla has assembled a small team to attack the tower directly, and rescue Genevieve. They should be along anytime now."

"Mmmm," Reave said. "That's a drawback to being so settled in this world now. I can't just take my tower away on a whim. We're more or less rooted here, so I suppose she knows where to find us."

"Yeah, I love the locale, by the way. The junkyard is very postapocalyptic." She wondered if Reave was even capable of recognizing sarcasm. If so, he didn't show it. "We should expect Marla, and that turncoat Zealand, and one of the city's big sorcerers, Ernesto."

"Thank your master for the information," Reave said. "And tell him I will have Marla's head on a spike in my front entryway soon."

"Second verse, same as the first," Nicolette said. "We'll believe it when we see it. You want me to hang around and give you some help repelling the invaders?"

"I do *not,*" he said, and Nicolette shrugged and blew him a kiss. He flinched as if she'd slapped him, and she laughed and turned to leave. Reave would kill her, she knew, if he ever decided he didn't need Gregor's help anymore. But Nicolette wasn't too worried. She was bursting with power now, and she had ideas for all kinds of contingencies. Just because she loved chaos didn't mean she never made plans.

Now, *this* was flying. No nausea, no risk of permanently pissing off one of the fundamental forces of the universe, no sense of lost control. After a shaky start, Marla got the hang of handling the chimera. She'd never ridden a horse, unless you counted a pony ride when she was six, but it must be very different, trying to *convince* an animal to do your bidding. The chimera was an extension of her own body, and she felt the air pass over her powerful wings, the strength in her shoulders, the thrill of momentum.

The lights of Felport below were intermittent, some areas having lost power, and she glimpsed moments of battle. Her dual vision meant she could look ahead of her and down at the same time. She saw the Chamberlain's ghosts insinuating their way into a group of shadow-faced men, possessing them, and exploding their bodies in puffs of ash and smoke; Viscarro's silver-and-gold clockwork automata dispatching a huddled cluster of squid-crab-spider creatures; Granger summoning the spirits of old-growth trees from the park to stride through the streets and smash Reave's crawling, needle-teethed baby-things into paste. The walking nightmares were no match for Felport's most powerful sorcerers, but they had the unstoppable advantage of numbers. Marla had to cut Reave's power off at the head, or her people would win every battle but still lose the war.

They approached Ernesto's junkyard, giant towers of junked cars surrounded by fences of boards and barbed wire and iron. The spire of Reave's black tower rose above the massed scrap metal, its ramparts haloed by a dozen of the giant blackbirds Zealand had told Marla about. She banked the chimera lower and swung around to approach the tower from an oblique underside angle, in hopes of startling the blackbirds from underneath. Zealand had one of his pistols out, and he fired neatly into one of the bird's heads as they approached, causing the thing to squawk and fall a hundred stories to the ground. Amazingly, there was no alarm raised, even when they killed four more of the birds and flew in close to the tower; Marla had worried that the chimera's white fur and feathers would make it stand out in the dark. Zealand tapped her shoulder and pointed to the balcony at the top of the tower, so that must be where Reave's rooms were. She arrowed there, and the chimera landed on the balcony with a hard jolt. They waited for a moment outside the high archway that led into the tower's darkness, but no one came running. "We're doing good," Ernesto said, and climbed down. Zealand followed. Marla hesitated—she didn't want to give up the chimera's strength, but riding it inside the tower was impractical. She wished there was a way to make it fight for her, since the creature's beak was formidable, but Langford's bridle didn't come with remote control. She made the chimera lay down against the balcony's outer wall, so it could be hidden from patrolling blackbirds, and then climbed off.

The initial sensation was like having her arms and legs cut off, and she stumbled, feeling several feet shorter than she should have been, but after a few moments of kneeling and taking deep breaths and reacquainting herself with her own standard-issue limbs, she felt better. "Okay," she whispered. "Genevieve is in here somewhere, I *hope* through that doorway, so let's go get her." They crept through a stone archway into the tower.

Zealand was unsurprised to find Reave's personal chambers devoid of personality. There was a chair, and a hook with a long black coat hanging on it, and a table holding a wide array of long knives. Otherwise it was all bare black stone, with no bathroom, no bed, nothing to suggest that Reave had anything like normal human needs. There were two doors in the room. One had a doorknob. The other had a barred grate and a sliding bolt. "There," he said, pointing to the cell door.

"Ernesto, guard the other door," Marla said. He went, carrying the trident from Langford's lab. She slipped up to the cell door and stole a glimpse into the grate. "She's in here," she whispered, and beckoned Zealand.

He began to hope they might pull this off. Zealand looked through the grate, and there she was, his poor Genevieve, slumped in a hard chair in a bare cell. Her head hung to her chest, her hair a tangled mass hiding her face, her yellow blouse stained with dark splotches, her black scarf trailing the floor. A steel bucket rested by her feet, and Zealand felt a surge of profound hatred for Reave—he'd given Genevieve, his creator, a *bucket* to piss and shit in.

Zealand would take her out of here. She would rebuild her palace, and mass an army, and Zealand would lead her host of dreams against Reave's nightmares, and smash the king of bad dreams to nothingness forever. There was no lock on the door, just the sliding bolt, which Zealand pulled open. The door swung wide with a drawn-out creak, but Genevieve didn't move.

He hurried to her, reached out, and touched her shoulder.

Genevieve lifted her head—and it wasn't Genevieve at all, but a shadow-faced man dressed in her clothes and a wig. He scooped up the bucket and flung its contents at Zealand's face. Zealand lifted his hands instinctively. The contents of the bucket sizzled when they hit, and Zealand screamed. His skin was boiling off. No, not his skin—the mold. The contents of the bucket were killing the mold, and a pain in his back struck so suddenly that he fell to the ground. The mold writhed and tried to abandon his poisoned body, and he saw it crawling across the floor, only to sizzle and smoke and turn brown and die. His back ached, and something wet ran out of him from the place where Reave had stabbed him. When the shadow-faced man rose and stepped over him, Zealand knew it was over—he was no longer a threat. Zealand's eyes slid closed, and he left the world with nothing but his hundred thousand personal regrets.

The thing that wasn't Genevieve threw something at Zealand, and the assassin fell. Marla drew her dagger, horrified that she'd been taken in by such a simple ruse, and then she heard a curse and the sound of smashing glass from the main chamber, followed by a stink of raw sewage. She couldn't worry about that now, and when the shadow-faced man stepped over Zealand, Marla lashed out with her dagger of office, tearing through his face like it was cloth, and he dropped. She was about to check on Zealand when Ernesto cried out for help. Marla spun and went back into Reave's chamber, where Ernesto stood shoulder to shoulder with a roiling thing of black smoke and dripping sludge—his pollution-golem, released and fighting. A crowd of shadow-faced men pushed through the door, and the golem and Ernesto fell back before them.

"Reave!" Marla shouted. "Why are you hiding behind your goons? Too scared of getting your ass kicked by a girl? Trying to wear me out a little so I won't spank you quite so hard?" She was *damned* if she was going to face his mindless shadow-killers—she wanted another shot at the man himself, and hoped his pride and misogyny would make it impossible for him to ignore a challenge from a woman.

The shadow-men hesitated, and Ernesto and his roiling golem took the opportunity to step back and get some breathing room. Marla looked over at Zealand, still on the floor of the cell, but when she saw the pool of blood running out of him she made herself give up hope. Zealand had gone from trying to kill her to dying for her.

No, to be fair, he'd died for his own cause—for Genevieve—and Marla would do her best to see he didn't die in vain.

Reave entered the room, his men making way for him to pass. He sniffed. "I smell a dead man. Poor Zealand. Though, to be fair, killing him wasn't really *homicide*, it was *herbicide*. Amazing what a bucket of weed killer will do to someone who's more mold than man. I'll have to kill the rest of you more conventionally."

"Where's Genevieve?" Marla said.

"Not far, just on one of the lower levels. I did keep her up here in my chambers at first, it's true, but a little bird told me I might have visitors, so I thought it better to remove her. Now I'll remove your head."

Marla, Ernesto, and the golem backed toward the balcony. "Ernesto," she said. "Leave the golem, but you get out of here."

"No way. This is my fight, too. This bastard's on my *land*."

"Ernesto," she said quietly. "I'm going to reverse my cloak, and I don't want to hurt you."

"Shit," he said. "Okay." He ran for the balcony and vaulted over the side with a grunt. Marla didn't worry about him. It was easier to land gently than it was to fly, and he was leaping into his own junkyard, where he knew every fold and cranny of hidden space; he'd be okay.

Marla didn't want to reverse her cloak. Letting that killing rage overtake her meant giving up a little of her humanity, and each time she used the cloak she got that much closer to full-on monsterhood. But it was a sure way to rip through Reave and his men, a pure desperation move, but better than no hope at all.

Marla reversed her cloak, and all her human concerns fell away. The alien intelligence that lived in the cloak flowed into her mind, and she saw everyone before her as targets, each holding equal weight. She didn't see friend or foe, only victims, and she leapt into the midst of the shadow-faced men with her arms extended and her teeth bared. A shadow of purple darkness clung to her like a bruised aura, and when she lashed out with her hands, she struck with purple talons. When she snapped her teeth, jaws of darkness leapt from her face like the muzzle of an animal, biting through throats. The shadow-men fell before her, and the one with the pale white head fled. She didn't pursue him. She'd reach him eventually, of course. She'd kill everything that moved across the world. Why had she bothered with mercy, with diplomacy? She should take what she wanted. Why didn't she wear this cloak every day? Why was she so afraid of her own power? The pollution-golem fought on, too, swarmed by shadow-men, and she ignored it for the moment, focusing her cold killing intent on more active attackers. She ripped her way through the men, clawing over them and out the door, into the twisted corridors of Reave's tower. Women in bloody wedding dresses fell before her, and she crushed the skulls of fanged infants underfoot. This was the purpose of life: to exterminate life.

The enemies all fell away, eventually, and she made her way halfway down the spiraling length of the tower, finally reaching a room with a throne made of skulls and bones. Reave sat upon the throne, gazing at her with some expression Marla couldn't read—facial expressions conveyed no information to her anymore, not in this state. She leapt toward him, moving faster than a cheetah.

And only stopped when a great crushing weight fell from the ceiling upon her. Reave had triggered a collapse, dumping heavy ceiling stones on her. She fought and scrambled and dug her way out, feeling bones snapping in her limbs but not slowing until she saw light from the smoky torches that lit the room. She willed herself forward, to kill, to fight, but her body was overwhelmed, and without her conscious will the cloak reversed itself, from violent purple to healing white.

Marla moaned. God, she'd almost lost it. If she hadn't been so catastrophically injured, the purple would have overtaken her mind completely, and she might have been lost forever to the strange parasitic intellect that lived in the cloak. The purple hadn't always been so powerful, but every time she wore the cloak, the urge to kill and kill forever became harder to resist. Now the white was repairing her broken body, and what had she achieved? She'd murdered a few disposable nightmare monsters. Hardly worth the effort.

"Ah, Marla," Reave said. "I didn't expect to use my collapsing ceiling quite so soon, but you seemed worth it."

Marla couldn't see him. She was buried in rubble, her neck twisted at an odd angle, with nothing but torches and a bit of the collapsed ceiling in her view. A booby-trapped ceiling. This guy was a real piece of work.

"I brought Genevieve to see you," he said, and Marla's neck healed itself with a pop. She turned her head and began dragging herself from the rubble. Reave stood with his arm around a cringing, glassy-eyed Genevieve, her head shaved, probably to make a wig for the decoy that had killed Zealand. "See, Genevieve? Zealand is dead, and Marla can't help you now. Your champions are broken."

"Genevieve, don't listen," Marla said. She could move again. Adrenaline and shock kept the pain from her broken-and-reset limbs from overwhelming her. But she couldn't reverse her cloak now, not with Genevieve in the room. She could kill Reave, yes, but she'd surely kill Genevieve, too, and then die herself for breaking her oath. The death of Reave and Genevieve would save Felport, she supposed, in the short term, but the other sorcerers would bicker and infight after Marla's death, and a war of succession would result. None of them were devoted enough or as qualified to run things as she was. She couldn't sacrifice her own life to save the city, then—her city *needed* her. Which meant she had to pull back and regroup. But how?

The pollution-golem saved her. It had never stopped fighting, apparently, and it burst into the throne room and went for Reave. Marla finished digging herself out of the rubble and prepared to grab Genevieve and spirit her away. But a horde of faceless men boiled from the shadows and seized Genevieve, dragging her to the back of the throne room and through some hidden passage. Marla cursed, but she couldn't go after the woman. There was no way Marla could face the combined might of Reave's army without reversing her cloak, not even with a few magic rings, magic boots, and her dagger of office. Without the element of surprise, she was outmatched. But for now, Reave was busy fighting off the pollution-golem, whipping his knives through its oily smoke, and that meant she could get away.

She made her way back up to Reave's rooms, kicking through a few of the shadow-men on the way. She reached the balcony and jumped onto the chimera, which her enemies had either ignored or never noticed. The harness of vines had disintegrated into fine dust, which gave her a pang—Zealand had been a good fighter, and dedicated to this particular cause. She had to squeeze tight with her thighs; thank the gods she'd kept up with her squats. She took the reins and the extra strength of the chimera flowed into her. Reave shouted behind her, and the smell of burning rubber wafted onto the balcony. The pollution-golem was being pushed back. Marla sent the chimera flying off the balcony and into the night, racing toward her home base. Rondeau's club was well defended tonight, turned from a public place into a fortress. If she could just make it back there, she'd be safe, and there would be time to regroup and . . .

What? Lead another attack? Reave would be even *more* prepared next time. How had he known she was coming? He'd mentioned a "little bird," but it was possible Gregor had just gotten lucky with his divination. Marla had tried to shield their plans from future-telling, but on such short notice her efforts had been limited. Or, much as she hated to consider it, she might have a spy. Hamil and Rondeau were both above suspicion. As for Ted or Joshua . . . Ted had saved her life when Zealand attacked her, and—quite apart from their love affair—Joshua had stepped in during her battle with Reave to let her escape. If either one of them was working for the enemy, why would they have helped her that way? To keep up appearances? She couldn't believe it. Trust came to her only with difficulty, but she'd been through a lot with both of them in the past couple of days, and unless she found real evidence to the contrary, she'd keep trusting them.

The giant blackbirds pursuing her cawed. She was over Fludd Park, where tree spirits still battled nightmare monsters, when the birds caught up with her. Something struck her shoulder, almost knocking her off her chimera, but she bent low and clung to its neck.

Her white cloak began healing the wound in her shoulder—was it from a bullet or something else? Whatever it was, it had gone clean through. She mumbled a painkiller spell, which made her hands go a little numb, but that was better than being laid low by shock if she took a more severe injury.

Her pursuers changed tactics, though, and some projectile struck the chimera in the side. The chimera screamed, the cry emerging from Marla's throat, and she instinctively swooped down closer to the park, trying to lose the pursuit by weaving through the treetops. Her cloak *didn't* heal the wound in the chimera, of course, but while she held the reins Marla felt the injury, as she felt the next ones—the painkiller didn't help with the transmitted pain, either. Something heavy struck one of the flailing bull's legs, and then a hot pain ripped through the left wing, severing the wing tip and sending her into a spin. The edges of her vision darkened with agony. The chimera fell fast toward the park, and Marla gripped the reins, pulling up at the last moment, hooves dragging in the snow. The chimera lost its footing and slid to a stop on the edge of the duck pond, and a tremendous pain ripped through Marla's—no, the chimera's—body. Marla fell numb from the chimera's back. The creature's rear legs were broken, bent at horrible angles, and Marla moaned and crawled a little bit away in the snow. The blackbirds were circling, and they landed in a ring around her, shadow-men dismounting and approaching warily. Marla twisted the rings on her fingers and struggled to her feet. *Now* she could reverse the cloak. They might kill her, but she . . . she would die pointlessly, killing disposable and easily replaceable enemies. The idea depressed her utterly.

Then the pond rose up, a thing the shape of a bear but made of water, and came lurching from the banks. Marla danced back, out of the way, as the thing silently waded onto the land and struck at the blackbirds and the shadow-faced men. This was one of Granger's many elementals, an avatar of nature trapped here in a city park, and sworn to defend it. The elemental recognized Marla as a fellow champion of Felport, apparently, because it paid her no mind, but struck viciously at Reave's men. The tree-spirits arrived a moment later, completing the rout, and soon most of the birds lay broken and dead in the park along with their riders, both already melting into viscous puddles. The water elemental slouched back into the pond when the last of Reave's men were killed, and the tree-spirits went about their business as well.

Marla sat down, and reached out to pet the chimera's head. After she'd stroked it half a dozen times, she saw that the bridle had fallen from its beak, straps broken during the fall. The creature turned its head to her, and its black eyes looked not dead now but soulful, and its tiny tongue flickered out pitifully. Marla went to the pond—which was just liquid again—and scooped water into her hands. She returned and held her hands out to the chimera, and it flickered its tongue into the water. The poor thing. It had been ridden hard and broken, and it had never sipped water, nor eaten food.

The chimera drank two more handfuls of water before it died.

Marla sat by its corpse, under the dark sky, huddled in her cloak. She needed to rise, and move on, and try to salvage things, but she'd never felt more defeated. Hamil said she always won because she was too stubborn to lose, but the idea of just curling up in a ball and sleeping had never seemed more appealing. Sleep was a wonderful drug. She understood for maybe the first time why Genevieve spent so much of her time in retreat from consciousness.

Marla wasn't sure if she was crying, or if it was just snow melting on her face. After a while she got up, and found a few fallen branches, and laid them across the chimera. "You were good," she said, petting its head again. "Better than we deserved." The branches were wet, but she conjured a hot and all-consuming fire, though she had to sacrifice some of her own body heat to do it. Soon there was only a blazing pyre where the chimera had been, and even under the protection of the spirits of the park, Marla was hesitant to stay for long by such a beacon. Watching the chimera turn to ash was too depressing anyway. She pulled her cloak around her and began the trudge back to Rondeau's club, sticking to side streets and avoiding confrontations. When she was two blocks away, she called home. Ted answered. "Tell the other sorcerers the attack failed," she said. "I'm almost home. They should pull back their forces, try to hold their own positions, and wait for further instructions."

"Oh, Marla. I'm so sorry."

"Yeah. Listen, when I get there, I'm going up to my office. I want to be alone for a few minutes. I need to think. I can't explain everything yet. Just . . . give me a little time, okay? Nobody bother me unless there are barbarians at the gate. You can do that for me?"

"I'll make sure of it," he said. "That's what I'm here for."

16

Nicolette came in quietly. Gregor sat with the Giggler, watching him draw pictures on a whiteboard with a hunk of runny blue cheese. The Seer drew something that looked like a tower, and a few M shapes that might have been birds.

Gregor looked at her, and she didn't say anything, and he shook his head. "Tell me," Gregor said to the Giggler, "is it safe for me to go outside?"

"While Marla Mason lives, there's nothing outside this building but your death," the Giggler said, as he always said, more or less. He threw the cheese at the wall, where it stuck with a plop, then he rolled over to his pallet and crawled beneath a dirty baby-blue blanket.

"I'm sorry, boss," Nicolette said. "I just heard from one of Reave's runners. He managed to kill Zealand, but Marla and Ernesto escaped."

"All right, then. Time to tip our hand. Have our spy kill Marla."

Nicolette shook her head. "I don't think he can. They're hunkered down, and in close quarters . . . the time isn't right. He's with us to a point, but he's not dedicated to you the way I am—he won't kill Marla unless he can do it without getting killed himself. With Hamil there, and Rondeau . . . it would be a death sentence. Assuming he could even succeed. I mean, Marla just got out of Reave's tower in one piece. She didn't die when I set her on *fire*. She's a tough broad, you gotta give her that."

"If I have to stay in this tower for much longer, Nicolette, I may walk out and take my chances with death." She'd never seen Gregor like this, so pale and demoralized, and she felt something like contempt. She was bursting with power now, and he seemed weaker than he'd ever been. "I never went out much. I was always content to stay here with my studies, but now that I *can't* leave, I want nothing more. You know, I never wanted the crown—heavy lies the head, and all that. Nor do I much look forward to being Reave's administrator. He will not be a popular ruler. But I was pushed into this situation by circumstance—I always took the path that wouldn't end in my death. Now look at me—right-hand man to a maniac with power based on subjugation and torture. I don't pretend to be a nice man, Nicolette, but I've never seen the point in being evil. Now I am in an evil man's employ. Reave's reign will be monstrous, and he has imperial ambitions. We may have nuclear bombs dropped on us before everything is said and done."

Nicolette shrugged. "Nuclear detonations cause a lot of disorder. I can deal with all that."

He waved his hand. "I know. But is that how we want to spend our time? For decades I've studied all the ways to see the future, and I've come to believe there's no such thing as fate. I always hated that old saying 'Fate leads him who will, and him who won't it drags.' But just because there's no fate doesn't mean there are no inevitabilities, and for all practical purposes, the result is the same. I may not be fated to serve Reave, but I have no other choice. When the Giggler said an alliance with Reave was my best chance of killing Marla, I took it. I did what I had to in order to survive. I am being dragged."

"I'm not too fond of Reave myself," Nicolette said. "Maybe once he disposes of Marla, we can get rid of him. The more successful he is at sowing discord, the more powerful I become, and we can model various coup and assassination scenarios until we find one that works."

"It's a thought," Gregor said. "But I fear he will be too powerful for us to stop by then. In a way, Marla is our best hope for defeating him. She might manage it, too. But if she does, if she defeats him and lives . . ." Gregor shook his head. "If I wasn't doomed before, I would be then. A collaborator with the enemy. Marla would execute me, and the other sorcerers of Felport would applaud. No, her death and Reave's success are the least bad outcomes for me. We'll have to keep supporting him." Nicolette frowned, and Gregor sighed. "For the time being, at least. We'll discuss the future when the future comes. All right?"

"You're the boss," Nicolette said. *For now.*

Marla opened the door to Rondeau's club, and the bar area was deserted, as she'd asked. They'd all be hiding out upstairs in Rondeau's apartment, probably, waiting for her to calm down. She didn't think she was a particularly bad boss, but she wasn't a good loser, and they were probably glad to be out of her way. The deference wouldn't last forever, though. They'd be looking to her for the next plan, and she'd run out of ideas. She'd tried a few times now to stop Reave, and slammed headlong into a wall each time. Now lives had been lost. How long before her people stopped following her, before the other sorcerers declared her unfit to save Felport and forcibly removed her from office, letting the Chamberlain or Viscarro take over?

A pizza was waiting in her office. She didn't believe for a minute any deliverymen were taking orders at the moment—it was after midnight, during a state of emergency, and there were monsters in the street—which meant Ted had reheated some of the food from this morning for her. He was a good assistant. She hoped there was enough left of her to be worth assisting when this was all over. As she ate, she slumped on the couch, and tried to think. She looked at the chessboard, paused in the middle of the last game she'd played with Ted.

What had Ted said? That tactics always lost to strategy in the long run? She'd disagreed at the time, but maybe he was right. Her tactics had been fine—she was in good fighting form, and so were her allies. But Reave, with the help of Gregor, had managed to outthink her at every turn. They were perpetually two moves ahead. She'd been thinking of making another frontal assault—because what *else* could she do? She dealt with problems by attacking them! But maybe it was time for a different approach. She rose and stood by the chessboard, moving a couple of pieces, then moving them back. The game wasn't a perfect metaphor for life, but she could learn something from it, maybe. She opened the door and said, "Guys, come out here!"

The door to Rondeau's bedroom opened, and he emerged, followed by Hamil, Joshua, and Ted. They all looked exhausted as they gathered around the battered table.

"Reave was ahead of me," she said. "He knew I was coming—I can only assume Gregor made a good prediction, or else I'm just naturally that predictable." *Or else one of you is a traitor,* she thought miserably, but all she could do about that was watch for suspicious behavior. "Zealand gave his life trying to save Genevieve. Ernesto got away, and I assume he's gone to ground in his junkyard. And I'm here." She spread her hands. "Tactics have failed me. We need some strategy." She went into the office and returned, dropping the pizza on the table. "Let's all eat, and talk. I need some lateral thinking here. My brain has some good moves in its repertoire, but I need people who can think in different circles, and that's you guys. Think about our situation. What the hell can we *do*?"

"We could give up the city," Hamil said, and at Marla's startled stare, he shrugged. "I'm just talking. We *do* have last-resort contingencies in place. We can teleport the entire populace a few miles away and seal off the city entirely. The border guards can jerk the whole place several dimensions out of phase. Cutting out a cancer is sometimes the only way to save the body, even if it means sacrificing some surrounding healthy tissue."

"No," Marla said. "I'd kill Genevieve and take my *own* death as punishment for oath-breaking before I'd give up this city. It's *my place*. Other ideas?"

"I can go to Reave and offer to be his, ah, boy bride," Joshua said. "It would at the very least distract him."

Marla considered. "I don't want to send you into that kind of danger. He'd never let you go, and then he'd have *two* hostages whose lives I value, so that's not really a win. Besides, we don't know where Gregor and Nicolette are in all this, but I believe they're still a factor. Distracting Reave only helps up to a point." She looked at Ted, who was silent, and the horrible worry that he might be a spy returned. Why wasn't he contributing? Didn't he *want* them to succeed? "Ted," she said finally. "I've seen you making a lot of phone calls lately, and you've been distracted. What have you been working on?" Surreptitiously, she touched a few wads of chewing gum stuck in a specific pattern on the underside of the table, activating a short-lived tattletale spell. If Ted told a lie, the table would knock and rock and tilt like a prop at a séance.

"I had a surprise for you," he said, and the table didn't move. "I thought it would be a nice way to celebrate your defeating Reave, but now I feel like an idiot for wasting the time."

"What kind of surprise?"

"You mentioned that you wished you could get Terry Reeves—the man who assaulted Genevieve—so you could make him pay for what he'd done. It seemed reasonable to me that if he'd raped one woman, he might have raped another, so I looked on the sex-offender database, and found a man by that name who was recently released from prison, and who still lives in Felport. I found a photo, and he even looks like Reave a little—bald, dead little eyes, ugly teeth. I was going to send a couple of your pet police to pick him up and bring him over. I thought it could help Genevieve's therapy, to know that her *real* rapist had been punished. I'm sorry I took on a project like that without—"

"Wait," Hamil said. "You found her rapist? You know where he is *right now*?"

"Well, yes," Ted said. "I guess he was never apprehended for the attack on Genevieve because she was catatonic. She never told anyone his name before—she still hasn't, St. John Austen told us. Genevieve probably can't even bring herself to *say* his name, though she was inside his mind, so it's no surprise she knew it."

"Marla," Hamil said. "I had no idea that man was still at large. But if he's local . . ."

"Holy shit," Marla said, rising. "Ted, you're a fucking *genius*. You're also an idiot for not mentioning this sooner, but even subtracting that idiocy from your score, you're *still* a genius. Where is this guy? We need him."

"Why?" Joshua said. "I don't understand."

She patted him on the head. "You don't have to understand, sweetheart, you just have to know it's *beautiful*. Ted, what's the address?" He checked his PDA and read it out. The place was in a shitty part of town, but they weren't too far from the shitty part of town, so that was all right. "Ted, you and Joshua stay here, man the phones, let me know if anything develops. Hamil, Rondeau, come with me."

"This could really work," Hamil said. "I need to give it some thought, figure out how exactly to proceed. . . . We should go to Langford's. He'll have anything we'd possibly need."

"Done," Marla said. Real hope was surging in her now.

"I'm glad I could help," Ted said. "Will you tell me *how* I helped?"

"After we've saved the city from devastation," Marla said.

"Can I come?" Joshua said.

Marla hesitated. She didn't want to leave his side, either—she'd missed him. "We'll have a celebratory romp if this works, Joshua. For now, I need you here. The bad guys might come knocking, and you're the only one who can sweet-talk them away from the door."

"If you think that's where I'd be most useful,"

Joshua said, sounding a little put out. She almost relented, but damn it, she was *right*. She could nurse his hurt feelings later. While wearing a nurse uniform, if that's what he wanted.

"We'll call when we finish," Marla said, and hustled Hamil and Rondeau toward the elevator. For once, Hamil moved faster than any of them. And why not? He was the one with the skills to take advantage of Ted's fortuitous find, though Marla would have to handle the tricky bits. That was okay. She liked the tricky bits.

In the car, on the way to Terry Reeves's house, Hamil leaned forward from the backseat and touched Marla's shoulder. "I want to make sure you understand how dangerous this is," he said quietly. If Rondeau could hear, he pretended not to. "If it goes wrong, if Reave doesn't react as we hope . . . you and Genevieve could *both* die, simultaneously."

Marla nodded, reaching back to pat his knee. "I know, big guy. But that's the kind of situation we're in. Finding Terry Reeves, having him in town . . . it's almost enough to make me believe in providence. At the very least, it's big luck. If it comes with big risks, well, so it goes. At least this will be decisive."

"True enough," Hamil murmured, and sank back into the seat.

Marla kicked in the door of the shitty little house on Rampart Street. Terry Reeves sat in a recliner in dirty boxer shorts, watching TV with a beer in his hand. His eyes went wide. "Get the fuck out of my house!"

"Terry Reeves?" Marla said, though there was no question—he was a less pale but equally bald version of Reave, with bushier eyebrows and an older face.

"It's none of your business who I am, bitch!"

"Oh, good, you are a total asshole," she said. "I won't feel bad about doing this, then." She tossed a fist-sized river rock at him, and he threw up his hands to ward it off. When it touched him, though, he dropped like a stone himself, totally unconscious. "He'll have a monster headache when he wakes up, and I can't say I mind."

Rondeau came in and sighed. "I always wind up doing the heavy lifting." He dragged Terry toward the door, wrinkling his nose. "Man, he stinks." Marla picked up Reeves's feet, and they hurried toward the waiting Bentley. Hamil took up most of the backseat, but that was okay, because they were sticking Terry in the trunk. They dumped him on top of the spare tire and the jack, and Rondeau hesitated before closing the lid. "Uh, Marla, are you really planning on killing this guy?"

"It could go that way," she admitted. "I'm not sure, but if it's a choice between him dying or having to kill Genevieve, who should win? A serial rapist, or one of his victims *and* me?"

"No argument there," Rondeau said, and shut the lid. "The cold-murder thing never sits well with me, but I understand having to make bad choices. I just . . . I kinda worry. . . ."

"I'm not looking forward to doing it, if that's what you're thinking," Marla said. "I think this guy should be castrated and put in a box forever, but I don't believe in killing anyone unless there's no other way to protect the innocent, you know that. And unless you're a sorcerer, a supermax prison is a pretty good way to make sure you never fuck over another innocent."

"You're doing good," Rondeau said. "I haven't had a chance to say that, and I know a lot of things have gone sideways these last couple of days, but you're doing good."

"Me and you should go have some breakfast when this all blows over," Marla said. "You can buy me a danish and tell me how awesome I am some more."

"It's a date, boss."

Langford opened the door and ushered them in. "Ted called and told me you were coming, though he wasn't certain *why*." He cleared off a long autopsy table so they could lay Terry Reeves down. "Who's our friend?"

"This is the man who assaulted Genevieve," Marla said. "The original flesh-and-blood inspiration for Reave, king of nightmares."

"Oh," Langford said, raising his eyebrows, which meant he was very impressed indeed. "That's clever."

"I should get to work," Hamil said, and set about collecting coils of wire, copper nails, vials of salt, and other tools of his trade. He'd seen the possibilities even faster than Marla had, probably. This idiot rapist Terry Reeves and the dark overlord Reave were fundamentally connected on a deep level; they weren't just similar, they were the *same*. They could make Terry Reeves into a living, life-sized voodoo doll for Reave. Whatever Terry Reeves suffered, Reave would suffer. If Reeves died, there was a chance—not a certainty, but a chance—that Reave would die, too.

But Marla and Hamil had more complicated ideas.

"Will you just be cutting off his head, in hopes that will finish Reave?" Langford said.

"Nope," Marla said. "I think the only way for Genevieve to really get rid of Reave is to *believe* she can beat him. He's grown to tremendous proportions in her mind. She needs to realize the *real* Terry Reeves is a sad piece of shit she can squish like a bug, not the monster she's built him up to be. She needs to see the inside of his head again and realize it's a squalid, nasty place, not worth her fear. Which means . . ." She went to the box of Genevieve's possessions, which Langford had used to track her. There were alligator clips attached to the photograph, the silk scarf, the hairbrush, the book. "We've got hair and clothes and beloved items, and that means we can set up a sympathetic resonance between Genevieve and whoever has these possessions. At the same time, we'll set up a resonance between Reave and Terry Reeves, and make the big bad guy a little bit more mortal and vulnerable."

Hamil came over and began lifting items from the box. "Marla's mind will enter Genevieve's body, and because Genevieve is such a powerful psychic, her consciousness should flow into Marla as well. There should be no danger of rejection. Thanks to the resonance, Genevieve should apprehend Marla's motives quickly, and though she's unbalanced, we think—or more truthfully, we hope—she will let us proceed. They'll essentially switch bodies. Marla will be able to deal with Reave, and Genevieve will be able to confront this man, and, perhaps, gain some closure. Or possibly slit his throat, depending on her temperament."

Marla took off her cloak. "You better lock this up, though, Langford. When I switch places with Genevieve, she'll be riding around in my body, and I don't want her having access to a weapon quite *that* badass. Who knows how she'll react when she recognizes this guy?"

Marla sat down. Hamil wound Genevieve's scarf around her throat, and wove strands of hair from the brush in with Marla's own. He tucked the book and the photograph into her pockets. "What do you think?" Marla said.

"It's fine," Hamil said. "I think it's good enough." He lit candles and began his incantations, and Marla did her best to meditate and empty her mind.

"I don't think anything's happ—" she began, and then, suddenly, something was.

Another bench, in another park, on a summer day. Not the dream world, exactly—the edges of this place blurred, nothing quite solidifying unless Marla looked at it directly. She was in some tiny corner of Genevieve's mind—or else Genevieve was in a corner of Marla's mind.

Genevieve sat beside her, twisting a scarf in her hands. "Marla. I can't keep you straight. Kill, save, help, harm."

"Definitely help now," Marla said. "So let me help, would you?"

"He can't be defeated. I've tried. He killed my knight."

"At the very least, I owe you a break, then. Let me take your place for a while. You can sit out the next round of the torture decathlon, okay?"

Genevieve cocked her head. "And what waits for me if I rest for a while in your body?"

"It's better if you see that for yourself." But of course, there was no keeping secrets from Genevieve—

even asking the question was just a courtesy on her part, the type of kindness polite psychics learned early on, and it was heartening that Genevieve was still sane enough to bother.

"You have . . . Reave? The man who attacked me? But he's here, in this tower—"

"Not exactly." Marla hesitated. It was hard to diplomatically tell someone they were bat-shit insane, especially when that someone could read your mind. "Reave is a nightmare you had. We've got the cause of the nightmare. Terry Reeves. Do you understand?"

Marla's mind was spread out before Genevieve like a rummage table at a garage sale, but Genevieve seemed to have trouble comprehending. "But he—I don't—what will he . . ." She trailed off, her face a twist of anguish.

"Look, you'll be safe. And I'll take your pain for a while. Let me do that? To make up for that whole planning-to-kill-you thing?"

Genevieve nodded, and the bench fell away.

Marla found herself in a small cell with black walls, sitting on a chair. She wasn't bound—why would Reave bind Genevieve, when she was so broken? The body was sore, but not abused. The torments would be mostly psychological, of course. Reave couldn't risk actually hurting Genevieve. She was his power source. Marla stood, stretched, and tested the body's capabilities. Genevieve was no martial artist, and she was physically weaker than Marla, but Marla wasn't expecting to brawl. She had other plans. She'd hoped that taking Genevieve's body would give her access to the woman's vast reality-altering powers, but no such luck—maybe she could have used those powers, but she had no idea *how,* anyway, any more than taking over a nuclear physicist's body would let her know how to build an atom bomb.

Marla could see, as with the vividness of a dream, the world through her own body's eyes, now inhabited by Genevieve. It was profoundly disorienting, but Marla's recent experience piloting the chimera helped. Genevieve stood up, and Hamil and Rondeau gave her reassurances, and Marla felt some strain in the back of her head as Genevieve read their minds. Marla's brain, of course, was no good at reading minds, so Genevieve had to reach back through their psychic link to her *own* brain to do so. Marla was impressed with the woman's range—Langford's warehouse was across town, and Genevieve was able to pinpoint particular minds there with great accuracy. Genevieve went to look at Terry Reeves, still unconscious on an autopsy table. "But he's so old," Genevieve said, and Marla grinned. That was as good a cue as any. She turned her attention away from Genevieve to the situation at hand.

"HEY!" she shouted, and a faceless guard appeared at the barred grate in the door. "Call your boss, I need to talk to him. Don't just stand there, shadow-face, get him! Unless he's afraid to speak to a *woman*." The guard disappeared, and Marla grinned. The muscles in her face felt strange. Genevieve didn't smile much.

Marla picked up the waste-bucket and stood by the door. In a moment the door creaked open and Reave entered. He was close to seven feet tall now, his bald head more gleaming than mushroomlike, his stupid shiny coat cinched tight at the waist.

Marla threw the contents of the bucket into his face, and laughed when he stumbled back. One of his guards handed him a handkerchief, and Reave wiped the worst of the smears away. "Have you gone even *more* mad, woman? You will pay for that."

"Why do you have guards with you, Terry? Too afraid to talk to me one-on-one?"

Reave frowned, then waved his hand, and the guards withdrew, shutting the door after them. "You know how I feel about women who talk back, Genevieve. You know what *happens* to them."

"Oh?" Marla said, pretending to cringe, then stepping forward and kicking him as hard as she could between his legs. Reave's eyes widened, but that was all, and Marla grinned. "A real man would have doubled over when I did that, Terry. But you don't even have balls, do you? You stand there all menacing, but you couldn't fuck me if I *begged* you, much less against my will. How is it you think you can threaten me when the closest thing you've got to a cock is this big stupid tower?"

Reave spat at her feet. "You are not Genevieve. This is Genevieve's *body*, but . . . Marla?"

She curtsied. "You're pretty slow on the uptake for the lord of nightmares, Terry."

"You think this is clever? You found some hair, some piece of her clothes, and decided to give Genevieve a respite? You think I won't *hurt* you?"

"Of *course* you won't, you moron. Genevieve is the source of your power. You won't touch a hair on her head."

Reave sniffed. "There are torments that do not result in death, Marla."

"Yeah, and I'm sure you're good at inflicting them on a traumatized woman in a state of semicatatonia. But I'm a little more feisty. You don't like feisty women, do you, Terry?"

"Don't call me *Terry*!" he roared, and Marla just laughed in his face. She loved this part.

"Oh, that's right. Terry's just the true story you were inspired by, right? Oh, and incidentally—we have him. The real original you, asshole."

"You lie."

Marla just snorted.

"Even if you do, it doesn't matter. He is not me. He is only a man. I am the king of nightmares—"

"Oh, what*ever*. I know you'd like to believe that, but you should know better. That drunk rapist is exactly what you are, when you strip away all special effects. A nothing who gets off on hurting people. And we've got him. Which means we've got *you*."

"Nonsense," Reave said. "I'll have my guards bring up a board, and a bucket of piss, and I'm going to strap you down and pour urine across your face until you decide to leave this body and—"

"Hold that thought," Marla said, and reached back in her mind for the connection to Genevieve, who was still staring at Terry Reeves. *Gen,* she thought. *Why don't you give that bastard a slap?*

What? I can't. What if he—

He can't do anything but take *it.*

She felt a little surge of glee from Genevieve, who drew her hand back and slapped Terry Reeves hard across the face.

Reave, who'd been unspooling more threats, suddenly staggered back and clutched his cheek. "What—how did you—"

"Genevieve just slapped Terry Reeves. Felt that, did you? Guess you guys do have some connection, huh?"

"I—I'll send my armies, and they'll find her, find

you, and Reeves, too. I'll install him here in palatial comfort, he will never want for anything—"

"Try it," Marla said. "My people are there, and Reeves will *die* if you make a move."

Reave shrank visibly before her. From seven feet to six, then down to five and a half feet tall, no taller than the real Terry Reeves. The hem of his long black coat dragged the floor now. "What do you want?" he said at last. "A place in the new regime? Something can be arranged."

"Oh, yeah, sign me up for a seat on the ruling council of the rapeocracy. Fuck you, Reave. All I want is for Genevieve to see you for what you are."

Reave whimpered.

Back in Langford's lab, the slap had awakened Terry Reeves, who tried to sit up, but was held down by his restraints. "Fuck is this? Head hurts," he slurred, and Reave's lips moved in the same words, though he didn't actually speak. Now that Terry Reeves was awake, the connection—strengthened and reinforced by Hamil's sympathetic magic—between Reave and himself was more noticeable, and Reave was probably seeing through Reeves's eyes as well as his own.

Hamil stepped toward Reeves. "Terrence Reeves. Does this woman look familiar to you?"

The man narrowed his eyes. "Never seen her before in my life."

Genevieve shuddered, a wave of revulsion passing through her and into Marla, but that revulsion was better than fear.

"You raped her in an alley not far from here, fifteen years ago."

"Some vigilante bullshit, always harass me. I did my time, I never touched her," he said, his mouth running on autopilot, and now the same words were coming from Reave's mouth. Somewhere, far off in the black tower, bits of stone began to crumble and fall with distant crashes.

"You remember me," Genevieve said slowly. "I see it in your mind. Why did you hurt me?"

"Fuck you, bitch, I'm innocent, let me go!" Terry yelled.

She shook her head. "You don't even know why. You just . . . do these things. Because you like them. I wasn't even a person to you."

"I got rights," Reeves said.

"Not today," Rondeau said, flipping his butterfly knife nonchalantly open and closed.

"He's only a little *nothing*," Genevieve said. "In his mind that night he was so strong, unstoppable, a force of nature. But he's just *crazy*." And there was something in her mind like a dam breaking, like long-closed windows being thrown open, like a flipped circuit breaker being switched back. It was like light came pouring into her head, and just as suddenly, the ceiling of Reave's tower room broke open, and by the gods, it was dawn in Felport already. "He's *afraid* of me," Genevieve said, real wonder and relief in her voice. Genevieve leaned close to Reeves, and then just shook her head. "We don't need him anymore. Let him go back to his rot and ruin."

"You're not worried he'll hurt someone else?" Rondeau said.

"Oh, no," Genevieve said, and did something Marla didn't quite understand, though she felt a twinge in her borrowed brain. Genevieve reached into Reeves's mind and did *something*, and Reeves began to whimper and twitch. "I fixed that. He'll never hurt anyone else. I gave him a little bit of what *I* have. He can never hurt anyone without feeling that hurt tenfold on himself."

"Ha!" Marla said in the tower. "You hear that, Terry? You got a megadose of empathy. Suck on that, you fuck."

"Put him out in the street," Genevieve said, and Rondeau and Langford untied Reeves, took his unresisting form to the door, and pitched him into the snow.

Genevieve sat down in the chair. "Let me back to my body," she said. "Marla. I want to see him. The *other* him."

Marla looked Reave over. He was shrunken, just a sketch of a man, and so she withdrew from Genevieve's mind, and felt Genevieve withdraw from hers. They passed in that dark space between, and Marla felt something like the touch of a gentle hand on her cheek, something like a "Thank you."

"Marla?" Rondeau said, back in the lab, and she hushed him quickly. The connection was still open between her and Genevieve, and she wanted to see.

Genevieve knelt beside Reave's twitching, quivering form. The nightmare king stared at her with eyes wide and terrified. "I would hate you, but I made you," Genevieve said. "I made you to punish myself. I gave you all the power you have." She shook her head. "But you don't have a place in my mind anymore, or in the world." She poked him in the cheek with her index finger, and his flesh gave way like the skin of a mushroom. A little puff of dust rose up, and then his head collapsed on itself, his eyes rolling free, transformed into marbles. His black coat and clothes liquefied into a puddle. Genevieve let out a little sigh.

Marla wondered if she should send some guys over

to the tower to make sure Genevieve was okay—Nicolette and Gregor were still at large, after all—but Genevieve just laughed in her mind. *The tower will be nothing but a puddle of blackness in a few minutes, and then I'm leaving this world for a while*, she said. *I have to set some things in order. I'll be in touch.*

And then Genevieve broke the connection, an act that should have been impossible given the potency of the sympathetic connection Hamil had created. But Genevieve could do lots of impossible things. That fact was *slightly* less scary now that she didn't appear to be insane.

"Ding, dong, Reave is dead," Marla said, and the others clapped their hands and whistled and cheered. "And Genevieve is sane enough to get the hell out of town. I'm going to go home, and eat some steak and eggs, and fuck my lover."

"Rondeau and I will get in touch with the other sorcerers, and tell them what's happened," Hamil said.

Marla stood up and patted him on the arm. "See, I count on you to make me look good. Yeah, go around and see them in person, would you? Smooth all the ruffled feathers, let them know we're cool, get the border guards to ease off on the blizzard, and all that. See if anyone has any suggestions for how to deal with the fact that much of the ordinary population of Felport saw impossible towers, monsters, and other weird shit on the streets, too." She unwound the scarf and put down the photograph and book. "Hold on to Genevieve's stuff. We'll give it back to her, if she doesn't disappear into a more pleasant dreamland forever."

17

"We won!" Marla said, bursting into her office, where Ted and Joshua—beautiful Joshua, such a welcome sight!—sat playing checkers on her antique chessboard.

"Hamil called us, it's wonderful," Ted said, rising. "He also explained about the sympathetic magic. I'm sorry, if I'd realized, I would have told you about Terry Reeves earlier—"

Marla grabbed him and gave him a hug. "Shut up, Ted. You did great."

"So what happens next?" Joshua said.

"Hmm? Well, things are chilling out all over the city. The monsters are gone, Reave's tower went kaput, the sinkholes are disappearing . . . I walked here from Langford's, and everything's getting back to normal. The sun's not shining, but I don't mind winter, when there are no monsters coming out of the snow. There are lots of loose ends—for one, I have to call Kardec and tell him Zealand didn't make it out alive. If Zealand had survived, I'd be smuggling him out of Felport and trying to send the slow assassins off on a wild-goose chase in the other direction." She shook her head. "I wish that's what I was doing."

"What about Gregor and his people?" Joshua said.

"Oh, Gregor's going to die," Marla said. "The other sorcerers will call for his execution for collaborating with Reave, and we'll all together kick his door down and drag him out into the daylight, but I'll be the one to carry out the sentence. I don't know what he was thinking, betting against me. He should know better. We'll pull him out of his spider hole and take off his head." She shrugged. "Executing traitors isn't exactly the *fun* part of my job, but it's necessary sometimes. As for Gregor's people, well, 'I was just following orders' doesn't go too far with me, but we'll take it on a case-by-case basis. All that's for later, though. Who wants breakfast?"

"Should I call down to the diner?" Ted said. "I heard on the radio that a lot of businesses are opening again this morning. You know, mixed in with the stories about mass hysteria and unexplained animal sightings and organized bands of looters."

"No, Ted, you're our resident hero, so *I'll* order the food. Steak, eggs, hash browns, juices all around—we'll have a big old greasy feast. And then, Joshua, you and I will go celebrate in *private*." She went to the desk, picked up the phone, and dialed.

A gurgle and cry behind her made her turn, and she saw Ted spitting blood, eyes wide. He fell to the floor, and Marla dropped the phone. Joshua held a long knife, and began nonchalantly cleaning it with a handkerchief. Who even carried handkerchiefs anymore? He was so classy.

"Joshua?" Marla said, bewildered. "What—why

did you do that?" The only possible explanation came to her. "Was Ted the spy? Was he working for Gregor? You killed him before he could attack me? Right?"

"No, you silly bitch," Joshua said. "*I'm* the spy." He shook his head. "Ted's just an insufferable little man who wouldn't even let me win at checkers, until I *told* him to. Some people have no manners."

"Joshua," Marla said, numb, conflicted. He was beautiful, her golden boy, but he'd just killed Ted, he was working with her *enemy*—gods, what a magnificent plan, how flawlessly he'd pulled it off! She wanted to applaud.

"And even now you love me," Joshua said, shaking his head, stepping over Ted's body as it emptied itself of blood. "You're *impressed* with me, you're admiring how I played you. As well you should. Gregor hired me before you even interviewed me. He saw the future, knew you would approach me, and so he came to me first. He offered me more money, more power, more of everything. Not that I care much about power and money. But he also offered me a chance to pretend—I always wanted to be an actor. I think audiences would love me. You certainly thought it was a command performance."

"But you saved me," Marla said. "You stopped Reave from attacking me in Gregor's office. You . . . I don't understand." She didn't. His brilliance was clearly beyond her ability to comprehend.

"I only stepped in because I thought you might actually *defeat* Reave, and Gregor didn't want that." Joshua shrugged.

"But you could have killed me anytime—in bed, I

was totally exposed, in your power . . . why didn't you?"

Joshua sniffed. "I'm a lover, Marla, not a killer." He glanced at Ted's body. "Well, usually. Gregor said he was hiring a professional to kill you, and he just needed me on the inside to provide information, and to keep you distracted from your proper business. Of course, things have become more desperate recently. Today Gregor called and told me to finish the job, if I could do so without dying myself. If I murdered you in front of Rondeau and Hamil, well, they would have ended me. They find me loveable, but not as loveable as *you* do. My power only becomes irresistible when I fuck someone. You know what they say about lovetalkers. As soon as I took you to bed, I knew I could do anything I wanted, and you would only stand there, gazing at me in wonder." He laughed, and it was still music to Marla. "This seemed like the right time, with no one here but Ted. I knew he'd be easy to take by surprise. And you, well, I can walk up to you now and put this knife in your heart, and your last word will be 'Bravo.'" He approached her, holding the knife inexpertly, but even an amateur could kill someone who didn't bother to defend herself.

"You tricked me at every turn," Marla said. "I'm humbled. And making love to you was the sweetest experience of my life. You're the worthiest adversary I can imagine."

"Yes, well, you weren't half bad yourself, Marla. It wasn't a *bad* job. I'll be a little sorry to kill you."

"One last kiss?" Marla said. "Before I go?"

"Oh, why not?" Joshua said.

Marla leaned in close. She took his face in her hands. She kissed him.

Then she put one hand on his chin, one on his cheek, and jerked his head around as hard as she could, snapping his neck and killing him instantly.

He fell, and she looked down at his body. He was still beautiful, even though the supernatural glamour had faded with his life. "Oh, Joshua," she said, and there were tears in her eyes. "I did love you." But he'd made the mistake of thinking she wouldn't kill someone she loved, and of course she would, if that was the only way to save her city.

She went to Ted, hoping he might have held on, but he was gone, bled out. Marla sat with him for a while, holding a vigil in miniature, gripping his hand in hers. They'd never play chess again. She wouldn't be able to see him settled in his own apartment, or show him her inherited library of books on magic. He would have liked that. She would have liked it, too.

Marla opened her mouth to tell Ted she was sorry, but he was dead, and couldn't hear her, and it was her fault. She'd told herself she was falling in love with Joshua, but she'd only met him less than a week ago. He'd been a stranger. She'd been bewitched and enchanted, just like the farm girls who pined away for the love of a Ganconer. Her fundamental mistrust had deserted her, and she'd let herself be tricked, mind and heart hijacked by Joshua's poisonous magic. She'd been careless, and now her friend was dead.

Marla closed Ted's eyes and trudged out of the room to call Hamil.

Nicolette came to Gregor in his underground safe room. "Boss, I just called Joshua . . . and Rondeau answered his phone. He says Joshua is dead, and Marla is coming for us."

Gregor covered his eyes. "That's it, then. I'm dead. All because I wanted to leave this fucking building."

"Yeah," Nicolette said, making a decision. "I actually feel really bad about that."

Gregor looked up. "What do you mean?"

"Oh, well. It wasn't a real prophecy, that's all. The thing about how Marla would kill you if you left the building. It was a lie."

Gregor stood up. "The Giggler told me. He's the most potent seer I've ever met, what do you mean it was a lie?"

"The Giggler will say anything for a cookie." She shrugged. "I told him what to say, and he stuck with it. For a bughouse lunatic who rolls in his own filth, he's a stand-up guy."

"Why would you *do* something like this?" Gregor said, shaking with rage.

Nicolette fingered the ends of her braids, where beads and feathers clacked, hoping Gregor would sense the implicit threat and keep his distance. "Just trying for a little upward mobility, boss. Like you said, you never wanted to be in charge. But I didn't want to be right-hand woman to somebody with no ambition. I figured, if I made you believe Marla was going to kill you, you'd kill *her,* and in the power vacuum that followed, I'd be able to move you into the top spot. The Chamberlain doesn't want the job, and the other sorcerers don't trust Viscarro, so you were the obvious choice for top man."

"This is madness," Gregor said. "When Marla finds out, she'll kill you, not me."

"Oh, I imagine she'd kill both of us. She's not one to worry about complexities, you know? Anyway, she'd kill me for trying to bust Elsie Jarrow out of the Blackwing Institute anyway, if she ever found out I was the one behind that."

"You *what*?" He looked more horrified than angry now. "You weakened the seals on Jarrow's prison? Gods, you weren't in the city back then, you don't know what it was like when she went mad, it was worse than the things Reave did! Jarrow is pure floating death!"

"I figured she'd stir up a lot of chaos, that's for sure," Nicolette said. "And distract Marla, which would make killing her easier. All the disorder in the city would make *my* powers grow, so I'd be able to help you take over more easily." She shrugged. "It didn't work out, but Jarrow woke up Genevieve, and her appearance caused as much chaos as I could've hoped for. I'm still feeling strong."

"Yes, well, your plan didn't work, did it? Marla survived our assassination attempts, and now she's defeated Reave, and you and I are *dead*."

"Yeah. About that. I mean, you're the only one who knows I tried to free Jarrow, and you're the only one who knows I tricked you into trying to kill Marla. So if something happens to *you* . . ."

"Traitor," Gregor said.

"Nah," Nicolette said. "I'm no traitor. I've been true to the only one who counts—myself. I had a little chat with Marla when I called just now. I told her I was really pissed about you working with Reave, since he was such a woman-hating fuck, and that I regretted everything, and would do anything to redeem myself in her eyes. She didn't want to believe me, but then she came up with a test of my loyalty."

"Oh, shit," Gregor said.

"Yeah. I'm supposed to kill you. So, bye, boss." She plucked a few beads from her hair and tossed them at her mentor and master.

There wasn't much left of Gregor when her spell was done, but the dental records would prove it was him. Nicolette went upstairs, whistling. She'd cut a pretty nice deal with Marla. Gregor's building belonged to her now. She couldn't wait to start redecorating. Especially since Marla was going to make Rondeau help Nicolette paint and move furniture and do a month's worth of shitwork to pay off his debt. She planned to clog every toilet in the place and make the little prick fix them. Life was sweet.

Marla opened her eyes in a strange bedroom. Genevieve sat beside the bed, working on some knitting, of all things. "Can't you just, like, wish complete sweaters into being?" Marla said.

"Yes, but it's more satisfying this way. Besides, it's a scarf. For you. For those harsh Felport winters."

"I didn't think we'd ever see you again," Marla said, sitting up. "Is this your palace?"

"As good as new. And a bit less, ah, architecturally eccentric. The past fifteen years were a sort of never-ending bad dream, and you helped wake me out of it. For that, I thank you. Without Reave's constant assaults, my mind is much clearer."

"Dr. Husch says you can come back to the Blackwing Institute, if you want. She's got some rooms for you—not a cell, just rooms. She thinks you could help with the therapy for the other patients."

Genevieve grimaced. "Marla, given the things I can do . . . I'm not sure it's such a good idea for me to do more than briefly *visit* the world outside this dream. There have been other people with my power in history, and most of them disappear at some point. I think because they realize it's better for everyone that way. There are probably a lot of floating bubble universes out there, ruled by little gods like me. I'm happy to have visitors, but I should stay away from your world. I just wanted to thank you for not killing me."

Marla laughed. "Don't mention it."

"And . . . I'm sorry for the loss of your friends. Ted. Joshua, even though he proved to be a villain."

"Yeah. Thanks. And Zealand, too. He died trying to save you."

"Well," Genevieve said. "As to that, I have something to show you." She beckoned, and Marla followed her into a hallway lit with skylights.

"You should rent this place out for corporate retreats," Marla said, and Genevieve laughed—a sane, comfortable laugh, which did good things for Marla's battered heart.

Genevieve opened the door to her library, and there was St. John Austen, restored to life—and Zealand, his hands crawling with green, his face as lined and strong as ever.

"Holy *shit,*" Marla said, and turned to Genevieve. "You—he—is it really *him*?"

"I feel like me from the inside," Zealand said, approaching and clasping her in a hug. "Though I'm not sure how I'd be able to tell the difference. Genevieve spent a lot of time inside my head, getting to know every snap and crackle of my neurons, and she managed to resurrect me here, just as she did with St. John Austen. I won't be taking any trips to the world I knew, alas—I'm not quite *that* real. Such a provisional existence could be disturbing, I suppose, but I find such epistemological dilemmas irrelevant when the alternative is nonexistence."

"You sure sound like Zealand," Marla said. "The slow assassins were pissed when I told them you'd died for a good cause, too."

"I wish I could have gotten to know your Ted better," Genevieve said, "and given him a sort of life here, too."

"He was a good guy," Marla said, but she'd save her memories for when she was alone, and could mourn him properly.

Marla chatted a bit longer, and embraced St. John Austen, but declined the offer of a drink, even when Genevieve mischievously assured her it wouldn't make her sleep for forty years or have any other fairy-food-like consequences. "I should really get back," Marla said. "Everyone's still a little freaked out, and I have to do some damage control. But, ah, before I go . . ."

"I see what you're thinking," Genevieve said. "And, yes, of course I can do that. But you're thinking it's a *boon,* a gift I might deign to grant you. That's not true at all. It's the least I can do, after all you've done for me."

"So it's not, you know, too big an undertaking? I mean, I don't want you to strain yourself, after all you've been through. . . ."

"Consider it done," Genevieve said, and draped the

finished scarf around Marla's neck. She grinned. "Even that last personal favor you want. And if you ever wish to see me, just call my name, all right? You're always welcome here."

"I'll send you a Christmas card next winter," Marla said, and Genevieve sent her home.

Rondeau and Marla sat at Smitty's diner in a corner booth, the torn red vinyl seats mended with strips of black electrical tape. They ate their pancakes and hash browns and eggs without speaking for a while. "Ted's funeral was nice," Rondeau said finally. "Who was that cute girl with the glasses? His daughter? She wasn't standing with the rest of his family."

"I don't know," Marla said. Ted had been ashamed of his liaison with the girl from the chess club, and there was no reason to embarrass him in death, though Marla had been a little surprised and pleased to see the girl at the funeral, along with Ted's family. She'd been pissed, too, though. They'd all shut Ted out, made him live on the streets, but once he got knifed—in what was, officially, a random and unsolved bit of street violence during the chaos of the blizzard—they all came to his funeral. Ah, well. Loyalty these days wasn't what it used to be. Look at the way Nicolette had turned on Gregor. Marla didn't trust the chaos magician any more than she could eat the moon, but she didn't trust most of the other sorcerers in Felport, either, so what did it matter? She'd rewarded Nicolette by giving her some of Gregor's holdings, after divvying up the rest of his estate and Susan Wellstone's more substantial assets among the sorcerers who'd helped her during the battle with Reave. Nobody was happy with what they'd received, everyone arguing that they deserved more for their service, and Marla hadn't exactly been diplomatic, snapping that they were lucky to even *have* a city. Only the fact that she'd just saved Felport from destruction staved off open revolt, and there were a lot of simmering resentments toward her now. Marla had actually offered Langford the bulk of Susan's assets, because he'd done so much to stop Reave, but he'd refused—he liked doing research, without any responsibilities beyond following his own interests. If he'd actually taken Marla up on her offer, the other sorcerers probably would have hollered for her head. She owed Langford a new laboratory in exchange for that drop of Gorgon blood, though.

"So the rumor is you did some crazy giant magic damage control," Rondeau said. "The common folk sure aren't *acting* like they just saw the city overrun by monsters."

Marla shook a blob of ketchup onto her plate and stabbed a forkful of hash browns. "Well, I don't mind if people give me the credit, but it's all Genevieve's doing. I asked her if she could smooth the waters. She's a powerful psychic, after all. So she reached out to every ordinary citizen in Felport who saw something they couldn't explain, and tweaked the experiences into short-term memory, so they faded like the memory of dreams. There are some state investigators here, responding to early reports, but the mayor's chilling them out, telling them people just went a little nuts during the blizzard, and the witnesses don't have much to say. It'll blow over."

"Damn," Rondeau said. "That's big stuff. I'm glad

Genevieve's one of the good guys. Well, I mean, basically. *Eventually.*" He eyed Marla's last uneaten strip of bacon, but apparently had the good sense not to reach for it. "So how are you handling, you know, the Joshua thing?"

Marla shrugged, looking down at her plate. "It doesn't make me eager to go out and start dating again, that's for sure. But Genevieve helped me with that, too."

"How so?"

"I didn't want to forget about Joshua entirely. Getting betrayed by a guy because I was too besotted to be suspicious? That's a valuable lesson. But Genevieve did help me forget one thing."

"What's that?"

"The experience of fucking him. Because they say when you sleep with a lovetalker, you can never really enjoy sex with anyone else again. They just don't measure up. Why would I condemn myself to a life of disappointment? So I don't remember a thing about sleeping with Joshua now. I don't even remember enough to miss it."

Rondeau laughed. "If you ever want to, you know, make *sure* you can still enjoy sleeping with other people, my door is always open."

"In your dreams, Rondeau. Only in your dreams."

ACKNOWLEDGMENTS

As always, I had a lot of help with this book. My first readers, who provided valuable advice and insight, were Jenn Reese, Sarah Prineas, Michael J. Jasper, John Sullivan, Greg van Eekhout, and, of course, my beloved partner, H. L. Shaw. My agent, Ginger Clark, gave great advice and encouragement, and Juliet Ulman is the best editor I could hope for. Thanks to Nick Mamatas for the Skatouioannis, and to my copy editor Pam Feinstein for keeping me from looking like an idiot. In terms of general support for my writing, I must thank my coworkers and boss at *Locus,* the best day job a writer could have, and my friends Scott and Lynne, who always give me a place to stay and provide great company when I need to get away from life for a weekend.

ABOUT THE AUTHOR

T. A. Pratt lives in Oakland, California, with partner H. L. Shaw and their son, and works as a senior editor for a trade publishing magazine. Learn more about your favorite slightly wicked sorceress at www.MarlaMason.net.